The Bunker

Eleven Down

By
Timothy King

Words Matter Publishing

P.O. Box 531

Salem, Il 62881

www.wordsmatterpublishing.com

ISBN 13: 978-1-947072-37-4
ISBN 10: 1-947072-37-4

Library of Congress Catalog Card Number: 2017960700

DEDICATION

I dedicate this book to my loving wife, Mary; for without her love, support, and patience, I would never have endeavored to express myself through the written word.

Thank you, princess, I love you beyond all words.

TABLE OF CONTENTS

ACKNOWLEDGEMENT
ℭ ℬ

The completion of this first book of 'The Bunker' series would not have been possible without the loving support of my precious wife, Mary; for without her understanding, encouragement, and assistance during this undertaking, this book would not have been finished.

And to my son, Austin, who encouraged me through prayer and guidance when I needed it the most.

And to my grandson, Levi, who not only pushed me to finish this book, but has now challenged me to make it into a trilogy because it was so 'awesome' (his words, not mine).

And to my nephew, Matthew Davenport, for through the encouragement in seeing him succeed as an author, I took on the task.

And to my loving, caring, and obstinate mother who refused to give up on me even though I had given up on myself early on in my life; through her constant prayers, the seeds that were planted when I was young took root and grew.

And to my Aunt Diane Tuggle, through her unfaltering love and support, she has helped me through some of my toughest times, even though she did not know it.

And to my heaven-sent publisher, Tammy Koelling, who saw the author in me, and through faith, believed in who I could be.

And to all my friends for their encouragement and support, it means more than one would know.

And above all, to the One who not only gave me the ability to place my jumbled mind upon the paper in an organized way, but who also placed the Holy Spirit in me when I accepted His Son as my Lord and Saviour; for without the Almighty God, I am but another rebellious soul travelling the wide path to destruction.

CHAPTER 1

ᘒ ᘓ

As Anthony nervously sits in his car staring across the parking lot at the small office building, with a sigh, he says aloud, "I can't believe I am doing this, but I need the money." *It doesn't look anything like a research facility; it is just a small office building with a sign on the door,* he thinks while picking up the piece of paper he had pulled off the dorm bulletin board:

Wanted:
Twelve students are needed for a research project.
You will be fully sequestered for fourteen days and will
be paid $2,000 upon successful completion of all tasks.
Only The Serious Need Apply.
Applications will be accepted on August 7 from 8:00
am to 5:00 pm only. Apply in person at Harrison
Research and Analytical Facility, 1213 Manufacturers
Road, Suite A. If accepted, sequestering will
begin immediately.

Anthony looks at his watch, 4:02 pm, and then he looks around the parking lot and says, "The parking lot's full, I probably don't even have a shot." Anthony sits for a minute as he anxiously drums his fingers on the steering wheel and finally says, "Well, the only way to find out is to go in," and with that, Anthony gets out of his car and heads to the door.

When Anthony enters, he is greeted by a stern looking

woman in her mid-forties, "Hello, my name is Ms. Camron; are you here in response to the flyer?"

"Yeah, are there still spots left?"

"Two more. Have a seat and fill out this basic questionnaire; once done, place it in the orange slot on the left wall."

"Thank you," Anthony says as he takes the clipboard and heads to a seat, all the while thinking that Ms. Camron is a little too cold to be a receptionist; she missed her calling, drill instructor is what Anthony thinks her job choice should have been.

He sits down and looks at the clipboard Ms. Camron gave him; as he flips through the pages, he thinks, *Basic questionnaire? This thing has at least ten pages. Okay, just keep your eye on the prize - two weeks, two thousand dollars; you can do this.* Anthony needs the money; without it, he will not be able to make his last semester's tuition. *Wow, they sure want a lot of information: allergies, phobias, prior surgeries, medication, military background, political affiliation, religion, next of kin; man, some of this is pretty personal. Two thousand bucks, don't forget that...two thousand bucks.*

Anthony is just finishing filling out the paperwork when a young couple comes in. He has seen them around the campus but doesn't know their names.

"Hello, my name is Ms. Camron; are you here in response to the flyer?" Ms. Camron coldly asks.

The new guy warmly pipes up, "Yes, ma'am, we are. My name is Roger Jackson, and this young lady is Rachel Moses. Are we too late?"

"No, there are still two spots available. Have a seat and fill out this basic questionnaire; once done, place it in the orange slot on the right wall," Ms. Camron says.

Anthony perks up at the mention of the right wall; didn't Ms. Camron tell Anthony the left wall? Anthony looks at the right wall, and there is an orange slot on it; he looks at the left wall, and there is also an orange slot on it. Anthony is just about ready to ask Ms. Camron which slot he is to use when the young girl asks her, "Ma'am, do we place it in that slot?" as she points to the one on the right wall.

Ms. Camron shoots the young lady a glare that is enough to make Anthony cringe, and then Ms. Camron says, "Yes, those are YOUR instructions," with that said, Ms. Camron goes back to typing on her computer while the couple sits down and begins filling out their questionnaires.

Once Anthony finishes making sure he has completed every question on the paperwork, he slowly walks over and places it into the left wall orange slot; he steals a quick look at Ms. Camron and sees a small smile on her face, he must have put it in the right slot. Anthony heads back to his seat with a sigh of relief, all the while wondering what he is getting himself into.

CHAPTER 2

Colonel Robert Johnson stares intently at the monitor; he only needs two more people for the test, and one young man is standing before Ms. Camron, maybe he will be one of the two.

"Doc, I can't believe it is all finally coming together," Colonel Johnson says to Doctor John Harrison, owner and driving force of the Harrison Research and Analytical Facility.

Doctor Harrison smiles at his friend, "It has only cost us ten years and more than a few million government dollars, but the knowledge gained from this test will be more than worth it."

Ten years ago, a retiring army psychologist approached his commanding officer with what he dubbed as the ultimate test for survivability training and the officer bit. You see, John knew that the one thing you cannot train for is the truly unpredictable; you never know how somebody is going to react until they are put into a real problem. So, John stepped out of the box; John was going to develop a test that would weed the weak from the great, and he was going to do it with civilians; unknowing green recruits actually. John decided to use civilians for the simple reason that military people expect to be tested. A recruit who thought they were still a civilian would never expect what was to come; thanks to the genius of Major Joanne Camron, the stack of authorization paperwork, and the interview process, they were becoming special government employees under the authority of the U.S. military without even knowing it.

The test idea was simple really, put a group of people into a controlled simulation, and then make them believe their simulation had become real due to a catastrophic event—in essence, fake doomsday and then unleash a doomsday upon them and see who excels, and who crashes.

John looks over at the monitor and sees the young couple come in; John definitely doesn't want couples for this test, as he figures they will not only skew the results due to protection and favoritism, but they won't be a couple by the end of the month.

"Hey Doc, two more; so now we have three for the two spots left," Colonel Johnson excitedly exclaims as he watches the monitor intensely, he wasn't his usual stoic self; he was giddy. Colonel Johnson earned this giddiness though, as he fought for seven of the ten years to get to this point; this was as much his baby as it was John's. You see, Colonel Robert Johnson was sent to take over monitoring the tests when the previous commanding officer moved on to a new assignment; the odds at the time was that the research facility would lose funding and close, but for some strange reason it has skated through funding each year untouched.

"Well, if we didn't have the issues from this morning, we would be done already," John says, referring to an earlier incident in the day concerning two of the possible recruits.

"Well, don't worry about them, they will be gone soon enough," Robert says as he tries to alleviate the concern of his friend.

While they watch the monitor, they see Major Camron admonish the young lady for her questioning of where to put the clipboard. "Well, Doc; she is a no-go; she questioned Joanne's directions," Robert says, referring to the way Joanne weeds out candidates: she will give somebody a set of precise instructions, and cull out the ones who fail to follow them to the letter.

"Good actually, you know I don't want any couples; or women," John says with slight relief.

"Doc, do you really think it could get that bad?"

"Who knows Bob," John says to the Colonel in a solemn tone. "As far as I am aware, nobody has ever done what we are about to do. Think about it: we are going to put twelve strangers in a bunker one hundred feet underground, and we are going to tell them that we are simply going to observe their interactions while they perform basic tasks for two weeks. Then we are going to fake a cataclysmic event followed by a complete disconnect for an additional two weeks while we secretly monitor their meltdown from inside. After two weeks of subliminal messaging, and with our guy inside feeding fear into them, they will think World War Three has happened, and they are the lone survivors trapped one hundred feet underground. Bob, how would you react?" John says to the Colonel.

Colonel Johnson stares at John for a moment, then quietly says as everything begins to come into perspective, "Two weeks of normal, and then two weeks of chaos; what if it gets really bad?"

"It will get bad, but if it gets too violent, Hank will pull the plug, and we will be in there in less than five minutes; and then we will all go home," John says solemnly.

Captain Hank McPherson was their inside man; an energetic young man that you would never have suspected to be a Green Beret. Captain McPherson is deceptively strong, fast, intelligent, and of average looks; he didn't look like a man who could take your life in the blink of an eye, he looked like an average thirty-something college guy.

"Doc, the single guy, finished his paperwork; do you want to bring him back now?" Colonel Johnson says as his enthusiasm comes back to him.

John looks over at his giddy colonel and smiles, "Have the major take him to interrogation room two; I will grab his paperwork."

As Robert sends a message to Joanne's computer asking her to send Anthony back, John steps out of the room and into the hallway where the clipboard is resting on the shelf below the wall slot. John flips through the pages and doesn't see any red flags; John sighs and speaks to the empty hallway, "Time to talk to Mr. Anthony Parker."

CHAPTER 3

As Major Camron finishes entering her observations of the newest candidates into the computer, the instant messaging screen pops up with a message from the Colonel, "Major, send the single gentleman back to interrogation room two, please."

Major Camron slides off her stool and walks over to Anthony, "Sir, they are ready to see you; please follow me."

As the Major walks past the young couple, she coldly states to them, "I will return shortly."

At the doorway to the hallway, the major directs Anthony, "Go to the first door on the left, enter, take the far chair on the opposite side of the table, and wait please," with that said, Anthony complies and enters the small room. The room is only about 8-foot by 8-foot with a 2-foot round table in the center, which has a small black microphone extending out of its center. Two chairs are at the table, and Anthony seats himself at the back one as he was directed.

After about five long minutes of apprehensive waiting, the door opens and a middle-aged gentleman, his salt and pepper hair cut short, comes in and warmly extends his hand, "Good afternoon Mr. Parker, I am Doctor John Harrison, owner of this facility, and the one conducting this research project. So, why do you want to be one of my guinea pigs?"

Anthony stands and nervously shakes the doctor's

hand, "Hello Doc, nice to meet you; please call me Anthony."

"Please, have a seat and relax, son," John says with a smile as he sits in his chair.

As Anthony sits back down, he relaxes a little and continues, "Why do I want to be a guinea pig? Well, Doc, I need the money to pay next semester's tuition so I can finally graduate; balancing a checkbook is not my strong suit, and I and have fallen a wee short of funds."

John smiles; at least the kid is honest, "One more semester to go? Ah yes, I see here that you are finishing up on your AA in Psychology—why psychology?"

"Well, I always wanted to know what makes people do the things they do; I figured psychology was the way to go," Anthony says as he relaxes.

Anthony's answer is the same answer John would have given an eon ago when he was out to save the world one mind at a time; John smiles, "So, is it the way to go? Have you figured out what makes people tick?"

Anthony gives a little laugh, "All I have figured out is people are unpredictable. Don't get me wrong, we all follow set patterns and habits, especially when scared; but sometimes, people break all the rules of predictability for no apparent reason."

"Very true," Anthony's words resonate deeply in John's head, *we all follow set patterns and habits, especially when scared,'* and that is what Doctor John Harrison is banking on. "Time to get to business; I am going to ask you a series of questions, and I only want yes or no answers."

"Okay," Anthony says as he straightens up.

John turns on a switch at the base of the microphone, "Candidate number 5-32, single male, age 24, psychology major, Anthony Parker."

"Mr. Parker, will you be mentally capable of being

housed underground?"

"Yes."

"Mr. Parker, will you be mentally capable of being sequestered with eleven other people for an extended period of time?"

"Yes."

"Mr. Parker, in the event of any injuries, including death, which may arise out of this study, do you hold all parties harmless?"

'Death' what am I getting myself into? Remember the money, you need this money, Anthony thinks to himself, then says, "Yes."

"Thank you, Mr. Parker, the interview is over," John switches off the mike and says, "Okay, Anthony, go down to the door at the end of the hall, enter, and wait there please."

Anthony gets up apprehensively, "That's it Doc?"

"Yes, for now; we will fill all the recruits in on the rest of the project once we have finished recruitment," John says as he leads Anthony out of the room and into the hall.

Back in the waiting room, Roger and Rachel have just finished their questionnaires. Roger takes their clipboards and places them in the right orange slot. After Roger sits back down, Rachel takes his hand in hers and quietly says to him, "Ms. Camron said there were only two slots left, and that guy hasn't come back yet. Roger, I don't want to do this without you; if only one slot is left, you take it, please."

"Don't worry hun; all will work out. Once we do this, we will have the rest of the money we need for our house. In two months, we will be married and in our first home. God has blessed us baby; we must never forget to sing His praises. His plan for us is all that matters," Roger says as he squeezes Rachel's hands as he comforts his future bride.

"I know; everything must be done for His glory," Rachel smiles as she says this; she knows their heavenly Father will take care of them no matter what.

"Mr. Jackson, they are ready for you; please come here," Joanne sternly directs Roger from her perch.

"Yes, ma'am," Roger gives Rachel's hands one last squeeze as he gives her a light kiss on the forehead, "I love you, Mrs. Jackson to be."

"I love you, Mr. Husband to be," Rachel says with a giggle as Roger heads over to the door where Joanne is standing.

At the doorway, Joanne coldly instructs Roger, "Go to the second door on the left, enter, take the far chair on the opposite side of the table, and wait please."

"Yes, ma'am, and thank you," Roger heads down the hall, enters the small room, and seats himself in the far chair.

After about five minutes, the door opens, and John comes into the room.

As Roger stands and extends his hand, John grabs it and says, "Good afternoon Mr. Jackson, I am Doctor John Harrison, and I am the one conducting this study; please, have a seat."

After Roger sits, John says, "So, why do you want to participate; what brought you here?"

Roger replies, "Well, sir, my fiancé and I came down here hoping to earn the final money needed for the down payment on our first house. You see, we will be getting married November first, and if we enter escrow on October first, we will be able to spend our first night together in our new home."

As John listens to Roger, a twinge of remorse sets in, "So, that is your fiancé with you?" John had hoped they were only boyfriend and girlfriend, not an engaged couple.

"Yes, sir," Roger states with a gleam in his eye and a smile on his face.

"Well, Roger, we only have one slot left; this means only one of you has a chance of going through. Will this be a problem; will you still be able to afford the down with only one of you going through?" John asks as he lays the facts before Roger.

"Yes, sir, I will, I have figured in a little buffer; so no sir, it will not be a problem," Roger says with a smile.

"I see here that you are a theology student; any particular following?" John asks as he tries to get back on track.

"I am a Christian, sir; Jesus Christ is my Lord and Saviour," Roger says as he sits tall.

"What denomination are you?" John inquires almost robotically as he waits for one of the usual answers.

"Non-denominational, sir; denominations are divisional, they are not biblical and only cause strife and confusion," Roger states in his calm and pleasant tone to John's surprise.

John muses on the thoughts of throwing a Bible thumper into the mix, especially this confident one; things just might get interesting, "Very well," John smiles at Roger and continues, "Let's get started. I am going to ask you a few questions, and I only want yes-no answers please."

"Yes, sir," Roger says as he straightens up and fixes his gaze upon the Doctor.

John turns on the mike, "Candidate number 5-33, single male, age 25, theology major, Roger Jackson."

"Mr. Jackson, will you be mentally capable of being housed underground?"

"Yes," Roger says as he twinges at the thoughts of being underground for two weeks.

"Mr. Jackson, will you be mentally capable of being

sequestered with eleven other people for an extended period of time?"

"Yes."

"Mr. Jackson, in the event of any injuries, including death, which may arise out of this study, do you hold all parties harmless?"

With the mention of death, Roger thinks to himself, *This study can't be that bad, this has to be a liability question.* "Yes."

"Thank you, Mr. Jackson, the interview is over," John says as he turns off the mike; he then directs Roger, "Roger, go down to the door at the end of the hall, enter, and wait there please."

"We are finished, sir?" Roger says as he thinks he must not have given the correct responses and is being sent away.

"Yes," John says with a smile as he gets up and walks out as Roger slowly rises. Once in the hallway, John walks over to his office as Roger heads out and to the end of the hall as directed. Roger stands in front of the door, not knowing what fate awaits him on the other side; he says a small prayer and opens the door.

CHAPTER 4

☙ ❧

Anthony walks down the short hall to the end door and enters the room. In the room, Anthony counts twelve others, nine guys, and three gals. As all stare at Anthony, the same bothersome thought runs through their minds, 'Twelve spots, but thirteen of us; one won't make it.'

"Howdy, my name is Karen." Standing before Anthony is a young lady, early twenties, curly blond shoulder length hair, and medium build.

"I'm Anthony," Anthony says with a smile.

A voice from the room pipes up, "We didn't expect anymore; we have the twelve." Anthony looks towards where the voice came from and sees a well-built man in his mid to late-thirties.

Anthony answers the man, "They said there were two more slots to fill when I got here."

A small-framed twenty-something redheaded boy curtly says, "They are probably expecting to weed a few culls out before all is said and done."

As Anthony decides not to feed into the little redheads trolling, he glances around and realizes he does not recognize anyone from his school, "Do you all go to UTC?"

Karen answers, "No, I am from Chat State."

"Virginia College." "No school; saw the flyer at the Y." "Unemployment office." The mixture of responses flies out as most answer at once.

"They got us from everywhere; we are diversified," Karen says with a smile.

Anthony gives a wry chuckle as he glances at the redhead, "Yes, yes we are."

Anthony surveys the room: a small podium at the front, three sets of chairs set five abreast; room for only fifteen people. Anthony takes an empty seat towards the front.

"Howdy, name is Hank. Any idea what we have gotten ourselves into?" Anthony looks at the man sitting next to him; it is the thirty-something who hollered at him when he came in.

"I have no clue, something about living together underground for two weeks. Oh, and if we die it's not their fault," Anthony says, somewhat tongue in cheek.

Hank gives a small laugh, "It never is. I think I have seen you around the campus; are you in the north dorm?"

"Yeah, I moved into it at the first of the semester; couldn't afford my apartment downtown anymore."

"I hear yah, rent is expensive around here; being a college town, they aim to milk the parents," Hank says as he quietly sizes up Anthony.

"And the college kid who is flipping his own bill," Anthony sternly states; he wants Hank to know straight out, that Anthony takes care of Anthony.

The door opens, and Anthony recognizes the young man from the waiting room, "I wonder if his girlfriend made it," Anthony says aloud.

"Huh?" Hank says as he looks over at the clean-cut kid who just walked in.

"He came in with his girlfriend right after I got here. Nice guy, quiet; one of those religious types. The Drill Sargent said only two slots were left, but three of us were in the room; if he and I are here, she is gone," Anthony says as he justifies his observation.

"Oh, okay," Hank waves Roger over as he quietly laughs under his breath – if he only knew that Drill Sargent.

As Roger comes over, Hank says to him, "Howdy. I am Hank, this is Anthony, and the lady behind you is Karen. Welcome, and have a seat."

"Thank you, my name is Roger Jackson. I am hoping my fiancé will be coming soon," Roger says as he glances over to the door.

Hank breaks the obvious news to Roger, "Roger, I don't think she will be coming. With you and Anthony here, the slots are full; we actually have two extra people here right now. According to Red, they plan on culling out the herd," Hank says as he glares at the redheaded boy.

Roger sighs, then smiles and says, "Well, all for the better. Rachel can take care of things outside while I take care of this. Two weeks isn't too long. We must always remember, all things according to God's plan."

Hank slaps Roger on the knee, "That's the spirit!"

CHAPTER 5
ᘓ ᘔ

As Rachel sits in the waiting room, alone, she quietly prays for strength. Rachel knows she won't be chosen, but she feels they will pick Roger. Two weeks away from Roger will be hard; they have been inseparable since they met two years ago at church.

Rachel lets out a little giggle as she thinks of that first meeting; a blind date AND in a church, two things she swore she would never do - go on a blind date, and step foot back in a church. Rachel's friend Donna had been painting Rachel a picture of the perfect man: levelheaded, smart, good-looking, hard worker, not a player, and a man with a life plan; he was the exact opposite of all the losers Rachel had been dating. The only drawback that he had was that he worked at a church; he was the youth pastor and the groundskeeper. You see, Rachel didn't trust religious people. When Rachel was young, her grandmother took her to a church where the preacher spent the whole sermon screaming at everyone that they were going to die and go to hell if they didn't give him money; Rachel didn't want any of that, so she swore off religion. Rachel figured if she ignored it, it wouldn't affect her; only after meeting Roger did she realize how wrong she was, in so many things.

After countless hounding from Donna, Rachel finally agreed to go out on a date with Roger. Donna said Roger did have some rules: she had to sit through one of his sermons, they had to go out as a double date, and the date would end by 9 p.m. since he had work and school the next day. Rachel still does not know why she agreed, but she did.

On that first date, Rogers sermon was based on John 3:16, and Roger presented it with such love and conviction, Rachel was moved to the point that she started questioning her earlier thoughts about religion. After the sermon, Rachel watched as Roger prayed with a young couple; they had come in bitter at their relationship and were now holding each other and saying how sorry they were.

On the date, Rachel was at first taken aback because Roger would hurry to open doors for her and pull out her chair. She told Roger she was a big girl and didn't need him or any other man doing that for her, but he told her that she deserved to be treated with respect and love at all times, and he would not demean her by not treating her like the lady she is. At the end of the date, Tom and Donna drove Roger and Rachel back to her apartment. Roger walked Rachel to her door, thanked her for such a great evening, and asked if he could see her again on the next Sunday; Rachel agreed, and Roger left.

Rachel remembered thinking how different this date was compared to the countless dates she had been on in the past; Roger was a gentleman, he was considerate of her needs, and he was there to serve and take care of her, not him. Roger was different, Roger was special, and that specialness scared Rachel.

Rachel then remembered back to the second date between her and Roger; that was the date that started Rachel to really begin thinking about what she was doing with her life.

Roger had geared the children's sermon to be a lesson on how to read the Bible; he covered things like the difference between LORD, Lord, and lord, and when you see a pronoun like Him and Me capitalized in the

Bible it is referencing God. Roger was adamant that we were always to read the Bible in context, not just a verse or two at a time. After that Sermon, Rachel asked Roger if he would teach her more later; she didn't know why she asked, but she did, and he happily agreed.

Rachel remembered going out to dinner; Roger was ever the gentlemen and let Rachel talk as much as she liked, and talk she did, much more than she had ever talked on a date, for Rachel was comfortable being with Roger, for it felt right.

Rachel remembered that Roger was happier, but more nervous around her on that date, only later did she understand why.

Rachel let out a little giggle and replayed the end of their second date in her head:

As Roger walked Rachel to her door precisely at 9 p.m., he handed her a present and thanked her for such a great date. Rachel asked if he wanted to come in, and he graciously declined with, "No ma'am, that would not be proper."

Before Rachel knew it, she blurted out, "We will spend next Sunday together. Goodnight Roger, thank you for the great night."

With that, Rachel turned and went into her apartment and headed to her room; she had one thought on her mind that scared her half to death, "I am going to marry that man."

Once inside, Rachel went to the bathroom and shakenly stared at herself in the mirror, "Rachel Marie Moses, what did you just do? Did you just act like a schoolgirl and ask Roger on a date? Girl, are you mad? Two dates and you are smitten beyond belief? Shame on you!" With that little outburst of emotion, Rachel went and lay on her bed.

While lying on the bed, Rachel realized that she still

had the present in her hand, so she slowly opened it. She knew it was a book by the way it was wrapped, and she had an idea it was probably a Bible, and low and behold, she was right. It was a beautiful brown leather Bible with three embossed crosses on the front, and on the front right bottom was Rachel's engraved name; just her first name, but room had been left for the last name, a last name longer than Moses. Through the goosebumps that were forming, Rachel wondered why Mr. Jackson might have done this.

Rachel cautiously opened the Bible, and there was a note just inside the cover:

'Dear Rachel, I pray that this Bible helps bring the true word of God into your life. I have bookmarked some key passages I think you should read, as they have helped me a lot these last few years. If you have any questions, please do not hesitate to ask; let me walk beside you on your journey to our heavenly Father. Forever yours, Roger.'

"Forever yours; really, Mr. Jackson, aren't you being a little presumptuous? This is only our second date," Rachel said out loud as she looked at the little slips of paper sticking out of the Bible: John 3:16-18, Ephesians 2:8-9, Romans 10:9-10, Romans 8:38-39, Romans 8:26, James 4:7, and much more.

Rachel stared at the Bible, and before she could stop herself, she said, "Rachel Jackson."

Through the butterflies dancing in her belly, and the explosion of goosebumps, Rachel smiled, looked up, and said, "Well, Sir, should I?" Then Rachel curled up and began reading her new homework.

As Rachel sits quietly in the waiting room, Joanne studies her. Joanne has tried to harden herself from feeling anything for the candidates; she knows that she must stay impartial; however, there is something about this young lady that makes Joanne want to yell at her to run back and grab her boyfriend and run out of this place, never to look back. However, Major Joanne Camron doesn't yell at her, she just silently makes the notation in her file,

'Does not follow directions, timid and meek – not recommended as a recruit.'

Joanne is mad at herself; she recommended this girl's fiancé; hopefully, he is not changed by the turmoil that is to follow.

As soon as Joanne enters the information on Rachel, a message pops up on her screen, "Major, please send Ms. Moses to room one."

"Miss, they will see you now," Joanne calmly says to Rachel from her perch.

Rachel snaps out of her daydream and walks over to the door to the hallway, "Thank you, ma'am. Ma'am, I know they didn't choose me, but that is okay; I have a wedding to plan."

Joanne smiles at Rachel, "Please go to the first room on the left. And good luck on your wedding."

Joanne realizes she is holding back a tear; this is not the 'stern Major' that she had fought to become.

Joanne goes back into the waiting room and begins straightening things up; soon this room would be back to its drab normal.

As Rachel enters the room, Doctor Harrison is waiting for her, "Miss Moses, I am Doctor Harrison."

"Hello sir, it is a pleasure to meet you. Please call me Rachel," Rachel says as she holds her hand out for him to shake as she stands tall before the Doctor.

"Thank you Rachel; you may call me John. It is my pleasure to meet you," John says as he gives Rachel's hand a gentle shake.

"Thank you, John. Let me save you some trouble; I know you are going to say I didn't make it, that is okay,

I feel it is for the best."

John suddenly feels a weight come off of him; he has sent many packing during this process, but he has silently dreaded the hurting of Rachel's feelings, "Why do you say it is for the best, Rachel?"

"Well, with Roger going through, I will need to get things ready by myself. Also, if I went through with him, it would probably mess up whatever study you are doing since he would be like a mother hen about me," Rachel says with a slight chuckle.

"You are right; thank you," John says, fighting to stave off the sadness he was feeling, "Well; I will not hold you up, as I know we both have a lot to do. I will ask that you do not tell anyone about this study," John pauses and holds out his hand, "It has been a pleasure to meet you Miss Moses; please, let me show you out."

"Thank you, Doctor, it has been a pleasure to meet you and Ms. Camron, you are good people," and with that, John shows Rachel out. When they pass Joanne, Rachel and Joanne share a smile and say goodbye.

As Rachel walks to her car, John goes over to Joanne, "That is a good kid," John says.

"Yeah, I feel sorry for her," Joanne says as they watch Rachel get into her car.

John raises an eyebrow, "YOU feel sorry for her?"

Joanne turns and scowls at John, "YES, I do. I hope this test doesn't change her boyfriend."

Solemnly, John says, "I hope not too; it will all depend on who he is inside."

As Rachel sits in her car, crying lightly, she knows all will work out, but she is scared of the unknown. Rachel takes a deep breath and wipes her tears away as she looks up and says, "Lord, let Your will be done, but please keep my man safe." Rachel starts her car and heads back to her apartment.

CHAPTER 6

ಛ ಝ

Jung Yong-chul tosses his keys down on the workbench just as his cell phone rings, "Hello?"

Cho is hiding in the bathroom, hoping Ms. Camron does not hear her, "Jung, this is Cho, Park's sister; we met at his wedding last May."

"Oh, hello Cho, what can I do for you?" Jung looks at his watch, 8:30 am.

"I remember you and Park talking about a traitor that you were trying to find; a Frank Jones. Are you still trying to find him?" Cho quietly says.

Jung straightens up; he definitely wants to find Frank Jones, "Yes, we are trying to find Frank. Do you know where he is?"

"Yes; he is trying to get signed up for a two-week study. If they accept him, he will be hidden for two weeks, and you will not be able to speak with him until we get released."

Jung's fury is rising; Frank only did half of what he was paid for, "Where are you at?"

"I will tell you if I can join the cause," Cho says as she refers to the main reason her family came to America.

"Of course you can; please, where is he?"

Cho is excited; finally, she will be allowed to be part of something important, "Grab a pencil and paper."

"Got it; now for the Supreme Leader's sake, address please!" Jung insists as his fights to keep his calm.

"We are at the Harrison Research and Analytical

Facility, 1213 Manufacturers Road. The testing finishes at five today, and we will be immediately locked away after that," Cho quietly says into the phone as she stares at the bathroom door.

"Thank you Cho; go now before you are found out. When you leave there, you will need to drive well out of the way before coming here to make sure you are not followed. When you leave, drive to the downtown mall and then come by our shop on the corner of Hudson and Pineville. Come to the roll-up door and honk once," Jung sternly instructs.

"Thank you, Jung, all for our Supreme Leader!" Cho exclaims then disconnects the phone; after taking a deep breath, she heads back to the waiting room.

In the waiting room, Cho looks over at Frank as she comes back into the room and thinks to herself, *He last saw me back in January when I was a blonde; I don't believe he recognizes me now, but I better be safe.*

"Frederick Samson, please come here," Ms. Camron calls out.

As Frederick goes to Ms. Camron, she says to him, "Go to the second door on the left, enter, take the far chair on the opposite side of the table, and wait please."

As Frederick judiciously leaves the room, Cho sits on the far side of the room and hides behind a magazine so that Frank does not see her. "Soon I will prove to my brother that I am a good citizen, that I have not forgotten my people," Cho says to herself as she wonders where her brother Park could be.

CHAPTER 7

附 附

Jung yells out into the warehouse, "Daniel! Kim! Come to the office, now!" Jung is livid; every time he thinks of Frank Jones, his anger boils.

Jung goes into his office and opens a secret compartment in the back of his desk drawer; from it, he angrily pulls out a red flash drive and puts it into his computer. While Jung is accessing the flash drive files, Daniel and Kim come into his office.

Kim asks Jung in his broken English, "Something the matter, sir?"

As Kim asks, Jung points a shaking finger at the monitor on the wall, "We all remember Frank Jones and how he did not fulfill his promise to us, how he stole the people's money, and how he is the reason Park is dead; don't we?"

"Yep, he set us back six months. Have you found him?" Daniel asks calmly as he stares at the monitor.

"The traitor has been found. I have been told he is only a mile from here," Jung angrily says through clenched teeth as he glares at the picture of Frank.

"You have a plan, sir?" Kim asks, even though he knows his colonel always has a plan.

"Yes; we are going to have him delivered to us. Kim, get me the private number for General Mars; this is his case, he should have the honor of giving Frank to us," Jung smiles at the deviousness of his plan.

"Yes, sir!" Kim says as he heads out of the office and

straight to his computer; from there, he methodically searches the hacked military mainframe database for General Mars personal number.

"Daniel, prepare the van for a quick mission; and load up your rifle, with a silencer!" Jung orders Daniel.

"Yes, sir!" Daniel says with a hearty smile.

Jung continues to stare at Frank on the monitor, "I told you not to cross me Frank; now you will pay."

"Sir, I have General's number!" Kim yells out as he comes running to Jung's office while waving a piece of paper before him.

Jung reaches into his top drawer and pulls out an old cell phone while taking the number from Kim. After Jung powers on the phone, he dials the number and begins speaking as soon as General Mars answers, "General Mars, the man you seek called Frank Jones is hiding at the Harrison Research and Analytical Facility." Jung pauses as he is interrupted by the General, "My name is not important, Frank Jones is. Harrison Research and Analytical Facility," Jung hangs up the phone and tosses it into a 5-gallon steel bucket that Kim has equipped with multiple electromagnets; he then places the lid on the bucket and hits the switch on the side, neutralizing the phone inside.

"Bring me my traitor General Mars, bring him to me," Jung says while staring at the screen.

"Sir, we are ready," Daniel says as he stands in the doorway.

"Let's go," Jung commands.

CHAPTER 8

Ms. Camron calls out into the waiting room, "Frank Jones, please come here."

As Frank comes before Ms. Camron, her phone rings and she quickly says to him, "Go to the first door on the left, enter, take the far chair on the opposite side of the table, and wait please."

Frank casually heads to the door Ms. Camron indicated, enters, and takes his seat.

The door opens almost immediately after Frank sits down, "Hello Frank, I am Doctor Harrison, and I will be conducting this interview."

"Hello, Doctor Harrison," Frank says from his seat.

As John quickly sizes up Frank, he says to him while still standing, "Frank Jones, why do you want to be in my study?"

"Well, sir, the money of course. Some buddies of mine and I have been planning a trip down to South America, and I am a little strapped for cash; what better way to make money than to give yourself to science?" Frank says with an arrogant smile.

John doesn't like Frank's answer or his cocky attitude, and is just getting ready to scratch him off the list when there is a knock on the door, "Excuse me for one moment, Frank."

John goes to the door knowing it must be serious since the Major has strict instructions not to interrupt.

When John opens the door, Major Camron motions

him out, "John; I am sorry for the interruption, but we need to speak in your office immediately."

"Okay," John nervously says as he and Joanne go into his office across the hall; inside, Robert is leaning against the bookcase.

"John, two of our recruits have been flagged for arrest; we must keep them here till the authorities arrive," Robert says as soon as the door shuts.

"Who, why; is there a danger to us?" John asks shocked.

"Frank Jones is one; I do not know why, but the Air Force is sending two of their MP's for him. We are told not to let him leave under his own power," Robert states, then continues, "And the other one is Margaret Penske; she is suspected of killing her boyfriend. The sheriff's office is sending two officers for her."

"Robert, are they dangerous? I have Frank in the room across the hall," John says nervously.

"I don't know what Frank did, but I wouldn't turn my back on him; if General Mars is involved, guaranteed it is something big. For Margaret, she is only dangerous if you want to date her."

"Okay smarty-pants, I will push them through," John anxiously says to Robert; Robert always jokes when he is worried about something.

John looks over at Joanne, "Major, how many have we sent back so far?"

"Three; Hank, Karen, and Frederick," Joanne says, then adds, "Should we warn Hank?"

"No way to warn him, hopefully, he won't put the moves on Margaret when she heads back," Robert jokes; Hank has been known to be a lady's man, at least in his own eyes.

"Okay, I will put Frank through now; then send me

Margaret, and I will put her through. After them, we still need nine more; keep these two out of our count."

"I will send Margaret back in five minutes; room two?" Joanne asks as she reaches for the door handle.

"Yes, room two will work; I will be quick."

CHAPTER 9

⋗ ⋖

Back in the holding room, Anthony gets to know the basics about his new acquaintances: Hank McPherson, Architecture student; Karen Mars, Nursing student; Roger Jackson, Theological Student; Cho Sang, Humanitarian Arts student, Alfonso Martinelli, History student; Jack Ramona, Culinary Arts student; Margaret Penske, Criminal Law student; Frank Jones, Radiological Technician; Harry James, Financial Consultant; Kevin Sinclair, General Education student; Max Malcolm, Dental Technician; Frederick Samson, English Major student; and Chung-Hee Chang, Asian History teacher.

While everyone is chatting away, the door opens, and Major Camron enters and announces to the room, "Margaret Penske and Frank Jones, please come with me."

Margaret pipes up, "Me, why?"

The Major stares at Margaret firmly, "Because you have been directed to do so. Please come with me now."

Without any further words, Margaret and Frank go to the door and follow Joanne out and into the Colonel's office on their left. When they enter, two military police and two sheriff officers are waiting in the room; Joanne shuts the door behind them as Margaret stares intently at the officers. Colonel Johnson is sitting behind his desk, and he addresses Margaret first, "Margaret Penske, you know why these two officers are here for you; you are wanted for the murder of your boyfriend."

"I didn't do it! And if I did, that bum had it coming! He had more girlfriends on the side than I have shoes, and I have a lot of shoes!" Margaret blurts out through an explosion of rage.

"Officers, she is all yours," with that, the two sheriffs handcuff Margaret and take her out the back door.

After the officer's handcuff and lead Margaret out, the Colonel faces Frank and coldly begins to address him, "Frank Jones," but before the Colonel can say anymore, Frank cuts him off, "I know, sir, they are here for me. It is okay guys; my work is done, and I have no fight left," Frank says as he holds his hands out for the MP's to cuff. The MP's handcuff and shackle the subdued Frank, then lead him also out the back door.

After the office is empty, through the silence Joanne looks at the colonel and quietly says, "Robert, what did Frank do?"

"I have no idea; General Mars called and said not to let him leave. I do know that he had top-level security clearance and was assigned to the Air Combat Command at Arnold." Robert says as he continues to stare at the doorway.

"I wouldn't have suspected him as a bad boy type. What did he mean by his work is done? Or that he has no fight…" Joanne's questions are cut short by the banging on the back door of the facility. Robert quickly rises, and he and Joanne go to the back door and begin to open it; only to have both MP's burst in with their sidearms drawn, "Sir, we need to contact base," one MP says to Robert as the other shuts the door to only a few inches.

"Of course. Joanne, take him to my phone, it is secure," Robert commands to Joanne as he then turns his attention to the remaining MP, "What is going on? Where is Jones?" Robert demands of the MP who is peering through the sliver of the door opening.

"Sir, Jones is dead; sniper took him out," the MP firmly states without taking his eyes away from the unknown.

"Sniper? What is going on; what did Jones do?" Robert demands as his apprehension level hits a new high.

"I don't know sir, all I know is that he is dead," the MP says to Robert. As the MP finishes scouring the surroundings, looking for the elusive sniper, he stands and says, "I believe our shooter is gone," then shuts the door as he coolly faces the Colonel.

"Sir, a removal crew, is coming and will be here in about twenty minutes; we need to secure and sanitize the scene. Do you have a place we can put Jones?" The other MP states as he comes back from using the phone.

"Yes, we can put him in the storage building on the side, but what is going on?" Robert pleads as he looks at Joanne. In all of Roberts years, he has never had to deal with anything of this magnitude; this is Hank's area of expertise, not his.

"Sir, we cannot say; protocol, sir," the senior MP firmly states as he peers out the doorway. "Colonel, Sergeant Turner and I will grab Mr. Jones body; I will need you to open the storage building," Captain Gant says and immediately hurries out the door before Robert can say a word. As Captain Gant heads into the parking lot with Sergeant Turner besides him, Robert goes straight to the storage building where he unlocks the door and opens it; once it is open, he and Joanne quickly clear an area for Frank. As the MP's carry Frank's limp body over and into the storage building, Sergeant Turner says to Robert as they lay Frank down, "Sir, we will need a pail of water or a hose to wash away the blood before anyone sees it."

"There is a hose on the side, I will grab it," Joanne says as she hurries out of the room, away from Frank's lifeless body.

"Sir, we need to secure this area if at all possible," the Sergeant says to Robert.

"Yes, of course, however, nobody inside can be bothered; today is the culmination of ten years' worth of planning, and it is being pushed by Congress; today must happen," Robert firmly states as he remembers his last meeting before the congressional oversite committee.

"Very well, sir," Major Gant says with a huff; how he despises the big brass.

As the MP's leave Robert and Frank alone in the shed, Robert looks down at Frank with pleading eyes, "Frank, who are you?" As the Colonel continues to stare at Frank, his fears and anxieties change to anger, and his anger rises to a point it has never been before; Colonel Robert Johnson is mad, for his house has been attacked, and he has no clue why, or by who.

As Robert goes back inside as the MP's finish cleaning up the scene, he says to Joanne, "I am calling General Mars, I need to update him and find out what is going on; you better update John, tactfully please."

Joanne goes over to John's office, and with a deep breath, knocks, "Hey, Joanne, just about ready to get the kids going. Did the cops take away Bonnie and Clyde?" John asks as he opens the door and lets in Joanne.

"Kind of; they took Margaret, but Frank is dead," Joanne says nonchalantly, still half in a state of shock.

"Dead?! What happened? Did she kill him too?" John exclaims in total shock as he quickly shuts the door behind them.

"No, Margaret didn't kill Frank, a sniper took him out as soon as he got outside. The MP's are cleaning up, and a crew is coming over; Robert is on the phone with General Mars trying to find out what was so important about Frank that he had to die. We have everything under control, but you need to continue with the mission,"

Joanne says as she tries to get John rooted back down.

Before John can answer, a knock on the door startles him; John turns and slowly opens the door to a tired looking Robert standing before him. As Robert silently walks into the room and plops down on John's couch, Joanne looks at him and asks, "Robert, did you find out anything?"

"Nothing … need to know is all I was told. John, General Mars seemed to know you and asked if you were okay," Robert says to John's lifeless expression.

As if a light clicks in John's head, life comes back into John's face as he looks at Robert, "General Frank Mars; he was my first commanding officer – two before you Bob. General Mars and I started this study, he moved up, Colonel Peterson came in for about a month and almost destroyed us, and then you came in and saved us," John gives Robert a smile; Robert has been the best commanding officer, and friend, John has had. "He is a good man, but definitely a 'by the book' guy. If General Mars is involved, this is major," John says, then asks, "Did the General say if we should be worried or not?" John knows if the General says to worry, he is to worry, if he says not to worry, then he can relax, for now.

"He didn't seem to think so, but he did say he was tipped that Frank was here," Robert says to his group.

"Tipped? I wonder who tipped him off and why?" Joanne asks rhetorically; so many questions are dancing through her mind, but there is nobody to answer them.

"Who knows? Oh, speaking of the General, you do know his daughter is a recruit, don't you?" John informs the Colonel and Major.

"What?! Wait a minute, Karen Mars," Robert says as he connects the last names.

"Yep, as soon as I realized it, I knew I had to push her through; it is a good chance she is a mole for him," John says as he remembers back on how General Mars liked to work all the angles.

"I was wondering why you pushed her through when I said no," Joanne says, agitated; she doesn't like to be second-guessed.

"I was going to tell you, but I haven't quite had the time yet," John says as he uncharacteristically sits on the edge of his desk.

The Colonel looks at the clock on the wall and then at John, "Doc, you better get your show going."

With a sigh, John says as he stands back up, "Yeah, time is wasting," John takes a deep breath and heads back to the holding room, "It's showtime," he sings out as he approaches the door to his remaining recruits.

As John enters the room, he hollers out, "Okay, everyone, please grab a seat and quiet down."

As everyone sits and settles down, Hank can sense something is wrong and pipes up, "Hey, where did the other two go?"

John answers Hank in his firmest of tones, "They have left. It was found they lied on their applications. This is a study based on trust; we will not have liars in this study."

John, now at the podium, grasps the sides of the podium top, squares his shoulders, and takes a deep breath as he fires off his sternest of looks, "You have all been chosen for a special study in long-term confined survival simulation. This study will see how a group of strangers will interact in a survival situation with minimal directions. You will be placed in a bunker 100 feet underground, and you will have basic survival grade food and minimal supplies, but that is all. You will be required to do all possible to extend those supplies out indefinitely. You will receive no interaction from me or anyone else upside; we will only observe and monitor from the surface. You will be simulating living in a nuclear fallout shelter post-nuclear blast. If anyone does not wish to proceed, please come up here as we will be heading down in five minutes."

Cho Sang sees her opportunity and stands up quickly and blurts out, "I didn't sign on to be buried for two weeks; you can keep your money!"

John is still rattled and just wants to get past what just happened, he doesn't have time for any garbage drama, "Cho, please come up here," John sternly directs in a tone that makes Hank take a double-look at John; John has his big-boy pants on.

As Cho comes up beside John, he firmly asks, "Anyone else?" With no answers, John instructs his recruits, "Okay; please stay seated, and I will return. Cho, come with me."

John leads Cho to one of the interrogation rooms; once inside the room, John says to Cho, "Please wait here, and I will get Ms. Camron to discharge you."

"Discharge?" Cho says surprised at the word.

"Yes, one of the papers you signed made you an employee of the federal government; your employment must be made void for you to leave," John snaps.

"Oh, Okay," Cho says as she fearfully lowers her head.

John heads out to the front and finds Joanne, "You win; Cho bailed," he says, exhausted.

"Really? The one time I wish I were wrong. The cleanup crew just showed up. Mr. Jones is heading to the land of 'need to know,' you know. Oh, they did bag his hands and feet, and they even used a Geiger counter on him; you figure that out. I do love our guys, they were quick and extremely efficient."

"They probably want to know where he has been," John says as he tries to fathom why they used a Geiger counter on Frank. "Can you discharge Ms. Sang?"

"Sure, it will be my pleasure," Joanne says sarcastically as she heads down the hall while cracking her knuckles.

As John walks back into the holding room, he heads directly to the back wall as all eyes stay fixed on his every move. As John walks towards the back, he reaches into his pocket and pulls out a small remote; he pushes a button on it, and a section of the wall lowers into the floor before him, exposing a series of twelve lockers. "Okay, everyone, take a locker; the number of your locker is also on the jumpsuit inside of the locker; this number is also your number down below. Take a jumpsuit from the locker, there are several sizes inside to choose from, and wait. Karen, once you have a jumpsuit and locker, come with me." With these directions, Karen goes over to a locker and quietly removes one that is her size, she then comes over and stands quietly beside John.

"Please remove all of your personal effects and place them in the locker; change out your street clothes with one of the jumpsuits; put your street clothes in the locker, and wait for my return," with that, John and Karen leave the room.

"Karen, you may use the restroom to change. Please bring all of your items with you, and we will put them in your locker," Karen goes into the restroom and changes; once changed, she comes back out, and they go back to the holding room.

Once John and Karen return, Karen silently places her personal items into her locker.

"You may bring one personal item with you; with some exceptions; no weapons, lighters, or drugs will be allowed," John tells the group. Roger slips his Bible into his jumpsuit as the others grab an item of their own; John and Karen walk off to speak quietly.

When John and Karen return, John pushes the button on the remote again, and the wall rises back into place, hiding the lockers behind them. John then pushes another button on the remote, and another section of wall lowers, revealing a set of elevator doors. John pushes another button and the doors open; he says, "Okay everyone, please enter the elevator and move as far to the back as possible, it will be a snug fit."

As everyone enters, John gives the final instructions, "When you reach the Bunker below, you will see a set of numbered housing pods; the number on your jumpsuit corresponds to which pod is yours. Now you will not see or hear from me for the next fourteen days. In fourteen days, the elevator doors will open in the Bunker; please enter, and we will bring you up. The elevator will only come down for two reasons: one, fourteen days have passed; or two, a severe emergency has been detected, and extraction is warranted. Remember folks that you are to place your minds into a state of survival where nothing above may exist; you are simulating that a major catastrophe has put you all down there for an unknown amount of time. You will need to grow food, interact as a cohesive unit, and pool your skills and resources; if you do not do this, you will not be paid. Heed all directions and survive folks," John shuts the elevator doors before anybody can say anything.

As the doors shut, Anthony says to Roger, "What are we getting ourselves into?"

As the elevator starts moving downwards, Roger attempts to comfort Anthony by telling him, "It's only two weeks, it won't be too bad; God will protect us."

Hank sees his chance to plant his first seed of doubt, "Unless they know something we don't know. Dude, never trust the government," Hank says with a smug smile.

Anthony and Roger look at Hank, who then says, "Just saying." The little-redheaded guy turns and stares at Hank with a leer.

"Don't worry Harry; you know I am only joshing you," Hank smiles at Harry James and thinks to himself, *Short, redheaded, freckles; this little guy is a firecracker waiting to explode.*

After a few moments, the elevator comes to a stop and the doors open, "Honey, I'm home!" Hank hollers out as he starts moving towards the front of the elevator, effectively ushering everyone out.

As the last person steps out and away from the elevator, the doors close and the elevator heads back up.

Anthony starts surveying his new home:

They are standing in a large cave, approximately 100 feet wide and 300 feet long. The room is actually well lit, with the light shining down from the ceiling; it does not appear to be from electric lights, but from multiple tubes funneling sunlight down. Along the right side of the bunker is twelve 8-foot by 8-foot buildings connected together; above the doors of each one is a small sign stating, Pod 1, Pod 2, etcetera, all the way to the last one marked Pod 12. Along the back wall where the elevator came down, is a series of buildings with signs above them reading, Supply Room 1, Supply Room 2, etcetera, all the way to Supply Room 9. On the left wall, there is a 12 foot, three door, raised building with a bicycle-like contraption on one end, and two large stacked drums on rollers beside the contraption. Above this large set-up is a sign stating COMPOSTING LATRINE. About ten feet past the latrine are two large upright round tanks with a small three-foot wide building between them with a sign above the door that says SHOWER, and another bicycle-like apparatus beside the tanks. On the right wall about ten feet past Pod 12, a channel of water is flowing out of the wall towards the center of the room, then it turns and goes straight into the far wall directly in front of them.

On the far edge of the large, well-lit expanse in front of them is two large sheds, one on each side of where the water flows back into the wall. Approximately 15 feet in front of them is a post with two signs on it:

"ATTENTION RECRUITS"

"Any illegal activity will be dealt with appropriately upon retrieval.

Compensation will only be paid in the event ALL of the Bunker Rules are followed:"

"BUNKER RULES"

- Each recruit will be housed in the pod living quarters that correspond to the number on their uniform.
- Only one recruit per pod.
- A garden shall be planted and tended. At the end of the stay, a self-sufficient garden must be present.
- All tools shall be kept in good repair.
- The composting system shall be fully utilized.

As everyone reads the signs, Jack Ramona voices what is on everyone's mind, "Now this just got real."

CHAPTER 10

03 80

As Kim parks the van across and down the street from the back of the research facility, Jung explains his plan, "In a few moments, the MP's will arrive. Once they go in, we must be ready. Daniel, as soon as they come out, you will remove the traitor's life, but only kill Jones." Jung sternly says as he looks down at his watch, 9:33 a.m.

"Yes, sir!" Both Kim and Daniel acknowledge in unison.

"Don't forget; Frank is the reason Park got killed," Jung says as he turns in the passenger seat and locks eyes with Daniel who stares coldly back at him.

As they watch people come and go, Jung looks at his watch: 4:45 pm, they have been here for over seven hours.

"Sir, are we sure of our informant?" Daniel asks as he watches out of the small side window of the van.

"Yes, it is Park's sister," Jung quietly says as he stares up the street. "Look, a police car is coming!" Jung exclaims.

"Unmarked car coming from behind," Kim says as Daniel chambers a round into his rifle and opens the side door just enough to fit the first couple of inches of his silenced rifle through.

"Wait; let us see what is going on," Jung commands; Jung knows that for this mission to work, there is no room for error.

As they watch the two cars park side by side towards the back of the building, they see two officers get out and speak with the two MP's, just as a woman comes out of the building and addresses all four, "Something not right; why all them?" Kim nervously says as they watch Joanne lead her party inside the building.

"Be ready," Jung commands.

Jung looks at his watch: 5:12 pm. When Jung looks back up, he sees a handcuffed younger woman walking out in front of the uniformed officers towards their cruiser. "Stations!" Jung commands as he hears Daniel take a deep breath while they watch the two officers put Margaret in the back seat of their car and drive off.

"Ready. As soon as you have a shot, take the traitor out," Jung commands. Jung is not worried about his men as they are the elite of the elite; the Supreme Leader wanted the best for this mission, and that is what Jung got.

Through Daniel's scope, he sees a solemn Frank being led out by the two MP's. Daniel sets the crosshairs right on where his old acquaintance's heart should be and squeezes off a shot just as the doors of the facility close. As Daniel watches Frank fall limp to the ground, he immediately places a second shot into Frank's lifeless body, "Done," Daniel says without an ounce of remorse as the two MP's dive behind their vehicle while drawing their sidearms.

"Kim, let's go," Jung commands as Kim slowly drives away.

"Definite kill sir," Daniel tells Jung as he puts his rifle away.

"Yes, I will confirm when I hear the report, but I agree the traitor is dead," Jung is pleased of his successful mission, but mad that it had to be done at this time, and in this way. Jung had planned to kill Frank from the beginning, but only after Frank supplied the arming codes to the warhead, he and Park had stolen. If Frank had complied, Park would not have been caught in the ensuing hunt and killed by the imperialists, and this inconvenience would have been avoided.

Kim drives several miles out of the way before returning to the warehouse about an hour later. Kim hits the opener on the visor, and the large roll-up door opens; Kim then drives in and shuts the door behind him.

"It is 6:30, secure everything and change the plates on the van. Oh, and Park's sister will be here shortly," Jung says to them as he walks towards his office.

"Sir, she is coming here?" Daniel warily asks.

"Yes, she will take Park's place," Jung says as he turns and faces Daniel, "Will that be a problem?"

"No, sir," Daniel says. Having Park's sister around will change things; women always change things, women are problems.

CHAPTER 11

❦

As Rachel parks her car in the apartment complex garage, she looks at the empty spot next to hers; Roger's place. Once Roger and Rachel had realized they were in it for the long haul and there was no turning back, Roger rented the apartment next to Rachel's as soon as it became available.

Rachel heads up to her apartment and goes in and says out loud, "Two weeks, I can do two weeks; I have a wedding to finish planning!" Rachel tosses her keys onto the breakfast bar and heads into the living room where she sits down on the small couch; Roger always teases her about her couch, he tells her it is a big chair and not a couch. As Rachel stares at the couch, she daydreams back to their third date, the exact turning point of her life:

Rachel, Donna, and Tom showed up at the church at 10:30, fifteen minutes before the service. As they walked in, Roger came over and excitedly greeted them, "Rachel, thank you so much for coming!"

"It is nice to see you, Pastor," Rachel says to Roger as she looks into his warm eyes.

"Please Rachel, call me Roger; I am only a youth pastor, I lead the 'wild ones,'" Roger says with a chuckle. "Rachel, you look lovely today," Roger says before he can stop himself.

As Rachel blushes, she says, "Thank you, sir, you look very handsome yourself."

"Why thank you. Donna and Tom, thank you for

coming also," Roger says as he tries to regain his composure.

"Come on Donna; they are getting all mushy on us; let's go grab a seat before we get stuck up front," Tom says to Donna as he looks towards the church hall entrance.

"Yes, sir! Rachel, will you be at our service or the 'wild ones' service?" Donna says with a Cheshire grin.

"Go ahead, I think I will go to the 'wild ones' service," Rachel says with a giggle.

"Oh my, please don't let anyone know I called their little angels 'wild ones', they will run me out of town," Roger says with a serious look on his face.

"Don't worry sheriff; your secret is safe with us," Rachel assures Roger as she holds her arm out for him to take.

"That's our clue Tom, lead me to the pews!" Donna holds her arm up for Tom to take as she stands there.

"Okay; hey, what's the matter with your arm?" Tom questions as he begins walking into the church while Donna stays back with her arm at half-staff.

"NOTHING is wrong with my arm, you are supposed to take it and lead me; a GENTLEMAN always takes a lady's arm!" Donna states adamantly.

"Oh, Okay," Tom says as he turns and grabs Donna's arm and drags her into the church.

As Roger takes Rachel's arm gently into his, he says, "Miss Moses, please come with me to the room of angelic children."

"My pleasure, Mr. Jackson," Rachel giggles as they head arm in arm into the children's room.

As Roger and Rachel enter the small classroom, some of the younger children run up to Roger and give him a hug. One little blonde headed girl with the biggest brown eyes looks up at Rachel and says, "Ma'am, you were here last week with our Mr. Jackson; are you his Mrs. Jackson?"

As Roger blushes to the point of a beautiful shade of red, Rachel bends down to the little girl and says, "No, ma'am, I am not Mrs. Jackson, but I am a good friend of his; you may call me Miss Moses. What is your name, hunny?"

"You may call me Miss Betty. Are you ever going to be Mrs. Jackson?" Miss Betty firmly asks while Rachel's heart melts as she looks into her eyes.

"That will all depend on Mr. Jackson," Rachel says as she looks up at him, "The ball is in his court," As the words flow out of Rachel's mouth, she is more shocked than Roger. Rachel looks up at Roger and sees a smile appearing on his face as his flush subsides.

"Mr. Jackson, Miss Moses wants to play ball with you, and it is your turn," Little Miss Betty says to Roger, her hands on her hips.

"Yes Betty, it appears so," Roger says, barely containing his laughter; out of the mouth of babe's the truth will flow, and this little one has quite the mouth.

"Okay everyone, let's get seated. Rachel, you can sit up here with me," Roger says with a warm smile.

"Children, today we are going to talk about the most dangerous weapon known to mankind; the tongue," as all the kids look at Roger with upraised eyebrow's, he goes on, "Think about it, how many times have you said something and immediately wished you hadn't said it? Once we say something, we cannot un-say it," Roger glances at Rachel to see her reaction, and she smiles at him.

"The Bible tells us that we can build up people with our words, or we can destroy them. Almost all wars and fights are because of what somebody says. Have you ever said something just to hurt the person you are talking

to? Was that a good, or a bad thing to do?" Betty slowly raises her hand.

"Yes, Betty?" Roger says to his star pupil and dating advisor.

"I have, and it was not good; they cried," Betty says as she hangs her head lowers her arm.

"No Betty, it is not good to hurt others. The Bible tells us that we have to watch what we say, always. When we hurt somebody, what are we supposed to do?"

"Tell them we are sorry and not to do it again," little Jimmy excitedly pipes up.

"Correct Jimmy; and remember to raise your hand," Roger says as he gently guides Jimmy.

"Yes, sir," Jimmy says with a knowing smile.

"So when we hurt somebody we are supposed to apologize and not do it again. Who do we apologize to?"

Little Jimmy's hand shoots up.

"Yes, Jimmy? And thank you for raising your hand." Roger says as he reinforces Jimmy's good behavior.

"To them!" Jimmy beams.

"Is it only to them? What about to God?" Roger asks the group as he lets his eyes float around the room.

A young teen, barely thirteen, raises his hand.

"Yes, Harold?"

"Why God?" Harold says with a worried look on his face.

"Well, Harold, I am glad you asked. When we hurt others, whether by what we say or do, we hurt God. To hurt others is a sin, and we know that sins hurt God." Roger says as gently as he can, for he does not want Harold to go silent on him.

Harold raises his hand again.

"Yes, Harold?"

"Does the Bible say that, sir? Does the Bible say sins hurt God?" Harold fearfully asks as he is barely able to *make eye contact with Roger.*

Roger can see that this lesson is actually getting through to Harold. Roger had heard that Harold has started bullying others; this is why Roger picked this subject for today.

Roger quietly reaches beside him and picks up his Bible and turns to his first bookmark. "First, thank you, Harold, for asking for Scriptural references; we must always remember to test all teachings against Scripture as is directed by the Scriptures; we must never add to or take away from the Scriptures, for that is a sin unto itself."

*As Roger lets that sink in to everyone, he takes a deep breath and says, "Now, let us open our Bibles to Genesis 6:5-6, where we read, **'When the LORD saw that man's wickedness was widespread on the earth and that every scheme his mind thought of was nothing but evil all the time, the LORD regretted that He had made man on the earth, and He was grieved in His heart.'** This says the sins of mankind grieved God's heart, it made Him very, very sad. Now later in the Bible at **Romans 4:25**, it says, 'He was delivered up for our trespasses and raised for our justification.' This verse is about Jesus. God became a man so that He could suffer for our sins; Jesus suffered for each sin you have done and will do. So, every time you sin, Jesus suffered for that sin," Roger sees that a few of the children are starting to tear up, so he looks over at Rachel and says, "Miss Moses, what does first John 1:9 say?"*

Rachel looks at Roger, not knowing exactly where to go. Roger reaches over and opens her Bible to 1 John 1:9, "There you go, I see I need to show you a few tricks on finding chapter and verse," Roger says with a smile.

"Yes, you do, sir. You promised to walk with me on my journey," Rachel says, smiling as Miss Betty giggles in

the audience.

Roger quickly says, "Miss Moses, what does first John, chapter 1, verse 9 say?"

*Rachel looks at the page Roger had turned her Bible to and sees a little nine before a verse. She cautiously reads the verse out loud, **"If we confess our sins, He is faithful and righteous to forgive us our sins and to cleanse us from all unrighteousness."***

"Splendid Miss Moses, splendid. Now, what does that mean to you?" Roger asks in his calmest of tones.

Rachel thinks for a moment and says, "Well, if we tell God that we sinned, and we are really sorry, He forgives us and wipes away our sins," Rachel begins thinking about this quite hard.

"Very good Miss Moses! If we tell God we have been bad and promise to do better; He forgives us. But we have to mean it; we can't cross our fingers behind our back when we talk to God because He sees all. So Harold, as you can see, sins hurt God. However, if we ask for forgiveness and promise to do better, God forgives us. Now, I want everyone to think of how they might have made God sad in the past. Once you remember, I want you to say a quiet prayer to God and ask Him to forgive you for each one of the bad things you have done. I want you to promise Him you will do better, but only promise Him if you truly mean it, for He will know if you do not mean it."

As the children all bow their heads in prayer, Roger looks over at Rachel; her head is down, her hands are tightly together, and a tear is hanging on the bottom of her closed eyes. With a lump in Roger's throat, he hangs his head in prayer also.

After a few moments, Roger looks up to see the children finish with their prayers. Roger looks over at Rachel and sees she is just raising her head; she looks fresh and new. As he smiles at the beautiful young lady next to him, he again addresses the class,

"Okay, so we see that what we say can hurt others, but the Bible also says it can help and heal others. How can it do that?"

Jimmy raises his hand.

"Yes, Jimmy?"

"By telling somebody, they did a good job on something," Jimmy says as he remembers a moment from his life.

"Excellent, Jimmy; most excellent," Roger gives Jimmy a big smile.

Betty raises her hand way up.

"Yes, Betty?" Roger says cautiously.

"By telling someone you love them," Betty says with a smile aimed at Rachel.

"Excellent, Betty. When we care for someone, we need to tell them before it is too late," Rachel says as she looks at Roger.

*Roger begins to blush and says through a gulp, "One last Proverb I shall leave you all with today, **Proverbs 16:24, 'Pleasant words are a honeycomb: sweet to the taste and health to the body.'"** Roger smiles at Rachel and then says, "So, what have we learned today?"*

Harold raises his hand as he looks Roger straight in the eyes.

"Yes, Harold?"

"We hurt God when we pick on others, but we make God happy when we build others up. We must watch what we say," Harold says with a heavy and convicted heart.

"Yes, Harold; when we hurt others, we are sinning. When we sin, we hurt God. We must always say we are sorry and ask for forgiveness, and we must pray that we do not do it again," Roger says with a compassion that almost makes Rachel cry.

From the middle of the group, little Billy's hand shoots straight up and begins waving frantically.

Surprised that quiet Billy wants to say something, Roger says, "Yes, Billy?"

"And you have to mean it; no crossed fingers!" Billy says excitedly as he enunciates each word with enthusiasm.

"Yes, sir, Billy, no crossed fingers!" Roger says back to Billy with his voice full of joy.

"Okay everyone, let's clean up the room and get ready to go," Roger says to his class with a smile.

As everyone gets up and begins picking the toys up and putting them away, Harold goes over to Roger, "Thank you, sir," he says through heavy eyes.

"You are welcome, but why are you thanking me, Harold?" Roger calmly asks.

"For showing me I was messing up, but that I can make it right," Harold says as he hangs his head.

"Thank you, Harold. It is a good thing to admit when you are wrong; it is noble to right the wrong, and you will be noble," Roger says as he single pats Harold on his shoulder while looking him straight in his eyes.

As Harold walks away with the knowledge that he was going to go and do the noble thing, Rachel says to Roger, "You are a good teacher; thank you."

"Thank you. But now why are you thanking me?" Roger says as he stares into Rachel's eyes.

"Because, you not only showed me how messed up my life has been, but you have shown me that now I have a real promise of a new life; I have the promise of eternal salvation. You have shown me that Jesus died for me, and He doesn't care how messed up I am," As Rachel says this, they both begin to tear up.

"Did you get all of that out of this little lesson?" Roger asks in a confused tone.

"No, from the verses you gave me to read, and things you have said, and the way you have acted. Roger, you are different than others, you actually care, and I don't want to offend you, but your care goes beyond any human care, it has to come from something greater," Rachel says as she stares at Roger with bright eyes.

"You are very right, my ability to care and love comes from the One who is greater than all, and you can have that same ability through His love for you," Roger says with a smile. *"Can we go for a walk in the park after Donna and Tom finish?"* Roger quickly asks Rachel.

"Of course; why don't you finish up with the 'wild ones,' and I will check on our chaperones," Rachel says to Roger as she regains her composure.

"Please, quiet on the 'wild ones,' they repeat EVERYTHING; especially Betty," Roger begs Rachel as he wipes his eyes clear.

Rachel smiles and walks out into the service hall; she turns and smiles at Roger and says, "You will be a good father also," she then turns, again shocked at what has come out of her mouth.

"Hey, you guys ready?" Tom asks Rachel as she comes out of the classroom.

"Yep, I was just coming to get you two to see if you wanted to go for a walk in the park," Rachel says as she shoots them both a beaming smile.

"Sure, we can do that," Donna says as she tries to read the joyous look on Rachel's face.

"Wait a minute, they can walk, and we will feed the pigeons," Tom says as he picks at the edge of his fingernail.

"Ugh, why do I keep you around?" Donna asks as she rolls her eyes at Tom.

"Because I am cute, manly, smart, humorous, fun to be around, cute, and incredibly modest," Tom says as he

stands as tall as he can while he continues to fidget with his finger.

"Oh my, how can I contain myself around you?" Donna asks as she rolls her eyes again, "Oh, and you said cute twice."

"That is because I am doubly cute; I am adorable, kinda like a fluffy puppy. Now, let's get these kids to walking so we can get our sit on," Tom says with a grin.

"Why don't we walk too, why sit and feed birds?" Donna asks as she stares at Tom.

"The human body has only so many steps in it; do you want me to waste mine without reason? I have already got the best gal around, I don't need to be wasting steps trying to impress you now," Tom says to Donna as he finally takes care of his finger issue.

"Wasted steps? Already have me? I don't see a ring on this finger, mister; you might want to waste a few more steps," Donna scolds Tom then says, "Tom, go wait outside, I need to talk to Rachel for a moment; girl issues."

Tom immediately heads for the door, "Say no more, I don't want to hear about any girl issues," Tom says as he goes outside.

"Okay, chicky, what gives?" Donna asks Rachel.

"What do you mean?" Rachel says, knowing full well what Donna is talking about.

"You have been on two and a half dates with this guy, and now you have that look about you; the look I was afraid I never would see on you. Your glowing, girl; have you fallen for Roger?" Donna asks as she hits Rachel with a piercing stare.

Rachel blushes and tries to look away before Donna sees her.

"You have!" Donna quietly exclaims as she grabs both of Rachel's hands.

""He is different. I am so relaxed around him; it is scary. When he talks, I melt. When he looks at me, I melt. When he plays with the kids, I melt. I know this will sound stupid, but I know I am going to marry him, and I think he feels the same way. He gave me a Bible with just my first name on it, but room for a long last name!" Rachel says with dancing eyes.

"Well, he is a great guy. And the kids love him, especially the little blonde," Donna says.

Rachel gives a little chuckle, "Do you think she is competition?"

"No, I believe he has enough love for you and all the kids," Donna says, smiling.

"Love," Rachel says quietly. "Okay, I will go get him; you go whup on yours," Rachel says as Donna spins and goes out the door cracking her knuckles.

Rachel heads back into the classroom, and Betty comes over and gives her a hug, "Miss Betty, did you want extra hugs?" Rachel asks Betty as she hugs her back real tight.

"Of course, I love hugs!" Betty giggles.

"Well, here, I better give you a super-duper, non-wearer offer hug!" Rachel tells her as she picks her up in a big hug.

"Thank you for making Mr. Jackson smile from the inside," Betty says as she leans back in Rachel's arms and stares into Rachel's eyes with her big brown doe-eyes.

"You are very welcome. But, I was just returning the favor; he has made me smile from the inside," Rachel says to Betty.

"I know that," Betty giggles as Rachel sets her back down.

"Miss Betty, your mother, is waiting for you," Roger says as he stands in the doorway with his hands on his

hips as he tries to appear stern.

"Yes, sir," Betty says as she runs over and hugs Roger. Roger looks at Rachel and sees her smiling at him, a smile that is more with the eyes than with the mouth. Roger smiles back and gives Betty a big hug back, "Go little one; I will see you later!"

"Love ya!" Betty hollers as she skips out of the room.

Rachel comes up to Roger and says, "Well, the kids are done with their fellowship and are ready to go sit while we walk."

"Sit?" Roger asks with one raised eyebrow.

"Tom made some statement about the human body only has so many steps in it before it dies. He says he has already gotten his girl, so he is not going to waste those steps with senseless walking," Rachel says.

"Did you call an ambulance for Tom?" Roger asks after thinking for a moment.

"No, but we might need to. But this does raise quite the question: if walking is a form of courtship Mr. Jackson, are you courting me?" Rachel says as she stares deep into Roger's eyes.

"Well, Miss Moses," Roger stammers and then pauses, "I would like that immensely if you will have me; but please do not answer till after our walk," Roger says with a pleading earnestness in his eyes.

"Okay, we will walk first, answer second," Rachel says as her mind tries to figure out what is going on.

"Thank you," Roger says with a smile.

"Hey, are you kids ready or not?" They both look over and see Tom and Donna standing in the doorway.

"Come on guys, Tom needs to sit on the park bench and practice feeding the pigeons," Donna says as she jabs Tom in the stomach.

"Yeah, what the love of my life said," Tom says with a wince.

Okay, let's go," Roger says as he gently takes Rachel's hand; Donna gives Rachel a smile that Rachel returns.

The drive to the park is quick, as it is only a few blocks away from the church. As the chaperones saddle up on a park bench and try to coax the pigeons over, Rachel and Roger begin the walk around the path, "Rachel, before I officially ask to date you, I think there are a few things you need to know about me," Roger says to Rachel.

Rachel thinks to herself, 'Oh man, I knew this was too good to be true; he is either gay or married.' Rachel looks at Roger as they walk, "Okay, start telling me about your other wives and children."

"Oh, nothing like that, but I do have a past," Roger says as he takes a deep breath and begins, "I grew up in a godless, loveless, angry home. Mom was never home, and when she was she was drugged up; she wound up overdosing when I was twelve. Dad is listed as John Wayne on my birth certificate, but the Duke was only in reruns by the time I was born. My sister was stabbed by a drug-crazed boyfriend and died in my arms when I was six; she was so out of it, she didn't even realize she was dying. I was put in the system and wound up spending time in foster care and juvie up until I was seventeen."

"Oh Roger, I am so sorry," Rachel says with tears in her eyes, "What happened when you were seventeen?" Rachel pleads.

"Thank you, but please don't feel sorry for me, I have done enough of that for both of us," Roger takes a deep breath and continues, "At sixteen, I died while trying to snatch a purse in this park; I was shot by a 65-year-old great-grandmother. She didn't mean to, the pistol was in her purse, and when I grabbed the purse, she instinctively reached in and grabbed it; she pulled the trigger as I jerked the purse towards me, it fired and put a bullet right into my heart." Roger pauses as he

remembers, then continues, "I spun around and fell flat on my back, dying; as I lay dying, I felt her hand on my chest as she began praying to this Jesus guy to save me. She said how she was sorry for what she had done; she asked for forgiveness for both her and me, she begged Jesus for my life.

As I lay there slipping away, she kept asking me if I was saved, if I knew Jesus. I told her, no, and she began to tell me about this great Man who died for my sins because He loved me. She was persistent; I am confident that she explained the entire Bible in about one minute. I fought her at first; the demons in me were dancing with joy since I was dying unsaved. But then I heard a voice that said, 'Roger, I love you; believe in Me, and you will be saved.' When I heard that voice, the calm that came over me was unbelievable. I remember looking up at this distraught Dirty-Harriett, and saying, 'I believe.' She asked me to pronounce that Jesus Christ was my Lord and Saviour and that I repent of all my past sins; and I did, at least in my head I did. When I did that, I felt a rush over my body, then darkness as I slipped away."

Roger paused a few seconds and then continued as they walked, "The next thing I remember was lying handcuffed to a hospital bed. I looked around the room, and beside the bed in a chair asleep, was Dirty-Harriett. I found the button for the nurse and pushed it; and when the nurse came in, I quietly asked her about my guest."

Roger smiles and continues, "The nurse told me that Dirty-Harriett had not only dialed 911 after shooting me, but she also applied pressure to my wound to keep me from bleeding out while praying for me. The nurse said she insisted on riding in the ambulance with me; she prayed for me all the way during the ride and all the way to the emergency room where they had to pull her away. One of the officers told her she would not be charged if

I died, and she said that she did not care about her life, she only cared about mine."

As Roger stifles a tear, he keeps going, "Spoiler alert, I lived. The doctors later told me that they only worked as hard as they did on me because of her; they said if she cared for me so much, then I must be mighty special to her. They got my heart patched and had to restart it a few times. They called it a miracle that I lived since the bullet actually lodged in the outer muscle of my heart; I later said it was because my heart had become so hardened, not even a bullet could penetrate it, only later did I realize differently."

Rachel feels Roger squeeze her hand; she knows he is thinking of something special, "Well, I healed up pretty fast; I had a great prayer team on my side that I didn't even know about. The nurse went on to tell me that I had been in the hospital for over a month, and Dirty-Harriett had been at my side every day. She said when she wasn't at my side; she was down at the courthouse pleading my case to anyone who would listen."

As Roger stifles back the tears, he says, "I tried to rob her, and she saved me. I didn't know her from Adam, and she fought for me," Roger pulls out a hanky and blows his nose, "How romantic," he chuckles.

"Well, the nurse left, and Betty woke up, and we talked for quite a long time. Miss Betty spoke of all the greatness of God, and I soaked it in. We talked, she read the Bible aloud, and we discussed well into the night until the nurse made us both go to sleep."

"Miss Betty?" Rachel asks with a questioning look as she thinks back to the little blonde in class.

"Yes, our little Miss Betty's great-grandmother, her namesake, put a cap in me," Roger smiles as Rachel stares in disbelief.

Roger takes a deep breath and goes on, "Well, it

was time for me to be transferred to jail, I had given a full confession to the officers; I told them about every crime I had committed that I could remember. They were shocked at my honesty, but like I told them, I must confess my sins. They charged me with burglary and robbery, several counts, and then I went to court. I expected to get the book thrown at me, to spend years in prison; I was ready to pay the price that I owed."

Roger takes another deep breath, "When I was led into court, I noticed the courthouse was packed, standing room only. I thought, 'Oh man, did I hurt all of these people?'

The bailiff called my name and read off the charges. The judge looked at me and asked if I had anything to say. I turned and faced the courtroom and asked for their forgiveness. I explained that the person who robbed them was the old me, and I was a new child of God now. I told them I deserved any sentence that the courts would give me, as a man must pay the price for his offenses. I then began speaking of the greatness of Jesus and how He had saved me; I spoke of Betty and her love for me, and mine for her; I then begged that the people in the courtroom seek the love of our heavenly Father and accept Jesus Christ as their personal Lord and Saviour. Then, the judge asked me to be quiet and face him. I turned and held my head down to him, and he said, 'Before I hand down judgment, I have been told that a few members of the court wish to speak.' This was when I figured I would be chastised, but it didn't happen that way. Miss Betty stood up and pleaded my case, and plead it she did. Once Miss Betty finished, the judge asked if there were any more wishing to speak; with that, each person in the courthouse came forward to plead for leniency; they pleaded for me, yet they did not know me."

Roger wipes away a tear, "After about a half-hour, the

judge stopped the pleadings and asked if anyone wanted to plead for anything other than leniency; nobody came forward.

The judge retired to his chamber, came back out about a half-hour later, and said, 'Roger, it says here you died on the operating table, is that right?' I said yes. The judge then said, 'Roger, you claim that you are born-again; do you know the true penalty you face if you are lying about this, and I am not speaking of a physical penalty,' I again said yes. He then said, 'Roger, since you died on the operating table and have been born-again as a new creation, and because of everything these great people have said for your sake, I am commuting your sentence to time served for all crimes except the attempted robbery of Mrs. Jackson. For that crime, you will be required to perform one-thousand hours of community service at the Haven Church; your new foster parent knows the location,' and with that, the judge slammed his gavel. As I stood there dumbfounded, he looked into the courtroom and said, 'Mrs. Betty Jackson, will you please come claim your charge; he is being released into your custody.' When the judge said that, I lost it and broke down and cried like a baby."

"Betty's great-grandmother became your foster parent?" Rachel asked in shock.

"More than that, she adopted me one month before my 18th birthday; Betty became my new mom. Little Miss Betty is my grandniece. Here is something you will not hear very often: if it weren't for a pistol-packing great granny killing me, I would never have found the Lord, a new mom, and a new life."

"Unbelievable, utterly unbelievable," Rachel stops and stares at Roger through tear soaked eyes.

"It is true, though, I will never lie to you," Roger says through teary eyes.

"So the Lord saved your life," Rachel says quietly.

"When I accepted the Lord, He saved my eternal soul," Roger says, and then adds, "I like to think He had a hand in stopping that bullet; a hand in guiding the surgeons; a hand in saving my physical life; I won't know until the day I am before His glory and splendor, and then I may not care. Ever since that day, I have had a feeling there is something He wants me to do for Him."

"Like what?" Rachel asks.

"I don't know, yet, but He will guide me and let me know when the time is right," Roger says with a smile.

"How can you be sure?" Rachel asks as she stares into Roger's eyes.

"Faith, my dear, faith. The Bible tells us that with the faith of a child, we are to believe in the Lord. Today, people have more faith in the brakes of their car than they do in the power of God," Roger says with a shake of his head.

"It shouldn't be that way; should it?" Rachel asks.

"No, it shouldn't. If you do not have faith that the Lord will take care of you, you do not truly believe in who the Lord is; if you do not truly believe, then you are not saved and will surely die," Roger says seriously.

"There is so much for me to learn, I don't know if I can," Rachel says as she hangs her head.

"You can if you believe. When you truly believe and accept Jesus Christ as your personal Saviour, He sends the Holy Spirit to help you on your journey to Him. God will also put other Brothers and Sisters in your life to help guide you, to show you the way to the Father through the Son," Roger says, smiling, glowing.

"Good, I need a guide," Rachel says with a smile, Rachel then adds, "Is there anymore gun toting grandmas in your past I need to know of?" Rachel asks Roger as they stand on the trail.

"No, I think that is it. Is my history too much for you? The old me was loaded with many demons, but the blood of Jesus has cast them away and made me new."

"It is not too much for me. I thank you for your testimonial," Rachel says as she looks away.

"Rachel, is everything alright?" Roger asks in a scared tone.

"Roger, my past is bad too," Rachel says as the tears form as she thinks of the things she has done.

"Rachel, when you fully accept Jesus Christ as your Lord and Saviour, when you confess it with your mouth and proclaim His greatness and that He defeated death, when you accept the gift He gives you freely, when you repent of your sins and ask His forgiveness; you are born-again as a child of God, and your old self is gone; you are a new creation. Rachel, will you accept Jesus Christ as your Lord and Saviour?" Roger says as he stares pleadingly into Rachel's eyes.

"I do," Rachel says between tears.

"If you actually mean it, then say it out loud, proclaim it for all to hear; but if you are unsure, don't do it yet," Roger says as he stands before Rachel.

"Jesus Christ is my Lord and Saviour, He died on the cross and rose three days later after defeating death, He is the Son of the Father, He is God. Jesus; please God, forgive me for all of my sins and forgive me for not knowing You. Please, Father, accept me as Your child and lead me," Rachel says through tear-filled eyes.

Roger grabs Rachel and hugs her tightly, not letting go of her as he feels her break down and cry, "It is okay Rachel, all will be better now," he says to her.

"I know it will, that is why I am crying; I am so happy!" Rachel says to Roger through tears and a smile.

Roger kisses her on the forehead and drops to one knee, "Miss Rachel," Roger starts to say.

"Oh no Roger, don't you dare!" Rachel says in a raised voice as she grabs his hands and tries to pull him up.

"Miss Rachel, I would like to ask permission to court you," Roger says sniffling with a wry smile.

"Oh, really? Well, Mr. Jackson, you will need to inquire my father on this subject; it is only proper," Rachel says with a half smirk as she wipes away the tears and tries to compose herself.

"Yes, you are correct. Miss Moses, do you happen to have his number available?" Roger asks as he stands back up.

Rachel, feeling Roger is only testing her, says, "Of course, let me call him for you," as she dials her father on her phone, Roger does not blink.

"Hi Daddy," Rachel says when her father answers.

"No Daddy, I don't need any money. Daddy, a young gentleman would like to speak to you," Rachel says as she hands Roger the phone; all the while expecting him to hang up on her father.

"Mr. Moses sir, my name is Roger Jackson," Roger says as he stares into Rachel's eyes, "Mr. Moses, I have called to request your permission that I may court your daughter."

Roger listens to Mr. Moses for a moment, "Yes, sir, I know courting is an old-fashioned thing; I believe we need more old-fashioned things," Roger says, and then listens some more.

"My intentions are to court your daughter until we both finish school in two years, to buy a home, and then to get married and give you many grandchildren, maybe twenty. And to answer your next question, sir, I do love your daughter," Roger says to the shock of Rachel.

"Of course, sir, when the time is right I will be requesting your daughter's hand in marriage personally

from you, face to face," Roger says as he smiles at Rachel.

Roger continues to listen as he reaches over and lifts Rachel's lower jaw to close her mouth that has fallen open, "Yes, sir, I am a presently a youth pastor who is studying Theology and Horticulture at Chattanooga State. My long-term goal is to be a pastor; however, I am currently employed by the church as the groundskeeper and youth pastor."

Roger listens for a moment, "Yes, sir, she is still standing here and has not run off or passed out yet," Roger says as he hands the phone to Rachel, "He wishes to speak to you."

"Hi, Daddy," Rachel says, still shocked.

After listening for a moment, Rachel says, "Yes Daddy, I love him too." Rachel cannot believe those words have left her lips, not only because this was only their third date, but because Rachel had never said those words towards anyone but her family.

Rachel hands the phone back to Roger, "He wants to talk to you," she says, still in shock.

"Hello, sir." Roger listens for a minute and then says, "Thank you, sir, I shall tell her. Have a good evening sir, and God bless you and your family."

As Roger hangs us, he looks at Rachel and says, "Daddy gave his blessings for me to court you; Miss Rachel Moses, may I court you now?"

"Yes, yes you may, Mr. Roger Jackson," Rachel says lovingly as they begin their walk back to Tom and Donna.

"Hi guys, do you have the pigeon feeding figured out?" Rachel asks as they come up to the two benchwarmers.

"Yep," Tom says with a smile as he throws a handful of feed at a single pigeon.

"Nope," Donna says with a sigh.

As Tom turn to speak, Rachel pops up and says

excitedly, "I gave myself to the Lord, and Roger and I are courting!"

"Congratulations, on both!" Donna says as she jumps up and hugs Rachel.

"Courting?" Tom asks as he gives Roger a bewildered look.

"Yes, Thomas, all things proper," Roger says through a faux British accent.

"Cool. And awesome on becoming a sister in Christ!" Tom says as he gives Rachel a hug. "Come on, let's go celebrate with dinner; I'll even buy!" Tom exclaims to the group.

"You'll buy?! This is a first," Donna says, shocked at her boyfriend's gesture.

"Well, it is not every day your friends start courting, and one gives herself to God. Rachel, this is your birthday!"

"Thank you, Tom," Rachel says with a light chuckle and a big smile.

"Yes, Tom, thank you. So where to; Mickey-D's?" Roger asks as he knows Tom is the cheapest human alive.

"Nope, pulling all the stops out tonight my Brother, girl's choice," Tom says, smiling.

"Thank you," Rachel says as she hugs Tom.

"Sweetie, you just got very cute; I forgive you for earlier," Donna says with a devilish look.

"Let's go, guys!" Tom hollers as he spins and heads for the car.

CHAPTER 12

CB ED

As Anthony begins to look around, his eyes pan over to the Pods, then he looks down at the number on his jumpsuit, "I am citizen 10," he half-heartedly chuckles.

"I appear to be citizen 11," Roger says with his own dry chuckle as he puffs his chest out.

"Look at me, I am citizen 4," Hank says staring down at his jumpsuit.

Karen, who is number 9, starts walking over to the door of Supply Room 1 that is next to the elevator, she hollers, "Hey, let's see what supplies we have."

As Karen opens the door, she sees it is full of boxes with Ready Meal – 12-day supply written on their sides, "Sounds yummy; MRE's boys," Karen says with a smile reminiscent of the Joker.

"How many boxes?" Hank asks, trying not to give away the fact that he knows exactly how many boxes are in the sheds, as he was the one who was in charge of their stocking.

"A full shed," Karen says as she turns to Hank as he approaches her.

Hank looks past Karen and into the shed and then starts moving his head back and forth as he attempts to give the illusion that he is actually counting the boxes.

"Let's look in the others," Alfonso, number 12, says as he walks over to the shed to the left.

"This one has boxes with Bedding, Toiletries, and Medical written on their sides," Chung-Hee, number 6, says.

"Boxes labeled socks, underwear, and boots," Alfonso says as he pulls his head out of another shed.

"Thank goodness for that," Karen says as she looks over towards Alfonso while opening the door of another shed. "This one is empty," Karen says as she closes the door.

"Yes! This one is full of toilet paper," Max, number 7 says excitedly.

"Zilch," Anthony hollers from one of the far sheds.

"This one has what looks like bicycle and plumbing parts in it," Chung-Hee hollers out from another shed.

"This one has a small workbench and tools in it," Kevin, number 5, calls out as he waves his arm towards one of the far sheds.

"These have gardening tools and seeds in them," Roger yells out from the middle of the field as he motions to the sheds on the far sides.

"Huh, some empty. Well, this place isn't well stocked for a survival bunker," Hank says as he inwardly laughs; it was his idea to keep things to a bare minimum just to put extra stress on the recruits during the last two weeks of the study. "But, we have ninety boxes of food which work out to about a three-month supply, and we will only be here for two weeks; I think we scored! I say we just kick back, pig out, and relax for the next two weeks."

As Roger comes back to the group, he says, "Hank, we are supposed to make that food last. The ground of the field appears to be composted topsoil, which is ideal for growing crops. We have sunlight, water, soil, and many varieties of seeds; we can easily start some crops, it will just take a little work."

"Work, are you crazy?" Hank asks in disbelief.

"Hank, Roger is most accurate; we are obliged to follow the rules as they are presented to us if we wish the compensation as was put forth in our contract. Also, I believe those cameras are watching our interactions and advancements," Frederick, number 1, says in a way that makes everyone look at him as if he spoke Greek to them.

"Yeah, what he said," Jack, number 2, says with a strained look on his face.

"Okay, but I don't have to like it," Hank says as he sticks his tongue out at the camera positioned over the elevator.

"I checked out the latrine; let's just say it is 'different,'" Karen says to the group as she comes walking back over to the group.

"How so?" Anthony questions.

"It says it is a composter. There are some instructions on it; I will leave it up to you college boys to figure out how to spin poo." Karen says with a crinkle of her face.

"There are two water tanks and a shower beside the toilet; it looks like some type of pedal crank pump system," Kevin says to the group.

"Well, all that is left to check out is our new homes," Anthony says looking over at the pods.

"Of course, we should go and investigate our new domiciles," Frederick says as the recruits head over to their pods.

"How… cozy," Harry says as he opens the door of pod 3 and peers in.

Inside the pod is a cot along one wall, a floor to ceiling shelf being used as a headboard that extends all the way across the far wall, a small table and chair, a trunk at the foot of the cot, and a shuttered light tube comes through the ceiling to provide lighting. Harry opens the trunk and finds a canteen, cup, bowl, plate, utensils, pencils, pencil sharpener, dynamo lantern, and a notebook, "Nice," he says as she takes the lamp out and closes the lid.

"Well, I guess we should grab some supplies and bedding and stock our homes before it gets dark," Jack suggests.

"Yeah, if all of our lighting comes from the tubes, it will be very dark soon," Anthony says as he glances up at the ceiling.

"I found a dynamo light in the footlocker, that will give us some light," Harry says as he holds up the lamp.

"I didn't see a bunch of tubes above, where do you think they go?" Karen asks.

"Probably to the top of the hill behind the building; one large central collector that octopuses the tubes out," Hank says as he envisions the system.

"You think?" Max says as he stares up at the tubes.

"Just a guess, we studied this type of setup in school when we were designing underground houses," Hank says. If only they knew he designed the elaborate sun tube lighting system himself.

"We better get moving before it gets dark," Chung-Hee says as he nervously looks around at their new 'town.'

The group heads back to the storage rooms, and each grab a box of bedding, toiletries, and MRE's; they decide they will go through the rest tomorrow. As Roger and Anthony get back to their pods, Roger says, "Good night Anthony."

"Good night Roger; and don't worry, your gal will be okay."

"Thank you, I know she will; she has the Lord to watch over and protect her," Roger says with a smile.

"I wish I had your faith man," Anthony says with a hollowness feeling forming in his stomach.

"You can Anthony; you just need to give yourself to Christ and accept Him as your Lord and Saviour," Roger says sincerely.

"Good night Roger, I will see you in the morning," Anthony says with a tone and look that means he doesn't want to talk anymore.

"Good night Anthony. If you want to talk, you know where to find me," Roger says as he takes the clue that Anthony is not ready to talk; and then Anthony and Roger go quietly into their pods.

As Anthony is putting his supplies on the shelves and making his bed up, he says aloud, "How can Roger believe in something that there is no proof of? What makes him think he is so right about God?"

As Anthony continues to put things away, he keeps thinking of how Rachel and Roger were so genuinely nice to each other and even Ms. Camron, *I bet Roger has never had it rough, he probably has never had to work for anything. He is probably one of those silver-spoon babies.*

If Anthony only knew.

CHAPTER 13

⚮

As John is settling into the observation room, Joanne comes in with a couple of cups of coffee, "Here you go John; I figured you could use this."

"Thanks; did you spike them?" John asks in a half-joking manner.

"No, but I do have another pot brewing," Joanne says with motherly sternness in her voice.

"Thanks. How are you doing?" John asks. He and Joanne have worked together long enough for him to know the iron-tough Major has a soft side, even though she doesn't let it show.

"I am okay; this isn't my first death to deal with, but it is my first assassination; at least I think it is. I have only one question: Why?" Joanne asks as she sits down.

"I don't know; hopefully, Robert finds something out. This is definitely not the way I pictured this study starting," John says as he finishes turning on the last of the monitors.

"Four monitors with four cameras per monitor; all should be covered down there," John says with a big smile as he changes the subject.

"Sound?" Joanne asks as she stares at the screens.

"Lots of sounds; every pod, shed, bathroom, field, and even the shower," John says, smiling.

"You wired the bathroom? You can be the one to listen to that feed once those MRE's kicks in," Joanne says with a disgusted look on her face.

"You always wire the bathroom; you get your best intel from there, as everyone thinks it is a safe place to talk," John tells Joanne.

"You can be the latrine monitor. Please tell me you didn't put a camera in there," Joanne says as she stares pleadingly at John.

"Just on the outside doors; I need to know when somebody goes in and comes out," John says as Joanne gives him a quizzical look.

"A person uses a bathroom for three reasons: normal bathroom duties, sick, or hiding. If sick, we need to know and monitor. If hiding, I need to know why; are they conspiring or snapping? Either one, I need to know," John says as he finishes checking the cameras.

"Well, it looks like they are stocking their pods; when do you plan on shaking them up?" Joanne asks, referring to the fake attack they have planned to weed out the weak.

"Day twelve we move to phase 2; lights will flash down the sky tubes, walls will vibrate, camera lights will go off, dust will blow down and around, and Hank will go into action – induced chaos," Robert says as he comes in and sits down.

"Hey, Robert; any news?" John asks as he turns to face Robert.

"Nothing yet; but General Mars is coming over," Robert says with a worried look as he grabs the chair next to Joanne.

"Bob, what is the matter?" Joanna asks; Robert is not a worrier, even though he has every right to worry now.

"Nothing; well, a little worried the General will pull the plug on us; and I am worried that whoever tipped off the assassin is still down below," Robert says as he searches the monitor screen looking for Hank. When Hank was sent to be part of this study, Robert felt it was a big mistake. Hank was not only arrogant and cocky, but he was a trained killer, and Robert felt that he was extreme overkill for this mission. However, after Robert got to know the real Hank, he knew he would work out fine, especially now.

"My worries too; I don't think anybody heard anything since they were in the holding room. And if the tipster is down below, I have faith in the Captain, he can handle anything we throw at him," John says proudly of Hank; John has grown to love him like a son.

"That is my hopes. We are outside of town in the industrial area, and it was late in the day, the rush was over. I don't see the 'hitters' calling the news, and the recruits were in the soundproof holding room. The only possible witness would have been Miss Moses, and I am sure she left a good ten minutes beforehand. And, yeah, the Captain can handle anything thrown at him," Robert says as he spins his wedding ring back and forth on his finger; it is times like these that his heart aches the hardest for his late wife.

"And everything had been sanitized by the time Cho left," Joanne adds.

"Robert, when do we expect the General?" John asks as he tries to get his friend back into the moment; John knows when Robert's heart pines hard for his wife, the ring spins.

"I would say about an hour, he is coming from the base," Robert says as he looks at the clock as he goes into deep thought.

"Robert, what are you thinking?" Joanne asks; she always can tell when Robert is thinking hard.

"Cho left right before everyone went down, but right after the event; I wonder if she is the canary?" Robert questions.

"Possible; we will let General Mars chase that bird,"

John says, then adds, "I should run down and get the General some lemon cookies; that will lighten up his demeanor," John says with a giggle.

"Lemon cookies; for real?" Joanne asks with a raised eyebrow.

"Yep, I think his wife used lemon cookies to get him to propose," John chuckles.

"John, take my car," Robert says as he holds out his keys.

"I got this," Joanne says as she hops out of the chair and grabs the keys while heading out of the door with John and Robert chuckling.

"Hey, it looks like the recruits are going in for the night," Robert says as he glances back at the monitors.

"Yep. With the only light shining into the courtyard coming from the light tubes, it will get very dark once the sun goes down," John says as he scribbles a quick note.

"That would be my Achilles heel; I hate being blind," Robert says as he watches Anthony and Roger talking by their pods.

"This is where they will be glad for the dynamos; not much light, but they won't be completely blind, and they can read if they brought a book," John says.

"Do you know what each one took down?" Robert asks.

"Of course; let me look at my list:
Hank has his watch.
Harry has a lucky coin.
Karen has a romance novel.
Jack has a book about spices.
Kevin has a picture of his girlfriend.
Frederick has War and Peace.
Roger has his Bible.
Anthony has a hankie.

Max has a toothbrush, but no toothpaste.

Chung-Hee has his watch, also.

Alfonso has a picture of his family."

"War and Peace? A toothbrush? Interesting choices," Robert says with a half-hearted laugh.

"Well, it was pretty much what they had on them, minus knives and lighters; oh, and Karen's mace," John says.

"Karen had mace?" Robert asks, shocked.

"Yep, and a butterfly knife. She didn't want to leave that or her lipstick," John says with a chuckle.

"You cad, a lady, needs to look nice while she protects herself," Robert says wryly.

"She will do okay; she has Hank. And speaking of Hank, time for his update," John says, referring to Hanks nightly update to be held precisely at 7 p.m. John turns up the volume for Hank's pod and does a quick rewind of Hanks camera, "All clear; no visitors."

Robert keys the mike, "Hank, are you decent?"

"Please tell me you don't keep that camera on twenty-four seven," Hank responds from his dimly lit pod.

"Only on standby, you know that," John says as he eludes to Hank knowing more about the Bunker than anyone else since he was one of the key designers.

"Yes, yes I do. Oh, thank you for the extra undies; I think that made Karen's day," Hank says as he pulls his boots off.

"I tried to keep things somewhat civilized," John says, "You better get to your report so that you can get some sleep."

"First, what was with the two rejects?" Hank says, referring to Frank and Margaret.

"Well, Frank was AWOL, and Margaret had boyfriend issues," John says as he gives Hank the micro-version.

"AWOL; is that boy stupid, or what? Man, that charge

doesn't go away even if you are toes-up," Hank says as he thinks back to a couple of young recruits he knew in Kuwait.

"Yep, but that is taken care of now," Robert says, trying to hide the emotions in his voice; he doesn't want Hank worrying, not yet at least.

"Boyfriend issues? What does that mean John?" Hank prods.

"Why are you asking me?" John asks as he is singled out.

"Because, you will give me the skinny on it," Hank says; he knows John likes to talk gossip.

"He liked the ladies, she likes shoes; he is dead, she is sitting in a cell," John says as he gives Hank the condensed version.

"She whacked him? That wasn't nice," Hank says with a hint of sadness in his voice.

"Oh, my goodness, you liked her!" John exclaims.

"No, well, she was my type," Hank says with a half stutter.

"Yeah, she was alive and of age," Robert says sarcastically.

"Hey I am offended; but, yeah, that is about it," Hank says with a quiet laugh.

"Let me set you up with my niece; she is perfect for you," Robert says.

"Colonel, you know I have sworn off all relationships beyond four dates; so, no thank you to your niece. Now, for the report; nothing much to report so far except Jo's pretty boy, Harry. Harry will be an issue; he is wound up tight and is itching for a fight. Oh, and what is with that Frederick guy? I can barely understand him with all of his highfalutin talk," Hank says melodramatically.

"Hank, Joanne will be offended; Frederick was her idea, she thought he would add levity," Robert says as he mulls over what Hank just told them.

"Well, send Jo down here to translate," Hank says with a grunt.

"Only four weeks; maybe you will learn something from him. Now, Harry is a worry?" John asks trying to bring Hank back on track.

"Harry is a worry. I will make him snap and see how others react," Hank says as he cracks his knuckles.

"Be careful; let's not wind up in the dark history books under, *Biggest Blunders of the 21st Century*," John semi-jokingly tells Hank.

"Yes, daddy. Bunk time, boys; Hank the Hunk out," Hank says, signaling his time to go.

"Goodnight, son, sleep well," John says to Hank as he turns off the mike.

As John sits staring at the monitors, the Colonel can tell he is worried, "John, don't worry, Hank the Hunk will keep them from killing each other."

"Robert, please don't call him that; his head is big enough without you validating him," John says, "I hope he keeps them tame; we can't blow this. Harry seemed so friendly and considerate when we interviewed him; Joanne even liked him!" Joanne was the actual clearer; if she said they were good, more than likely they were going through.

"Remember the Majors last boyfriend, what color was his hair? Or the boyfriend before him? Joanne has a weak spot for redheads," Robert says as the door opens and Joanne comes in with a tray of lemon cookies.

"Did you push carrot-top through because he was cute?" John blurts out to Joanne.

Joanne glares at Robert, "I have no idea what you are talking about," Joanne says to John while her eyes continue to burn through Robert.

"Robert, did I tell you I qualified as Expert with the

pistol the other day?" Joanne says to Robert in a not so veiled threat to John.

"Good for you! Oh, I see you went to the bakery for the General's cookies," Robert says, trying to divert Joanne back to the task at hand.

"Yes I did," Joanne says as she sets the cookies well away from Robert and John.

"Robert, do you think Harry is the mole?" John asks Robert as he tries to figure out why Harry was perfect above, and terrible below.

"No, I have a strong hunch it is Cho," Robert says as he looks at Joanne who shakes her head in agreement.

"John, can you pull up the parking lot camera? We can watch for the General from here," Joanne says to John with a big, fake smile; poor John knows he is going to pay for his comment.

John pulls up the camera just in time to see a white sedan pull up. As they watch the camera, they see the back door open, and the General slides out and stands.

"I will go get the General, boys; please be good," Joanne admonishes John and Robert as she heads out to get the General.

John looks at Robert, "Aren't you her commanding officer?" John says acutely aware of the answer.

"Yes, I am. However, I told her years ago; she gets one shot at me a month to keep her from snapping. I will take this shot compared to an Expert shot," Robert says, alluding to her recent pistol qualification on the range.

"Smart move," John says as the door opens to the General and Joanne.

"Frank, long time no see!" John says as he hops up and gives the General a hearty handshake and a hug.

"Robert, have you met General Mars?" John asks Robert enthusiastically.

"Yes, we have, John. General Mars, sir, I wish you

were here under different circumstances," Robert says to the General as he shakes his hand.

"Me too Colonel. Do I smell lemon cookies?" The General asks as he looks around, sniffing the air as he tries to zero in on Joanne's cookies.

"Yes, sir; Major Joanne Camron picked you up some fresh ones," John said with a wry smile as Joanne picks up the undisturbed plate and offers it to the General.

"Major Camron, thank you very much," The General says to Joanne, then looks over at John as he takes a cookie off the plate, "A bribe John?"

"Of course, I want to know what was so important about Frank Jones that he had to die," John says to the General in a serious tone.

"Need to know John, need to know," General Mars says.

"I totally agree, Frank, we need to know. Please tell," John sarcastically says to the General.

As General Mars grabs another cookie while Joanne hands him a cup of coffee, the General sits and takes a slow bite, "My weak link, lemon cookies. I will tell you some information only because of the situation. You all have a maximum security clearance, so I don't need to worry there. Major, please take a seat, let's keep this informal, please," General Mars says as he waves his hand towards the free seat next to him.

Once everyone is situated, General Mars begins, "Lieutenant Frank Jones was an integral member of the Air Combat Command. His primary duty was warhead inventory; at least up until earlier this year when he and Corporal Park Sang-Hun went AWOL," the General says as he finishes his cookie and takes a drink of coffee.

"Another cookie, sir?" Joanne asks as she holds the plate for him.

"Thank you, Major," the General says with a smile;

then his look turns deadly serious, "What I am about to tell you cannot leave this room."

"Yes, sir, of course," they all say in quiet unison.

"When Jones and Sang-Hun went AWOL, they took something with them; something that no one would have thought was possible," the General says as he locks eyes with Robert.

"What, Frank," John asks, fearing the answer he envisions.

"They made off with a nuclear warhead," General Mars says ominously as he lets his eyes scan across the others.

"A nuclear warhead; how?" Robert asks, shocked.

"Believe it or not, they drove it right out the front gate; they had found a chink in the dragon's armor so to speak, and they took advantage of it. We believe Park was the brains, but he got killed last month in a shootout where we thought we had them, and the warhead," General Mars says as he takes another drink of his coffee.

"General, do we know the who, where, and why's?" Joanne asks after taking a deep breath.

"We believe the who is the North Koreans. Park had documentation that he was a third-generation American with South Korean heritage; however, we are now sure that was all a lie, a multi-generational lie. We believe his entire family is actually a North Korean sleeper cell. His lies were good enough to get him top-level clearance," General Mars says as he finishes his cookie.

"More coffee, sir?" Joanne asks as she tries to digest this new information.

"Oh, yes, please. Thank you, Major." As Joanne goes out to grab the coffee pot, the General says, "I still can't believe how easy it was for them just to drive out with a 600-pound nuke."

"Okay, everyone, present arms," Joanne says with a

forced smile as she comes in with the coffee pot.

As everyone holds out their cup for a refill, General Mars continues, "As I said, the who is the North Koreans, the where is unknown at this time; a lot of speculation due to the warhead they grabbed."

"What did they get, sir; if I may ask?" Robert asks, not wanting to hear the sickening answer.

"W-87 Minuteman warhead, 300 kilotons of death packed in a six-foot package; enough power to vaporize a two-mile radius and burn everything for a four-mile radius. If they get the codes, we are talking about a death circle eight miles wide; and that is for a ground burst. Oh, and that is not counting fallout from the ground blast, or the EMP hit if they are able to get it airborne," General Mars says as he helps himself to another cookie.

"They don't have the codes, sir?" Robert asks anxiously.

"We don't believe Jones had them to give up. We were actually surprised they killed him; they must have known he didn't have the codes," General Mars says as another lemon cookie disappears, "Or they don't need them anymore."

"General, I thought all of our warheads require launch codes," Joanne asks.

"Yes and no. The safety interlocks which are built into nuclear warheads are extremely extensive and complex. To up and set one off without all the codes, interlocks, and parameters performed in the proper sequence and environment is impossible. If you have a warhead and want to use it for something besides a lawn ornament, you have three options: one, bust it open and use the nuclear material for a dirty bomb or your own bomb; or design a code breaker that can bypass all the safeguards and soft interlocks," General Mars says as he stares at Joanne.

"What are your thoughts on what they did, or plan to do?" John asks, trying not to show his worries.

"I hate to say this, but I am hoping for a dirty bomb; that is the least deadly alternative and the most viable to catch. If they make their own; well, we know they can and have, but that is a major venture that could take years on American soil. We would catch them before it is completed."

"Viable to catch, how so?" Joanne asks.

"We have radiation sensors everywhere; if they crack that warhead, we will know it unless it is shielded," the General says as Joanne tops off his cup.

"And the third option Frank, the magical key that bypasses all the safeguards?" John asks, trying to remove that option altogether.

General Mars pauses for a moment and stares at the dark monitors, "Before last week, I would have said no chance; now, if my info is right, I will say there is a chance, a good chance."

"Why, sir?" Robert asks as he leans forward.

"Kim Chang-hwan is why. From our intelligence reports, we know Kim spent over ten years reviewing our nuclear interlocks for one purpose, to override and hijack."

"Where did he get the Intel to work with?" John asks, shocked.

"We suspect he got it from Russian and Iranian spies, and a lot of our own unclassified information could have been used. All of the pieces of the puzzle are out there; you just need a puzzle master to put it all together," the General says as he looks at his feet and wiggles a foot side to side.

"And Kim is the master," John states the obvious.

"He is. He will have only one shot; if he messes up, it will break the strong link, and they will have to go with a dirty bomb or homemade," the General says as he offers the last cookie to Joanne, which she declines and he happily pops into his mouth.

"What are the odds, sir?" Robert asks in a monotone voice.

"I will give Kim a ten percent chance of success."

"That high? Any thoughts on targets?" John asks as he feels the pit of his stomach knot up.

"Too many, way too many. Think about it; if you set off a nuke anywhere on American soil, the ensuing fear would cripple this country for several years. And, if it is used in connection with an outside attack, I don't want to think about it," the General says as the last cookie is washed down with the last of the coffee.

"However, with the hit today, I would say they are within a hundred-mile radius of this location; that means the warhead is within a hundred miles of here," the General says solemnly.

"So, if the warhead is here, most likely their target is here, or within flight range," Robert says as he tries to focus his thoughts.

"That is my thoughts. Atlanta, Chattanooga, Nashville, Memphis; heck, maybe even a high-altitude burst over DC," the General offers up.

"What can we do to help sir?" Robert asks as he envisions the United States being knocked back to the dark ages.

"We will need to review all of your videos; did he talk to anyone or make any calls while here?" The General says as he looks at the monitors.

"He didn't talk to anyone that I saw. When you called, he had only been here about a half-hour," Joanne recalls.

"Only a half-hour? Who else was here at the time?"

"Let me check the log, I will be right back," Joanne says as she heads out the door.

"Do you think an accomplice is down below?" John asks as he perches on the edge of his seat.

"I don't know. My tip came from a direct call to my personal cell phone, a dead number. Male voice, slight Asian accent, said Frank was here."

"We have one fitting that description; he is below. But he came in after we had Frank in holding, so I don't think it would be him," John says, thinking of Chung-Hee Chang.

"General, three were in the room with Frank; Frederick Samson, Margaret Penske, and Cho Sang," Joanne says when she comes into the room.

"Cho Sang? Park's sister's name is Cho Sang-Hun; I wonder if she shortened her last name to Americanize it? Cho Sang is too close to be a coincidence. Where is she now; is she below?" The General asks excitedly.

"No, sir, she left right after Frank was killed; as soon as I got back in the room and told the recruits what they were in for, she bailed. Here, let me pull up the video so you can see." John says as he grabs the keyboard and pulls up the surveillance video.

As they watch the video of Cho in the waiting room hiding from Frank; Cho waiting in the holding room right after Frank and Margaret were taken away; Cho's actions in the room when John came back, and her subsequent departure; the General says, "She gave up Frank to someone. We need to find her. I am going to get her phone records, and I will need a copy of these videos," the General orders.

"Of course, sir," Joanne says as she makes a note of the timestamp on the videos.

"Frank, that was your daughter in the room; Karen is below," John tells the General.

"I know. I can't worry about that; she is safer down there than up here right now," the General says,

"Remember, this conversation never happened," with that, the General gets up and heads for the door.

"Frank. Go get 'em," John says as the General starts through the door.

"I will, or die trying," General Frank Mars says as he walks down the hall to the main door.

As they watch on the monitor the General get into his car and drive off, John says, "I will take the first shift if it is alright with you guys, I don't think I will be able to sleep."

"Sure, Doc, I will relieve you at midnight," Robert says as he starts to head for his bunk in somewhat of a state of shock.

"I guess that means I have the 4 a.m. shift. Goodnight boys," Joanne says as she heads to her room.

"Guys, please say your prayers tonight; we need all the help we can get," John says as his two friends walk out the door; as they leave him to the night, he turns back to the monitors and turns the volume up, and prays for the first time in years.

CHAPTER 14

◇

As Cho pulls up to the warehouse, her thoughts are racing all over the place; she is both scared, and excited. Cho honks the horn once, and immediately the large roll-up door opens; a young man steps into the doorway and signals her to drive in. Once Cho is inside, the roll-up door closes behind her; the young man is standing by her door, he motions her out.

"I am Daniel, you must be Park's sister, Cho," he boldly says as Cho nervously gets out.

"Yes, I am Cho. Do you know where Park is? Nobody has heard from him in months," Cho pleads of Daniel.

"Phone please," Daniel, firmly says to Cho with his hand outstretched.

"Why do you need my phone?" Cho says as she timidly hands her phone to Daniel.

"It must be sanitized; you can be followed off of it," Daniel states firmly as he opens the back of the phone and pulls the battery and memory card.

"Park worked on it a few months back; he said it was untraceable," Cho says, agitated at the disemboweling of her phone.

"We can never be too safe; I will change your phone out. Just do not call anyone unless Jung approves them," Daniel says sternly.

"Cho, welcome," a warm voice welcomes Cho from the other side of the shop before she is able to respond to Daniel's coldness.

Cho turns to face the voice, "Thank you, Jung," she says as she recognizes her brother's mentor.

"It is my pleasure. Thank you for the information, it proved very valuable to us," Jung says with a wry smile.

"No problem, I knew you wanted to talk to Frank. Jung, do you know where my brother is?" Cho asks as she glances at Daniel.

"Yes, we needed to see Frank," Jung says, pauses, and then continues in a softer voice, "Cho, come into my office so we can talk," Jung says as he motions towards his office.

"Okay, thank you," Cho says as her apprehension continues to build as she goes where Jung has motioned.

Once in Jung's office, Jung says to Daniel, "Daniel, please get Kim, I think we all need to be here for this. Cho, please have a seat," Jung says as he motions Cho to the chair across from his small metal desk.

Cho looks around the bleak office, no pictures, plants, or paintings; she thinks to herself, *cold, like Daniel.*

"Can I get you something; water, coffee?" Jung asks as he stands before her.

"No thank you, I am fine," Cho says as she musters a smile.

As Daniel and Kim come into the office and take a seat, Jung says, "Aw, good, we are all here; now we can get started."

As Jung leans back against his desk, he asks Cho, "Cho, do you know what your brother did for a living?"

"Something in the military; I believe he worked around nuclear bombs," Cho says with a faint smile.

"Yes! Very good," Jung exclaims with a smile.

"Now, you also know that your grandparents came from the Democratic People's Republic of Korea in 1954 for a special mission, correct?" Jung asks as he observes Cho's reaction.

"Yes, to prepare for the impending battle with the imperialistic Americans," Cho says as she sits up straight as if she was sitting with her grandfather again.

"Very good! Now, you also know that the directive your grandparents were working under is binding for all family members, correct?" Jung asks in a serious tone and a fixed stare.

"Of course, that is why we are sworn to secrecy as soon as we can speak. One day we will have our vengeance on America for what they have done to our countrymen," Cho says as she sits at attention with her head held up high.

"Very good! Yes indeed, we are at war with the imperialists," Jung takes a breath as he lowers his head, "Cho, with a heavy heart I must inform you that Park was a casualty of this war. Because of the actions of Frank Jones, Park was murdered by the imperialists," Jung says as he stares deeply into Cho's eyes.

As Cho slumps into her chair as if all of the air is let out of her, she is unable to speak as the realization sets in; Daniel says, "Cho, he died valiantly; he died fighting. Do not be sad, be proud of your brother."

Cho straightens up while taking a deep breath, "Jung, tell me everything; tell me why Frank killed my brother."

As Jung looks at Cho, he begins speaking, "Cho let me take you back to the beginning. After Park had been assigned to the Air Combat Command at Arnold Air Force Base, he was able to befriend Lieutenant Frank Jones. We knew from our intelligence that Frank was deeply in debt due to some gambling issues, so Park was able to use that to get close to him," Daniel gives a quiet laugh that Jung hushes him over.

"We wanted Park to be friends with Frank?" Cho asks, confused.

"Yes, we needed Frank to further our cause," Jung

says, "We needed Frank to get Park into position.

Once Park befriended Frank, the rest was quite easy. Park was able to secure the unit, and Frank was able to help him get it out. But Frank lied to us, he didn't give us everything he said he had," Jung says as his brow wrinkles.

"The unit? What did they take? What did Frank not give us?" Cho asks as she tries to follow along.

Jung stands up and walks around to his chair as Cho watches him intently; Jung sits, pulls himself all the way into the desk, places his elbows firmly down while bringing his hands into a fold at the bottom of his lips, and coldly says to Cho with a smile, "A Minuteman 3 nuclear warhead."

"A nuclear warhead?!" Cho squeals as she almost falls out of her seat.

"Yes, we have a nuclear warhead to use against the imperialists, and it is one of their own," Jung says as he watches Cho's reactions to see if she is really with them.

"Fabulous! Finally, we can take the war to them! But wait, what didn't Frank give us?" Cho asks as she remembers what Jung had said of Frank.

"The launch codes," Kim says with a lear.

"Well, we don't need to launch it. We can just drive it to the White House and set it off!" Cho excitedly says.

"It is not that easy. We must have the codes so that the warhead can be armed; no codes, no detonation," Jung declares.

"So, what now? If we can't set it off, what did Park die for?" Cho asks angrily as she hangs her head.

"Park died getting us the bomb that will bring anarchy and death to America. We had three options: dismantle the bomb and reuse the parts to make our own; dismantle and make a dirty bomb, or we make a special key that works as the codes," Jung says as his smile comes back.

Cho stares at Jung for a moment, "Can we make a key?" Cho quietly asks.

"Kim can, and has," Jung says as he smiles at a smirking Kim.

"So we can blow it up; what are we waiting for? Let's take it to the White House and destroy America!" Cho says as she gets out of her chair.

Jung motions her to sit, "The White House is not the target, too guarded and it wouldn't cause near the chaos of detonating in a city; we need the people of Washington to make the wrong decisions and destroy America from the inside as we attack from the outside." Jung smiles and continues, "Also, we cannot transport the warhead very far for fear of detection, and we cannot secure a plane, so that eliminates many targets. The Supreme Leader has given us two choices for the attack, and one choice for when to attack."

"You have spoken to the Supreme Leader? You have been greatly honored! Where and when?" Cho asks as she squirms in her chair.

"The Supreme Leader wants us to attack the imperialist on August 25," Jung says as Cho interrupts, "Day of Songun!"

"Yes, our Day of Songun holiday. The Supreme Leader feels it is the perfect time seeing as the Day of Songun marks our military greatness. After we take America, the Day of Songun will be our new independence day," Jung says smiling as he leans more towards Chung, "And the where is either Atlanta or Chattanooga."

"Atlanta will have more casualties; many more imperialists will die," Cho says as she thinks of her friends in Chattanooga.

"Yes, but Atlanta is farther, and we need to get downtown for the highest casualty count; Chattanooga is right here, and is considered to be a more wholesome town," Jung says as he leans back.

"Please let me be a part of this great event; please let me avenge Park," Cho pleads.

"Of course, you will be part of this," Jung says as he is reassured by Cho's eagerness.

"What can I do to help?" Cho begs.

"For now, nothing really; we have everything ready to go."

"The bomb is ready?" Cho asks, surprised.

"Yes, Kim has the key ready and attached; all he has to do is turn the key on and push the button," Jung says, smiling at Kim. "Would you like to see the death of America?" Jung asks Cho.

"Yes please!" Cho says excitedly.

"Daniel, show Cho the Supreme Leaders Fist," Jung says, referring to the pet name they have given the warhead.

Daniel smiles and walks over to an older blue van; he opens the back doors and motions Cho over.

As Cho walks over expecting to get into the van to drive to the location of the bomb, she looks at a large object in the back of the van, "Is that it?" She asks, shocked.

"That is it," Daniel says with a smile.

"It is smaller than I thought it would be. How many will it kill?" Cho asks as she turns and locks eyes with Daniel.

"If set off center of Chattanooga noon on Day of Songun, we expecting immediate death toll approximately seventy-five thousand with fifty-thousand wounded," Kim says in his broken English.

"That bomb will kill that many? Why did they ever build such things?" Cho asks, stunned.

"Greed, they want the world," Daniel says with a scowl forming on his face, "And this is one of their smaller ones."

"Daniel, close it back up. Cho, I need you to work with us here to keep our cover-up," Jung says as he brings Cho back to the present.

"Of course, sir. What will my job be?" Cho asks her new boss.

"We are a specialty import service, but most of our service is done strictly online. This way, it is not strange that we have no inventory. You will just take phone and internet orders," Jung commands.

"Of course! Anything for our leader! Anything for Park," Cho says as sadness comes over her, "Does Park's wife know?"

"Yes. She was sent to be part of his cover. She is back in Pyongyang," Jung states.

"Good, so good," Cho says as a few her grief lifts.

"Yes. Now, we must rest. Daniel, you have the first watch; Kim, you have second; I will take third; Cho, I will show you to your quarters," Jung says as he turns towards the hall.

"I can take a shift," Cho states emphatically.

"No, not yet; you have training to do first. Come, and I will show you where we sleep; tomorrow we will go get you some new clothes," Jung says sternly.

"Yes sir," Cho says as they walk to the sleeping quarters.

CHAPTER 15

$$\text{CB \& BO}$$

As Rachel pulls into Grammy Betty Jackson's house, Little Betty runs out to meet her, "Aunt Rachel!" Little Betty exclaims.

"Hey, little one!" Rachel cries as she sweeps up Little Betty and spins her around in her arms, "Are you and Momma visiting Grammy today?"

"Yes ma'am, Momma said Uncle Roger, and you were going away for two whole weeks, so we came by to cheer her up," Little Betty says while batting her big brown eyes at Rachel.

"Aww, that was very sweet of you two," Rachel says as her heart turns to putty.

"Where is Uncle Roger? Did you lose him?" Little Betty asks as she looks around.

"No, hunny, I didn't lose him; this time. Are Grammy and Mommy inside?" Rachel asks, not wanting to explain everything twice.

"Of course, you don't see them out here, do you?" Little Betty says with a little smirk and a tilt of her head.

"You are just like your Uncle Roger," Rachel says with her own little smirk.

"No, I'm not, I'm a girl!" Little Betty says with a huff.

"Very true, you are a young lady," Rachel says as she sets Little Betty down, "Let's go see Momma and Grammy," Rachel says with a smile as she holds onto Little Betty's hand.

"Okay," Little Betty happily says as she turns and

leads Rachel to the front door.

"Hello Rachel," Grammy Betty says as Rachel come into the kitchen behind her little guide who immediately turns and zips back out and into the house. "Pull up a seat, hun," Grammy instructs Rachel as Grammy sits at the kitchen table.

"Yes, ma'am, I don't mind if I do; but first, I need coffee," Rachel says with a smile as she pulls a cup out of the cupboard just as Little Betty's mother, Mary Parnell, comes into the room and sits down at the table beside Grammy Betty.

"Hello Mary, long time no see," Rachel jokes to Little Betty's mother as she finishes fixing her cup of coffee.

"Amazing how two weeks can fly by so fast! It seems like I just saw you this morning at breakfast," Mary giggles, referring to the going away breakfast they all shared that morning.

"Coffee?" Rachel asks as she holds up the pot.

"No thank you, I am floating right now," Mary says as she cradles her stomach.

"A little topping, please," Grammy Betty says as she holds her cup out for Rachel to fill, "Where is my boy at? Did he get that little side job you two were talking about?" Grammy asks as she shoots a glance into the other room as she tries to spy Roger.

"Yes, they picked him, but not me. He will be gone for two weeks," Rachel says with a pout as she tops off Grammy Betty's cup and then sits down at the table with Grammy and Mary.

"Two weeks without your man; girl, what are you going to do?" Mary asks in a concerned tone.

"It will be hard, but I do have the wedding to get ready for," Rachel says as she tries to muster a smile.

"Shopping therapy is some powerful medicine when one gets the blues; just watch out you don't get the addiction," Grammy says with a laugh.

"Well, maybe I need to take you with me just to keep me straight," Rachel says with a giggle.

"What about me?" Little Betty exclaims as she appears in the room.

"You better ask Momma," Rachel says as she pictures Little Betty throwing everything into the cart as she runs through the store.

"Momma, can I please? Without me, Aunt Rachel is lost!" Little Betty says to Mary in her most pleading voice.

"Really, she is lost? Oh, my, we can't have her getting lost. Rachel, when do you think you will need your little shopping guide?" Mary says as Little Betty beams.

"Well, it is too late now, and I am beat. How about tomorrow morning, if that is okay with you," Rachel says to Mary while shooting a smiling glance at Little Betty.

"That sounds good as long as Little Betty's chores are done," Mary says as she locks eyes with Little Betty.

"All my chores are done!" Little Betty says proudly as she snaps to attention.

"Really? Is your room clean? Everything put away? Laundry done? Chickens fed and cows milked?" Mary asks Little Betty.

"We don't have chickens and cows!" Little Betty exclaims.

"True, so what about the rest?" Mary asks with a stare.

"Let me go check," Little Betty says as she heads out of the room like a whirlwind.

"Well, that will keep her busy till bedtime; her room is a mess," Mary chuckles.

"Now, tell us about this study; they only took Roger?" Mary asks as she sits down at the table.

"Well, they were very friendly people, and it was in

a place on the other side of town down by the river," Rachel says. "They never told me what the study was about, just that they needed twelve people for a two-week study where you would have no outside contact; Roger was number twelve. So no Roger for two weeks," Rachel says, pouting.

"Poor Roger, he will not know how to function without his Rachel," Grammy Betty declares.

"Poor Rachel, she won't know how to function without her Roger!" Rachel exclaims.

"It will be okay; two weeks will fly by. We have a wedding to plan, and we have ice cream," Mary says with a gleam in her eye.

"Ice cream? Oh, yes please; I would love some," Grammy Betty says as she looks pleadingly at Mary.

"Rachel, could you help me grab some ice cream?" Mary says with a grin as she catches Grammy Betty's hint.

"Of course," Rachel says as she gets up with a giggle, "We must have ice cream to mend our battered hearts."

As they settle in with their ice cream, Rachel can't seem to shake the feeling that a darkness is around Roger right now; a darkness that means him harm. Rachel says a quiet, heartfelt prayer for Roger's safety.

CHAPTER 16

෪ ෫

As Rachel pulls into Grammy Betty's drive, Little Betty comes running out, "Aunt Rachel, are you ready to go shopping?" Little Betty impatiently asks.

"Yes, I am, but first I need to come say my good mornings to your Momma and Grammy," Rachel says as she gets out of her car.

"Okay, I guess so," Little Betty says with a pouting face.

"Now, now little one; as your Uncle Roger says, turn that frown upside down," Rachel singingly instructs Little Betty.

"Like this?" Little Betty says as she turns her head upside down.

"Not entirely, but I guess that will work," Rachel says with a giggle as she scoops up Little Betty and heads into the house.

"Good morning, Rachel," Mary says to Rachel as she takes the opportunity to tickle Little Betty in Rachel's arms.

"Hey, no fair!" Little Betty hollers and squirms as Rachel sets her down.

"All is fair in love and tickles, you know that!" Grammy says as she comes into the room and reaches for Little Betty, "Good morning, dear," Grammy says to Rachel as Little Betty barely dodges her wiggling fingers.

"Good morning," Rachel says to Mary and Grammy

with a big smile.

"Coffee?" Mary asks as she holds out a cup for her.

"Yes, please," Rachel says as she takes the cup Mary has offered her.

"So, what is the plan for the day?" Mary asks as she takes a sip of her coffee.

"Shopping!" Little Betty exclaims.

"Really, for what?" Rachel asks Little Betty.

"Wedding stuff for you and Uncle Roger, and a present for me!" Little Betty says with an excited look on her face.

"A present? Why do you need a present? And you know it is not nice to demand things," Mary says as she gives Little Betty a mild glare.

"Uncle Roger said when Aunt Rachel and I go shopping again, I get a present," Little Betty says while pouting after being admonished.

"Really? Rachel, do you think she is telling the truth?" Mary asks playfully, as she knows Little Betty has never lied.

"She is, Roger said that he thinks it is time for her to get a Bible," Rachel says with a smile.

"Well, he would know," Mary says, then asks, "Did he have an idea of which one would be best for her?"

"There are different ones?" Little Betty asks as she stands between them all in the kitchen.

"There are many translations and styles of Bibles, hunny," Grammy says as she puts her empty cup in the sink.

"Why?" Little Betty asks after thinking a moment.

"Well, some people like the old style Bibles like the King James type; you know, the ones where they say, thee, thou, verily, and those other funny words that confuse you. Some people like the ones that sound more like regular talk; sort of like what Uncle Roger uses.

But he wanted you to have one that is designed for little ones, a children's illustrated Bible; that way, we can read together," Rachel explains.

"I like it when we read together. Can I get a dolly too?" Little Betty asks with her big eyes in full beg mode.

"That depends on how well you cleaned your room," Mary says as she stares at an imaginary spot on Little Betty's forehead so that she is not taken hostage by her doe eyes.

"It is spotless!" Little Betty says as she grabs her mother's hand and drags her back to Little Betty's bedroom.

"You know, sometimes I swear she is related to Roger by blood," Grammy says with a shake of her head.

"I know, it is uncanny," Rachel says with a giggle as she puts her cup in the sink.

"Are you still using the Holman translation?" Grammy asks Rachel.

"Oh yes; I will always use that Bible; it is the one Roger gave me. And after Roger did his study on the history of the Bible, I don't think I could use anything but the Holman," Rachel says.

"So do I hunny, so do I; and I stopped talking in the old King's English back in high school," Grammy chuckles.

"You're not that old, young lady," Rachel admonishes Grammy.

"Sometimes I feel it," Grammy says with a laugh.

"Don't we all," Mary says as she and Little Betty come back into the room and hands Rachel some money, "The Munchkins room is actually pretty clean, she may have a dolly," Mary says as Little Betty stares up all a smiles.

"Okay, let's go little one; what are you waiting for?" Rachel says as she spins and heads for the door.

"I have been waiting for you! Bye Momma; bye Grammy!" Little Betty says as she races for the door.

"Bye Mary; bye Momma!" Rachel exclaims as she grabs the door and swoops out ahead of Little Betty.

"Bye!" Mary and Grammy holler out as the two shopper's race for the car.

CHAPTER 17

⋐⋑

As the morning begins to reveal itself through the light tube in Hank's pod, Hank jerks himself awake out of another nightmare; his past will not let him sleep. "Well, I guess that's my wake-up call," Hank says as he sits and stretches on the edge of his cot.

"Coffee, I need coffee," Hank says as he puts on his boots and opens the door of his pod.

Hank sees Roger come out of his pod, "Hey, Roger, you make the coffee, and I will whip up the bacon and eggs," Hank says to Roger through a scratch and a yawn.

"Coffee? Bacon and eggs? Are those in the meal packets?" Roger eagerly asks as his stomach growls at the thought of bacon and eggs.

"Nope, all that is in there is gruel, I just wanted you to get the taste of bacon in your head before you bit into floor scrapings," Hank says with a light laugh. "They say that they have stuff like pork and rice, pasta and garden vegetable, Asian style beef, and the like, but it's all gruel. Oh, there is coffee in them, though," Hank says as he tries to re-inflate Roger's bursting bubble.

"I take it you have eaten them before?" Roger asks as his stomach cries out in anguish.

"Yeah, I did a 4-year stint in the Army; all it did was pay for my schooling and teach me how to drink," Hank says with a big smile on his face.

"Hank, what am I going to do with you?" Roger jokingly asks.

"Gotta love me!" Hank exclaims.

"No, I don't," Karen says as she comes out of her pod.

"Howdy, Sunshine," Hank says to Karen with a big smile.

"Good morning, Karen," Roger says with a smile.

"Don't howdy me, cowboy. Good morning, Roger," Karen says with a smile back to Roger.

"Ouch, I am hurt. Well, if you kids will excuse my dejected heart, I need to go figure out the latrine," Hank says as he hurriedly walks over to the latrine he helped build a few months ago.

"Once you figure it out, let us know please," Karen says, "And quickly."

"Did you sleep well?" Roger asks Karen.

"So-so. I didn't have to worry about a light being on, that is for sure," Karen says, referring to the darkness of the night.

"I know what you mean; I figured for every two minutes of cranking, you get ten minutes of light," Roger says.

"Good morning," Anthony says as he walks over to Karen and Roger.

"Good morning," Karen and Roger say in unison back to Anthony.

"Excuse me as I try out the bathroom," Anthony says as he walks towards the latrine.

"Be careful, Hank is in one of the stalls," Karen says.

"Will do," Anthony says with a waved hand over his back.

"Good morning, Karen; Roger," Max says as he comes up to the two.

"Good morning Max," they say back to him.

"So, what is on the agenda for today?" Max asks as he stands near Karen.

"Well, I was going to start on the garden," Roger says

as he looks towards the expanse of bare dirt.

"I guess that is the only thing we have to do, make a garden," Karen says, referring to the instructions on the sign.

"And use the poo spinner," Max adds as Karen and Roger both crinkle their noses in disgust.

"I saw some folding tables and chairs over by the bathroom, maybe we should bring those over and set them up," Karen suggests.

"Then we can have breakfast before starting on the garden," Max adds.

"Sounds good, let's go get them," Roger says.

While Roger, Karen, and Max are setting up the tables, Hank and Anthony come back over. "The kid and I got the latrine contraption figured out, so whenever you all want, we can go show you what is involved," Hank says proudly as Anthony gives him an annoyed stare.

"Yeah, come on Anthony," Karen says as she ignores Hank.

"Ouch, second burn for the day," Roger says with a crinkled look on his face as Anthony and Karen head over to the latrine.

"No biggie, I am used to rejection; but, my offer on bathroom use still stands," Hank says as he sits in one of the chairs at the table.

"Bathroom procedure schooling, how quaint," Frederick says as he comes over to the group and sits down.

"Professor, it is not that bad," Hank says to Frederick.

"I am not a professor, yet," Frederick says to Hank.

"Maybe not, but that is your new nickname," Hank says with a smile as Frederick rolls his eyes.

As Roger looks around, he sees Jack, Alfonso, Chung-Hee, Frederick, and Kevin up and milling about. "Where is Harry?" Roger asks as he looks around for Hank's firecracker.

"Probably still sleeping; hopefully, it's charm rest," Karen says as she and Anthony come back to the table.

"Well, let's grab breakfast, then we can get the garden in; with all of us helping, it shouldn't take too long," Roger says as he looks back at his pod.

"Gotcha, Mr. Green Thumbs," Hank says to Roger.

"Do you think anything will grow?" Jack asks with a yawn.

"I believe so; they have actually supplied us with a vast assortment of seeds. And whoever designed these sky tubes, they did one heck of a job; all I can say is they are awesome. Think about it; we are a hundred feet underground, and we have as much light as if we were on the surface," Roger says as he looks over the area and sees it fully lit up with daylight.

"Awesome? Wow, I bet the designer would be tickled to hear you call it that," Hank says as he feels his chest grow.

"Do you know who did it?" Karen asks in a surprised tone.

"Me, no; just as an architecture student, I know the awesome compliment carries significant weight in the building community," Hank says, trying to cover his near giveaway.

"Good morning, Harry," Kevin says as Harry comes over to the group.

"Morning," Harry responds as he comes over to the group.

"We were just talking about eating breakfast and then putting the garden in," Karen says to Harry.

"K; should we divvy up the chow first? That way we can all store our own, so nobody winds up eating everybody else's," Harry says while looking at Hank.

"We could do that. You are the financial guru; what is 90 divided by 11?" Hank sarcastically asks.

"Eight and change," Harry says, still scowling at Hank.

"So, eight boxes per pod; sounds good!" Hank says as he gets up from the table.

"Let's move them over, then I can show anyone you all how the heater works in them," Karen volunteers.

"You know about MRE's?" Hank asks, shocked.

"When your daddy is a general, you learn these things," Karen says with a smile.

"Your pop is a general?" Hank asks as he tries to hide his surprised tone.

"Yeah, he jumps between Fort Campbell and Arnold Air Base; General Mars. Have you heard of him?" Karen asks Hank.

"No, I don't think I have. I have been out for a bit, though," Hank lies to Karen; he knows General Mars quite well, he actually served under him during his last mission; Hank realizes he needs to be a gentleman from here on out.

"Let us get our delicacies," Jack jokingly says.

"I will trade my brownies for any lemon poppy cakes," Karen says as they open the storage shed.

"Deal!" Roger says, letting his sweet tooth show.

After they have all put their boxes away, they set the last two boxes on the table, "Okay, twenty-four divided by eleven; each gets two pouches with two left over," Chung-Hee says as he shows off his math skills.

"Awesome, they do have a coffee packet!" Hank says ecstatically.

"Calm down, Hank. Now, this is all you have to do to heat up your meal," Karen says as she starts showing the recruits the basics of the MRE's.

After everyone heats up their meals and begins eating, Jack says with a sick look on his face, "Oh my, this is gag awful."

"You will get used to them, but they will clean you out," Hank laughs.

"Lovely thought," Frederick says sarcastically as he nibbles on his meal.

"Hank is right; the MRE curse hits about half of the people that have to eat them, but don't worry, it passes," Karen says with a giggle at her little pun.

"After breakfast, Anthony and I will show you the poo spinner," Hank says through a mouthful of food.

"Once more, another lovely thought," Frederick says as his complexion fades.

After everyone finishes eating and Hank and Anthony demonstrate the basics of the latrine to them, they head over to the field, "Well Green Thumbs, what is the plan?" Hank asks Roger.

"Why ask goody-two-shoes?" Harry says as he glares at Roger.

"Because he is the one with the agricultural background," Anthony says before he even realizes it. Harry moves his glare towards Anthony.

"Well, Green thumbs?" Max asks, backing Hank and Anthony as he automatically chooses his side.

"Well, I took a quick inventory of the seeds yesterday. Our best bet right now would be to make rows that we can divert the creek to water. We can stagger the rows based on germination rate, growth rate, and harvest rate; we should have a good start by the time we leave," Roger says.

"What will grow in two weeks?" Kevin asks.

"Radishes will be the first to come up; they will be up in about five days, and you can actually harvest them in a month," Roger says.

"And you can eat the greens also," Jack interrupts.

"Yes, we will be eating the thinning's before we leave," Roger says with a smile directed at Jack. "The

Swiss chard, lettuce, and spinach will take a bit longer, but they will be able to harvest them after we leave."

"I say we plant a mega garden, and maybe they will give us a bonus!" Hank says as Harry scowls at him.

"What first, Green Jeans?" Harry sarcastically asks as he draws out 'Green Jeans.'

"Get the tools out, mark off the rows, make the rows and the water channels; after that, we plant," Roger says matter of factly.

"Alright, you all heard the man; tool time!" Hank hollers as he heads for the sheds.

"Hank, best if we walk off to the side; we don't want to compact the soil," Karen directs Hank as he starts cutting through the loose garden soil.

"Yes, Mrs. Green Jeans!" Hank says as he cuts over towards the side of the Bunker.

"Hank, I know where you sleep, and I will hurt you, bad," Karen says as she too cuts over to the side so as not to step in the plowed soil.

"Yes, Ma'am," Hank says more subdued.

After about four hours of laboring work, an 80-foot by 80-foot garden sits finished with sixteen long rows divided into fourths, effectively giving them sixty-four 18-foot by three-foot rows.

"Now what, Brown Jeans?" Hank asks Roger as Hank pops his knuckles.

"Brown Jeans? I guess so. I will send them to the laundry later on," Roger says jokingly as he looks down at his dirty jumpsuit, "Now, we plant."

"Have at it, I am done," Harry says as he starts to head for the shed with his rake.

"Hey, we all have to do this," Hank says in a raised voice while puffing out his chest.

"That is okay, Hank, we can get it," Roger says as he tries to calm Hank down.

"What is that supposed to mean?" Harry says as he turns to face Roger.

"It means we can get the seeds in the ground if you want to sit out for a bit," Roger says as he realizes this situation is starting to head south.

"I can pull my weight," Harry says, puffing up on Roger.

"I know you can, you have been busting your tail out there all day. You worked circles around me, you deserve to take a break," Roger says trying to salvage the situation.

"You know it," Harry says as he stabs his shovel into the ground and grabs his water canteen and walks back to the tables.

Hank stares at Roger for a moment and says quietly, "Watch your back and block your door at night, he wants to hurt you, worse than Karen wants to hurt me."

"I know, and I will. Mostly I will pray for him, and for myself," Roger says as he grabs Harry's shovel and turns towards the shed.

"Green Thumbs, you will need more than a prayer against him," Hank says quietly.

"No, all I need is God; you need to have some faith, sir," Roger says as stops and turns to face Hank.

"Yeah, that and two bucks will get you a cup of coffee on the top-side," Hank says as he begins to feel uneasy.

"Hank, I see we need to talk," Roger says with a smile.

"Seeds, Mr. Green, we need seeds," Hank says as he crinkles his forehead at Roger.

"Yes, Captain!" Roger says with a quick snap salute that Hank almost instinctively returns.

"Seedtime?" Karen says as she comes over with Max, Anthony, and Frederick.

"Yep, let's go get them, and I will show you what we need to do," Roger says as they walk over to the garden sheds with tools in hand.

After a couple of hours, sixteen of the rows have been planted, "Why didn't we plant them all?" Alfonso asks as he stares at the empty rows.

"This way we can do succession planting; in four days we plant another sixteen, then four days later, another sixteen, and so on. That way you always have produce coming ready at different times. As it is, we are going to have LOTS of radishes," Roger says with a laugh.

"But we still have a big section not healed up yet; what is the deal with that?" Max asks as he looks at the empty section just as big as the one they just spent all day working.

"That section is for when we get this one finished; no sense busting ourselves up right off the bat," Roger says as he looks at the group.

"Time to water?" Chung-Hee says as he stretches his back.

"Yep, let's block off the end and let it flood up; once flooded, we can open the drain back up and let the water go back to flowing," Roger directs.

"I will go ahead and grab a shovel and block it," Jack says.

"Perfect," Roger says to Jack with a smile.

"Has anyone checked how the shower works?" Karen asks as she sniffs the air around her.

"From what I can surmise, one pedals the cycle which turns the gear on the side of the giant contraption to the rear of the unit; this contraption has three positions for the attached shifting mechanism which is located on the edge of the contraption. One position is marked: Shower Tank Fill, one is marked: Holding Tank Fill, and the last is marked: Shower Tank Heater. I must deduce that when one pedals the tank while it is in the Shower Tank Fill position, a pump is operated which fills the shower holding tank above the shower unit. After the vessel is full, I would construe that you maneuver the shifting mechanism to the Shower Tank Heater position, which must control some form of the heating element inside of the shower holding tank. From there I would conclude that you disrobe, enter the shower, and pull the handle inside which allows the water to flow over you," Frederick says to the bewildered group.

"Huh?" Anthony says, completely befuddled.

"You pedal, I shower," Karen says as she translates Frederick talk.

"Gotcha," Anthony says as they go over to the shower.

"Max, can you watch the door and direct pedal-boy for me?" Karen asks Max.

"Sure thing," Max says with a smile.

"There are eleven of us, and about four hours of light left; we need a pedal plan," Hank says as he looks at the group.

"Alphabetical, minus Karen since she is first?" Frederick says.

"That works. Hey, the tank is almost full; can somebody shift me?" Anthony asks as he pedals the machine. Harry comes over and moves the lever to heater for Anthony, "Thanks, Harry," Anthony says to Harry.

"No problem," Harry says with a type of smile that Hank has only seen one time before; from the time of where his nightmares come.

After everyone finishes showering, Hank heads back into his pod and latches the door. "Well, Hank, we saw that you were quite busy today; kudos sir, job well done," John says to Hank as Hank stretches out on his bunk.

"Geez, John! You scared me half to death," Hank says as he jumps up into a defensive stance.

"I made you jump? That is a first. Let me guess, Harry is bothering you," John says with a gleeful laugh, followed by a serious tone.

"Harry is an issue, a big issue. He worries me to the point I know it will get violent. That redhead is not a firecracker, he is a stick of dynamite, and Roger is the match," Hank says as he sits back down on the edge of his bed.

"How worried are you, Captain?" Robert asks as he sits down and stares at Hank in the screen.

"Sir, worried enough to tell Roger to block his door at night, and I am too," Hank says as he glances at the door latch.

"Do you think we should extract?" Robert hesitantly asks as he thinks of what an extraction would do to the mission.

"No, I will handle it; just be ready to stop recording," Hank directs them.

"No casualties, Captain," Robert says sternly.

"No casualties, Coronel," Hank reassures Robert.

"Garden is in; shower used; MRE's divided; latrine figured out and used," John says as he tries to change the conversation to something positive.

"Yep, and what is the deal with no soap?" Hank demands, remembering the hollering that came from Karen.

"Unnecessary item," John says with the sternest voice he can muster.

"Really? Okay, I want you to skip soap for the next month and see how unnecessary soap is," Hank says with a scowl towards the hidden camera.

"Hank, water is all you would have if you were down there for six months or more. Now get some sleep, and double check your door lock," John orders.

"John, you will be the first one I hug when I come out of here," Hank threatens.

"I will be waiting for it, son," John says with a smile.

"Goodnight, Pops," Hank says with a sigh as he checks the latch on his door and then lies back on his cot, hoping the demons of his past let him sleep tonight. As Hank lies there staring up into the darkness, he can't stop thinking about Harry; Harry is a problem.

CHAPTER 18

As the light shines into Anthony's eyes, he quietly curses the designer of these pods, "Why didn't they put the light tube over the table area? What idiot puts a spotlight over a bed?" As Anthony rises and puts on his jumpsuit and shoes, he grabs an MRE and opens his door.

"Good morning Anthony, come on over and eat with us," Roger says, motioning to the table Roger, Hank, Jack, Karen, and Max are sitting at.

"Thanks," Anthony says as he comes over and starts trying to remember how to make his coffee.

"Hold on, son. Go grab your canteen and fill it with hot water out of the shower, put two packets of coffee in it and you are set," Jack instructs.

"How ingenious!" Frederick exclaims as he comes over to the group.

"Yep, our little cook figured that out right off the bat," Hank says as Anthony and Frederick head back to their pods to grab their canteens.

"What is on the agenda today?" Karen asks as she sips her coffee.

"The rules say we must grow a garden and use the latrine, nothing more," Max says to Karen with a warm smile.

"We need to check the watering in the garden, but that will only take a few minutes," Roger offers.

"The Doc said we are simulating living underground

during World War Three, he said to survive, why would he say that?" Anthony asks as he and Frederick come back with their filled canteens.

"Maybe they are trying to work out the kinks in a system like this, or maybe they want to keep the next generation safe in the event of Armageddon; you know, keep a group down here every two weeks. With the way things are going in the world, Armageddon could happen tomorrow," Hank says as he plants his own little seeds.

"Well, they have a lot of kinks in this system; lack of soap is the main one," Karen says with a huff. "And if they are wanting to keep shuffling a group of repopulater's underground every two weeks, I see now why our government is in sad financial shape," Karen says as she stares at Hank.

"Repopulater's, cute title," Hank says with a laugh, "We are the unshaven phoneless mole-kids who will repopulate the earth after the zombie apocalypse."

"Don't mention the lack of phones," Karen says with a scowl at Hank.

"So, you think they are keeping groups of us underground just in case of war? I haven't heard of anyone else doing this; no other studies," Max says as his curiosity peaks.

"Perchance we are the first; hence why certain amenities have been overlooked," Frederick says in a voice of reason.

"And the fact that there are only a woman and ten men; that is not the way to repopulate the world after nuclear annihilation," Chung-Hee says as he comes over to the table.

"Exactly, so don't be getting any ideas that involve me," Karen says as she glares at each man around the table.

"Don't worry Karen, I have your back," Max says as

he unconsciously puffs out his chest.

"So, what is their plan?" Kevin asks as he also comes over to the table.

"I don't know, but this is quite the elaborate set-up just to see how well we can grow a garden underground for two weeks. Maybe it is all innocent, and the government is telling us the truth, and this is just to see how eleven people can get along," Hank says as he waters his well-planted seeds of doubt.

"Look, Hank is a comedian; government telling the truth," Kevin says with a light chuckle.

"But why in a grave?" Harry says as he comes up to the group.

"Maximum stress level; no way out, no outside interactions, minimal necessities, only raw emotions between people who do not know each other," Anthony states dryly as he looks at Harry.

"No emotions, no stress," Harry says as he stares at Roger; and Roger smiles back at Harry.

"Gentlemen, let me show you the miracles of the coffee canteen," Frederick says as he gets out of his chair and motions the latecomers to follow him, "We will head over to the magnificent shower system. I shall pedal, and you will fill your canteens once the water has come to the proper temperature," Frederick says as his group blindly follows him.

"Eyes wide open," Hank murmurs to Roger.

After Frederick brings his happy coffee sipping group back, and everyone is sitting around the table eating breakfast, Hank says, "Since we are supposed to be play acting about being stuck down here during Armageddon, how would that work? What would we have to do to survive for the next sixty years?"

"If it were the real Armageddon, being down here would not matter; but that is a different discussion,"

Roger says smiling at Hank.

"True, maybe I should say nuclear destruction," Hank says as he doesn't want to get Roger to preaching.

"We would have to get out of here; just saying," Karen says as she thinks of the ten to one odds against her virtue.

"Okay, escape is one; but how? And what else?" Hank says as he eggs the group on.

"Escape would be up the elevator shaft, that is the only way out," Harry states as he looks over towards the elevator doors.

"The what else; we have some food but need to grow more, we have water that appears to be good, temperature seems to be constant, only dropping minimal at night, clothing would be an issue later on as these wear out, but it wouldn't be a worry now," Harry says as he pulls his coveralls outwards with his thumbs as he inspects the cloth.

"What about medical?" Hank asks as he stares at Karen.

"I am in my last year of nursing so I can handle most everything, except surgeries," Karen says as she stares back at Hank.

"I am a dental tech, and I have pursued every additional bit of training I can so I can handle almost any oral emergency that pops up," Max says as he looks at Karen.

"So, with Max and me together, your health is not an issue," Karen says as she smiles at Max.

"Except for medical tools and medicine," Harry says as he points out the obvious.

"We would have to figure out something in that regard; a garden knife is not the best tool for extracting a rotten tooth," Max says to Harry.

"For food; will the garden be producing enough before

the MRE's run out?" Hank asks Roger in an attempt to distract Harry.

"Yes. We would be able to supplement the MRE's with radish greens around the fourteenth day, with radishes around the thirtieth day; all the other greens around a month and a half. For the protein source, the beans, figure two months. Actually, by two months everything will be coming in heavy," Roger says as he pictures a flourishing garden in his head.

"So, two months is where the MRE's would have to get us," Jack says as he stares at the barren garden.

"Yes. The main thing is crop rotation, succession planting, and composting; we don't want to deplete the soil in one area, and we don't want a hundred pounds of radishes all at once," Roger says flatly.

"Gotcha, and we can't preserve anything either," Alfonso states as he sits listening and thinking.

"Could we dry anything? Maybe set up something under the light tubes and dehydrate stuff?" Kevin asks as he tries to think of how a dehydrated radish would taste.

"Doubtful, I believe the humidity is too high down here. It feels like the temperature hovers around 70 degrees, but I can feel the dampness in the air so drying stuff would be hard," Hank says, impressed that Kevin was thinking outside the box.

"I wish we had some way to cook things, I am an excellent cook," Jack offers.

"That would be nice, but I think they left cooking out on purpose," Harry states.

"Yeah, we might burn the house down," Karen says sarcastically.

"Actually, cooking takes oxygen out of the air; we need all the oxygen we can get," Harry says in a serious tone.

"We could make soup in the shower pot," Anthony

says as he looks over towards the shower.

"Ewww, that is disgusting," Karen says as her complexion fades.

"Yeah, you say that now," Anthony says, teasing Karen.

"Raw vegetables have better nutrients," Kevin declares.

"With that mention, I am going to water the garden, anyone want to come?" Roger asks as he tries to change the subject.

"Sure, time to get away from the weird ones," Karen says as she looks at Anthony.

"I'm in, I just have to be back to wait for the cable guy; they gave me a 10 am to 8 pm window for him," Anthony attempts some humor, but it is lost on most.

"Har-har," Karen says as she, Max, Anthony, Kevin, and Alfonso head over to the garden.

As Hank stares at Harry as the others leave the table and meander away, Hank bluntly asks, "What do you have against Roger?"

As Harry watches Roger and his entourage walk over to the garden, he turns his stare at Hank and answers, "What do I have against a self-righteous, pompous fake who believes in a myth? What do I have against that hypocritical lacky that thinks he is better than all of us? I will tell you what I have against him and his kind, everything. They claim their mythical God is all about love, yet I only see death and destruction," Harry says as he gets up and heads back into his pod without looking back.

"Well, I was right, he does have issues," Hank quietly says as he gets up and walks over to join the garden group.

"Well, everything appears to be watering well," Roger says as he moves a shovel to divert some of the water flow to another set of rows.

"Where did you learn to do all of this, did you grow up on a farm?" Anthony inquires.

"Far from it, I grew up down on the Southside; the people at my church and books taught me everything I know about gardening, and that has only been since I was saved," Roger says as he leans on the shovel.

"You are from the Southside?" Alfonso asks, surprised.

"Yeah, I am glad I am not there anymore," Roger sadly says as memories start to trickle back into his thoughts.

"You don't act like a Southside," Anthony says, trying to figure out if Roger is lying to them.

"That is because I have been reborn as a child of God; my old is gone, and my new is on," Roger rhymes with a smile.

"What does that mean? I hear your type talk about being born-again all the time, what does that really mean?" Alfonso asks.

"Let's grab some chairs, and I will go get my Bible, it will help me explain what being born-again truly means," Roger says as he stabs the shovel into another channel.

"Bible class, really?" Karen says with a huff.

"What else do we have to do?" Max asks Karen.

"True; get your Bible, Preacher," Karen says reluctantly.

"Will do, and I am not a preacher," Roger says as he turns and runs back to his pod to grabs his Bible.

"Let's set up some chairs and a table over here," Alfonso excitedly says.

"Hey, what's up?" Hank asks as he comes over to the group.

"Preacher Green Jeans is having a Bible class," Karen says.

"Really? Have fun with that," Hank says as he starts to walk away.

"Why are you running, Hank; are you afraid of a little alternative view of your reason for existence?" Karen taunts Hank.

"Afraid? Hank McPherson ain't afraid of anything," Hank says as he turns and grabs a chair.

"Well, hello Hank, please have a seat," Roger says as he comes back to the group.

"So, Preacher Green Jeans, what is today's lesson; are you going to teach me how to walk on water?" Hank asks sarcastically.

"First, I am not a preacher; second, Alfonso asked what it means to be born-again, and third, you can walk on water if your faith is strong enough and the Lord asks you too," Roger says as he grabs a chair and sits facing the group.

"Well, Preacher, tell us," Anthony says, ribbing Roger with the preacher title.

"Okay, first, please forgive me if I act like you are all a bunch of pre-teens; I am a youth pastor and am not used to talking to anyone over the age of twelve," Roger says to his group.

"No problem Youth Pastor Green Jeans," Max says.

"Ugh," Roger sighs as he opens his Bible. "When someone says they are 'born-again,' they are referring back to what Jesus said in **John 3:3**, which states, **'Jesus replied, "I assure you: Unless someone is born again, he cannot see the kingdom of God."',"** Roger says as he reads aloud.

"How is someone born again? Mom had me once, and I guarantee you she won't do that again," Alfonso interrupts.

"Now you are talking just like the Jewish politician who was speaking to Jesus. In **John 3:4**, we read where the leader says, **'"But how can anyone be born when he is old?" Nicodemus asked Him. "Can he enter his**

mother's womb a second time and be born?"," Roger
reads aloud.

"See, I am smart like Nicky," Alfonso says to the
group with a smile.

With a light laugh, Roger says, "Yes, you are, Alfonso.
Now, Jesus answers Nicky, **'Jesus answered, "I assure
you: Unless someone is born of water and the Spirit,
he cannot enter the kingdom of God. Whatever is
born of the flesh is flesh, and whatever is born of the
Spirit is spirit. Do not be amazed that I told you that
you must be born again. The wind blows where it
pleases, and you hear its sound, but you don't know
where it comes from or where it is going. So it is with
everyone born of the Spirit.",**" Roger says as he reads.

"Huh?" Karen says with a raised eyebrow.

"To be born of the water means to be born as we
know it, from a mother without a choice of our own; to
be born of the Spirit means that we have been born as a
child of God by our choice through accepting the Lord's
gift," Roger says as he opens his Bible to another section
after thinking a moment. "In Romans 10, the Apostle
Paul states, **""If you confess with your mouth, "Jesus
is Lord," and believe in your heart that God raised
Him from the dead, you will be saved. One believes
with the heart, resulting in righteousness, and one
confesses with the mouth, resulting in salvation. Now
the Scripture says, 'Everyone who believes on Him
will not be put to shame, for there is no distinction
between Jew and Greek, since the same Lord of all
is rich to all who call on Him. For everyone who calls
on the name of the Lord will be saved.'",**" Roger
pauses a moment to let what he read sink into his group.
"When we believe, when we truly believe, that is when
our rebirth begins; when we confess out loud our true

belief, when we do away with our old life, when our old life dies away, and our new life comes, that is when we become Born-Again. To be born as a child of God means that we have turned from our sins and have asked for forgiveness. It also means that we have accepted Jesus Christ as our Lord and Saviour, that we fully believe in who Jesus is and what the Scriptures say about Him, and that we have accepted Jesus Christ as our Master; and as such follow all of His commands, not just the ones that we want to. When we do all of this, when we leave our old life fully, we become a new creation with God as our heavenly Father," Roger says to the group.

"Nobody is my master; I am my own master," Anthony says as he furrows his brow at Roger.

"Anthony, to have a master is not a bad thing, only in the last couple hundred years has the term master gained a negative connotation attached to oppression and pain. Back in biblical times, an upright master protected and took care of his workers just as if they were family members, sometimes better. To have a good master meant that you would be cared for and taken care of, and you had no worries. To say you are a slave for Christ and that He is your Lord and Master is to say that you will follow His commandments, and He will take care of you. He will give you eternal life, He will never leave or forsake you, He promises us this very thing," Roger says as Anthony stares at him.

"So, all I have to do to be born again is to say I am sorry for all the bad things I have done, follow the Ten Commandments, and tell everyone that Jesus is my Lord; and I will be saved?" Karen asks in a skeptical tone.

"Well, you have to truly repent of your sins; to repent is to ask for forgiveness and 'go and sin no more.' You cannot ask for forgiveness for adultery while you are in an adulterous relationship. You cannot ask for forgiveness for beating somebody up as you tell everyone how much you hate that person and that they had it coming. You must turn from the sin altogether," Roger says. "And it is not just to follow the Ten Commandments, those were God's original commandments to the Jewish people; we must follow the commandments of Jesus as is found throughout the New Testament. In essence, those commandments boil down to loving God with all of your heart and soul and showing love to all others. We can study all of Jesus's commandments later," Roger says with a smile. "And yes, we must tell others that we are a child of Christ, that is a commandment; we can't be ashamed of who we are," Roger says to everyone.

"So, you don't sin, Pastor?" Alfonso asks Roger with a doubtful attitude.

"I have sinned when in a weak moment, but when I do, I ask for forgiveness; for when I sin, that means I am walking away from the narrow path to the Lord. When a brother or sister in Christ walks away from the narrow path that leads to the Lord, their fellow Christians are commanded to rebuke them and bring them back to the path. That is another lesson in itself, though," Roger explains.

"You say if we do all of this stuff, we are saved; what does that really mean?" Anthony asks as he tries to drill down on what Roger is saying.

"To put it bluntly: to be saved means you have eternal life with God; to not be saved means you have eternal damnation in hell," Roger declares as he looks Anthony straight into his eyes.

"Why can't we all just have eternal life? Why is there a hell?" Karen begs of Roger.

With a sigh, Roger says, "Because of sin. In Revelations, it says that sin cannot enter the new heaven, nor the one who sins; only those who have been washed by the blood of Jesus can enter. God made humans without sin, but Adam chose to sin; that choice damned us all and blocked us from being able to dwell in God's presence, that is why we got kicked out of the Garden of Eden. That is, until the second Adam came, the Son of the Father, and gave us salvation. Because of the pure sacrifice of Jesus, we now have the choice of eternal life or eternal suffering; it is our free choice to make," Roger says, "We cannot live a life without consequences for our choices."

"Being a Christian is a lot of work," Max says after everyone sits quietly for a moment.

"Not really; ask for forgiveness, stop sinning, believe in God and let people know about Him, and be good," Roger says and then pauses. After a moment, Roger begins again, "I have one more lesson for you to think on, the message of the three crosses. When Jesus was crucified, He was crucified with two others beside Him; two thieves, one on the right, and one on the left. One thief tells Jesus that if He is the Messiah, he must save all of them. The other thief rebukes that thief and asks Jesus to forgive him, and he acknowledges that Jesus is the Son of the Father, that Jesus is God. This repentant thief then tells the evil thief that they both deserve their fate since they both did the crime, but the repentant thief tells the bad thief that Jesus has no sin and does not belong on the cross. Jesus tells the repentant thief that he is forgiven and will be in heaven, with Jesus. All the repentant thief did was believe in Jesus; he had faith, and for that faith, he had salvation. That thief didn't give an elaborate prayer, he didn't send anybody money, he didn't go to a priest and be told to say fifty Hail Mary's, he didn't burn any incense and chant. All he did was believe in Jesus and ask for salvation, that is it," Roger says with a pleading earnestness in his voice as his eyes travel from one to the other.

"That is a lot to think on Preacher," Karen says to Roger as she drops her stare to the dirt.

"Yes, it is. If you have any questions, ask; I can clear up some time on my calendar," Roger says dryly. "My one desire is for each and every one of us to give ourselves to the Lord; I want us all up in heaven when everything is said and done, God wants that, and I want what God wants. Remember this: Jesus suffered and died for each one of us, He wants you in heaven with Him. Jesus wants to forgive you of your sins, all you have to do is make the choice to believe, and to ask," Roger says to the group.

"Lesson over?" Hank asks as he feels the weight of conviction coming over him.

"For now, it is good to let things digest a little at a time," Roger says in his calmest of voices, "But like I said, my calendar has some free spots on it if you want to talk."

"Thanks, Preacher, good message for the day," Alfonso says quietly as he gets up.

"Yep, thanks, Preacher," Karen says with a smile as her head spins.

"You are all welcome, but I am not a preacher, I am a youth pastor," Roger emphatically states.

"Thanks, youth pastor Preacher Roger Green Jeans," Max says as they all begin heading back to their pods.

"Ugh," Roger says as he walks back to his pod to read his Bible and recharge his mind.

"Well, what do you think?" Karen stops and asks Max, Alfonso, Hank, and Anthony.

"I don't know, it is a lot, but eternal life sounds better than eternal death," Alfonso says.

"Hey, I am a good guy, I haven't killed anyone," Anthony interjects.

"Sin is not just killing, sin is all the things your mama yelled at you for," Max tells Anthony.

"And Roger said we have to be born again," Karen reminds them.

"A lot to digest; and besides, not all of us can be saved," Hank says as he pictures the thieves on the crosses next to Jesus.

"Yeah, a lot to digest; but it sounds like we can all be saved," Karen says to Hank as she and Max start back to the pods, talking amongst themselves.

"Time for a jog then a shower," Hank says as he starts jogging, and thinking.

"What do you think?" Alfonso asks Anthony.

"I ain't jogging, that is self-abuse," Anthony states bluntly.

"I meant about what the Preacher said," Alfonso asks.

"I don't know, too much to think on right now; come pedal for me, and I will pedal for you," Anthony says, effectively changing the subject as they start walking for the shower.

As Hank stretches out on his cot after his shower, he looks at his watch, "10, 9, 8, 7, 6, 5, 4."

"Hank, don't launch off," Robert says over the mini-intercom.

"Right on time, sir," Hank says back to the Colonel.

"How was your day? It looked like you all kept busy," John says as he feels Hank out; John had already reviewed the tapes of the day.

"Yeah, garden watered and mental seeds planted. Everyone thinks that you have them down here to repopulate the world after the 'big one.' Poor Karen is about ready to tunnel back up thinking you have her down to be the new Eve for the world," Hank says with a chuckle.

"Yeah, we caught a lot of your conversations today," Robert says cautiously.

"I never thought I would see you at a Bible study, Hank," Joanne says with a smile in her voice as she broaches the subject the others had been avoiding.

"Hey, Jo, nice to hear your voice; and it wasn't really my idea," Hank says as he begins to squirm.

"I know, they called you a yellow-bellied chicken," John teases.

"Not quite, but close," Hank says. They know him too well; call Hank a chicken, and he will do anything to prove you wrong.

"I caught the conversation with Harry," John says, "If we see an imminent threat, we will use the gas," John says as he leans into his microphone, referring to the sleeping gas delivery system that they installed in case of a riot.

"Only use the gas if I am incapacitated or about to be bested by Karen," Hank orders, "I mean it."

"Okay, but defuse the boy," Robert commands.

"I don't think he can be defused; he needs to blow," Hank warns as he stares at the ceiling.

"I hate to say this, but I agree; he has built up so much hatred for Roger, he needs to blow," John quietly says.

"Red will eat him up; Roger won't fight back," Hank says as he shakes his head.

"Keep an eye on them, please," Joanne pleads with Hank.

"I will, Momma; I won't let them hurt each other too bad," Hank teases the Major, "Goodnight everyone, it is time to sleep, I actually worked today," Hank says as he fluffs his pillow.

"Goodnight son," John says.

"Night-night, Hanky," Joanne says teasingly.

"Goodnight Soldier," Robert says with a stern, fatherly voice.

As Hank lays in the dark on his cot, he thinks back to what Roger was saying, and says to himself, 'Sorry preacher, my sins can't be forgiven.' Hank rolls over and waits for the inevitable nightmares to come.

CHAPTER 19

০৩ ৪০

General Mars is sitting at his desk, worried. It appears that every lead the General follows turns out to be a dead-end, and the General hates dead-ends. He knows two players on the other team, but that is all. Cho Sang and Kim Chang-hwan are two complete opposites when you look at them on paper: Kim is a well-known physicist, engineer, and spy; Cho is a college student who has never been in trouble, has a 3.8 GPA, in the school gardening club, and the child of a sleeper cell. Who else is there?

As the General sits pouring through the stack of papers, his phone rings, "General Mars," he says as he answers the phone.

"General Mars, sir, this is Corporal Martin down in the ballistics lab. Sir, we have a hit on the bullet used in the Frank Jones assassination," Corporal Martin states.

"You do? That is great, Corporal Martin; I will be right down," the General excitedly says as he hangs up the phone and heads out the door; this just might be the lead he needs.

As the General enters the lab, Corporal Martin snaps to attention and salutes the General, "At ease son; talk to me," the General says to the young Corporal as he returns the salute.

"Well, sir, the bullet we recovered is a 180-grain, full-copper, 300 Weatherby Magnum hollow point that had been modified to explode on impact; it is composed of a lacquer sealed aluminum tip with a lead azide center," the Corporal excitedly says to the General as they walk over to the Corporals workbench.

"Interesting," the General says, then asks in a confused tone, "If they were designed to explode, how do you have anything left to check?"

"Well sir, there is a flaw with explosive bullets, sometimes they don't explode and wind up leaving us a perfect specimen," the Corporal says, smiling.

"Well, do we have a perfect specimen?" The General questions the Corporal patiently.

"Oh, yes sir; sorry for getting ahead of myself. The first bullet exploded after entering the victim; because of that, Mr. Jones was dead instantly. The second bullet, the 'just in case' shot as we like to call it, it didn't explode. We checked the rifling on that bullet to ones we have in our database, and we connected it to an assassination of a high-level Russian mob boss in 2010," the Corporal says excitedly.

"A Russian mob boss? Do we know who did it?" The General asks, worried now that the Russian mob might somehow be involved.

"Yes sir, we do. The information we have, from the Russians no less, is that it was a hit performed by Kang-Dae 'Daniel' Dong-gun, by order of Jang Sung-taek," the Corporal says.

"Jang Sung-taek? Wasn't that Kim Jong-un's uncle?" The General cautiously asks, trying to remember his North Korean history.

"Yes, and it is rumored that Jang's wife, Kim Jong-il's sister, set up Jang's execution," the Corporal says as he is barely able to contain his excitement.

"So, this Daniel guy is a top-level assassin for North Korea," the General says quietly, trying not to let the Corporal hear the worriedness in his voice.

"More than that; according to the Russian report, Daniel is an elite North Korean Special Purpose Force member. Daniel is a very dangerous and evil man," the Corporal says as his excitement about dealing with assassins begins to get the best of him.

"Special Purpose Force member?" The General says as he stares into the Corporals eyes and pauses as he processes this new information, then the General goes on before the Corporal can reply, "Yes, he is a dangerous man. Thank you, Corporal; please send me everything you have as soon as possible," the General says as he starts walking for the door.

"Yes, sir!" The Corporal says, snapping to attention.

"At ease soldier, at ease," General Mars says as he walks out and heads back to his office without looking back.

As the General enters his office and locks the door behind him, he heads over to his desk, unlocks the bottom drawer, and pulls out a thick file marked: **Jones, Frank – 012.2017**. As he sits down and sets the file on his desk, he opens it up to a tab labeled:Associates. "So, Frank, now I need to add three new friends to your file: Kang-Dae 'Daniel' Dong-gun, Cho Sang, and Kim Chang-hwan," the General says as he stares at Frank's picture.

General Mars turns on his computer and logs into the secure section of the Defense Intelligence Agency website. Once in, he enters Daniel, Cho, Park, Frank, and Kim's information and begins the cross search; he knows if there is a connection, the DIA will find it.

As the General flips through Frank's file, he cannot help shaking the two fears that weigh on him; if they set that warhead off in downtown Atlanta or Chattanooga; one, the death toll would be unbelievable, and two, the ensuing chaos would be unfathomable. "Frank, I will find who the mastermind is, I will find that connection, and I will get my warhead back," the General says at the same time his computer beeps.

When the General looks at the computer monitor, he sees DIA has only given him one name: Jung Yong-chul.

As the General pulls up Jung's file, he begins to read it slowly so as not to miss anything: Colonel Jung Yong-chul, age 26, married, one child, North Korean Special Purpose Force commanding officer; suspected of murder, terrorism, sabotage, and espionage against Americans and her allies.

General Frank Mars quietly picks up his phone and dials a very rarely used number. "This is General Frank Mars, I need to speak to the President; it is a matter of national security," the General says as the full picture is laid before him; and now he is the most frightened he has ever been in his 58 years of life.

CHAPTER 20

Ω Ω

As Roger heads out of his pod, Anthony waves him over to the breakfast table.

"Good morning, Roger," Karen says as Roger sits down.

"Good morning, everyone, I hope you all slept well," Roger says to the group.

"Morning. Not bad, better than them," Max says through a mouthful of MRE while motioning to the crowd around the latrine.

"Excuse me, sir; coming through, I say, excuse me!" Frederick says aggressively as he hurries out of his pod and runs for the latrine.

Roger watches Frederick dash across the yard just as Chung-Hee comes out of the bathroom holding his stomach, "Oh, I think I have the flu; did you see any Pepto in the medical stuff?" Chung-Hee says to Kevin who is standing by the latrine.

"I think there was some in there, but you don't have the flu; you have the MRE curse Karen warned us about," Kevin explains.

"Great," Chung-Hee says as he spins and runs back into the latrine.

"How are you feeling?" Anthony asks Roger.

"Good. How about you guys?" Roger says, motioning towards the latrines.

"I feel fine; iron gut," Anthony says as he pats his stomach.

"Never better; I was weaned on MRE's," Karen says.

"I'm good. That stuff is better than my cooking," Max says half-heartedly.

"Note to self," Karen quietly says to herself as Max shoots her a raised eyebrow glance.

"So, what is the plan for today?" Anthony asks.

"Watering the garden is about it. It feels strange we don't have to weed or worry about bugs," Roger says as he watches the latrine group and wonders how the composter is going to hold up to all of the use.

"Less work, I like it," Karen says, then adds, "Hey, no bees to pollinate for us!"

"I know, but we won't have to worry about that since we will be out of here before pollination time comes," Roger says. "But they need to put a couple of beehives down here so that the future groups can have honey and open-pollinated plants, and honey for food and medicine."

"When will pollination time be, Green Jeans?" Hank asks as he comes over.

"Well, most things will be around the 45-day mark, but I saw that a lot of the seed varieties were self-pollinators; all we would have to do is shake those plants to help them out. For the other plants, I suspect that is why Q-Tips are in the garden shed," Roger replies as he fidgets with his empty canteen while staring over at their hot water supply.

"Boy, now you are talking work," Alfonso says as he sits down. "Oh, I think I will skip coffee for now," Alfonso says as he sees the crowd of belly-huggers around the latrine area.

"Good idea," Karen says.

"Time to check the garden," Roger says as he gets up and starts heading that way.

"Wait up, Preacher, you don't get all the fun," Anthony

says as the group gets up and follows him over.

"Hey, I see green!" Alfonso says excitedly.

"Ah good, the radishes are coming up; I didn't expect them till tomorrow," Roger says.

"Yeah, this is only day four; you are Green Jeans!" Max says with a laugh as he reminds everyone how long they have been in the Bunker.

"Prayer is powerful stuff," Roger says with a smile.

"You said after two weeks we start eating them?" Karen asks as she looks at the little green babies.

"Yep, the thinnings; we planted the radishes close together so that we could harvest the ones we thin out to make room for the actual radishes. We will eat the thinnings," Roger says.

"I like radish greens," Jack says as he comes up to the group.

"What do they taste like?" Karen asks with a curious look.

"Hint of radish, a little peppery," Jack explains.

"Cool, anything is better than gruel," Hank says, thinking of the MRE's, and the coming final two weeks of the study.

"Yeah, I figure we will have a few with our last meal," Roger says as he bends down to the row of green dots.

"Dude, never say last meal when we are a hundred feet underground," Alfonso says with a seriousness that makes the others take notice.

"Hey, this is the safest place around in the event of the impending global destruction," Hank says, seizing on his opportunity to water the mental seeds he has planted.

"You think?" Anthony asks as he looks up towards the roof.

"Yeah, methinks. Look around and take inventory. We are one-hundred feet underground which means that we are shielded from any nuclear blast except a dead-on strike. We have a constant flow of fresh water, garden soil, composting latrine for fertilizer, plenty of garden seeds, great light, and a person with gardening knowledge. I say if an attack occurred this week, we could live down here for quite a few years," Hank says as he gauges their reactions, just as he feels a cold chill run over his body; Hank has only felt that chill a couple times in the past, and it was never associated with anything good.

"Wouldn't the elevator shaft and light tubes be a weak link regarding radiation?" Max asks, bringing Hank's mind back into the mix.

"I don't think so, as long as the actual fallout doesn't come down, we would be okay," Karen says as she thinks about some of the dinner table discussions she had with her dad. "And what radiation does come down, the iodine pills would help keep us from cancer."

"What about air? If a blast seals us off, how will we breathe?" Jack asks as he looks over at the elevator doors.

"The moss on the walls and the garden will produce ample oxygen as long as it is green; that is why there is no fire source; fires eat oxygen. Like Brutus said, the only real worry would be from a direct strike, and we wouldn't have any worries then," Harry says as he comes over.

"Yep, we would actually be set," Hank says while looking at the seedlings and fighting the urge to pummel Harry.

"Farmer boy did good, he is a daddy," Harry says sarcastically to Roger.

"We all did well through the grace of God," Roger says in his calm tone that seems to always light Harry's fuse.

"Yeah, sure," Harry says as he turns and walks away.

"Punk," Karen says under her breath.

"No Karen, he isn't; he just needs our prayers and

love; he is hurting," Roger says as a sadness falls over him.

"Dude, watch him, or he will be hurting you," Alfonso says as he watches Harry head back over to his pod.

"Don't worry about me, I have God on my side," Roger says as he says a quiet prayer for Harry.

"How can you be so sure?" Jack asks with a stare.

"Because the Bible tells me so," Roger says smiling, "I memorized two verses early this morning; **Romans 8:28** says, **"We know that all things work together for the good of those who love God: those who are called according to His purpose."**, And **Hebrews 13:6, "Therefore, we may boldly say: The Lord is my helper; I will not be afraid. What can man do to me?"**, so, you see, I know I have God on my side," Roger says with a sincere smile.

"So God has never let you down? Everything always works out the way you want it?" Max questions.

"No, and no. God has never let me down, but usually, things don't work out the way I want them to; they work out the way God wants them to, which is the right way," Roger says to Max.

"That's messed up, God should make it work out the way you want it to, not the way He wants it," Alfonso says with an attitude.

"God knows best. You see, God knows the beginning and the end, He knows all. He knows all of the variables; that is why I let God drive while I ride shotgun," Roger says plainly.

"But if He is so great and powerful, why can't He make it all works out the way we want it to?" Max questions.

"Because, the employees don't tell the Boss what to do; the soldiers don't tell the General what to do; the servant doesn't tell their Master what to do; God takes care of us the way He sees fit, God knows best. God will take care of our needs in this life, and award us in our everlasting life with Him. And besides, if God let everything work out the way you wanted it to, what if that isn't the way Karen wants it to work out or the way Max wants it; God knows best," Roger explains.

"I wish I had your faith," Karen says quietly.

"You can, you all can; all you have to do is believe and accept Jesus Christ into your heart as your Lord and Saviour," Roger says as he stares at them all with pleading eyes.

"You make it sound pretty enticing Preacher," Max says as Karen looks at him.

"Eternal salvation is very enticing; the alternative is not enticing at all," Roger says.

"Come on Preacher, show us what we have to plant next," Alfonso says as he tries to change the subject.

"Okay, I see you guys want the lesson to be over," Roger says as they all start heading towards the second row.

"Yeah, better for now," Karen says with a smile as the group heads over to plant the second plot.

CHAPTER 21

Σ Ȱ

"Good morning Jo; I brought you some Joe," John says as he comes in with two cups of coffee.

"How original. Good morning John; is it that time already?" Joanne asks, referring to the end of her 4-hour shift.

"Yeah, it is almost eight o'clock," John says, "Any excitement last night?" John asks.

"The MRE's are taking their toll on Frederick, Chung-Hee, and Kevin," Joanne says as she turns down the volume on the monitors.

"Only those three?" John asks, surprised.

"Yes, luckily just those three," Joanne says as she remembers her bouts with the MRE curse.

"At least we let Hank pick the flavors, that might have helped," John says as he remembers back to the vivid discussions between Hank and the planning committee concerning the supplies. Hank was so worried about the MRE flavors that he changed out the committee's lunch with MRE's; Hank won that battle and was put in charge of choosing the flavors.

"Possibly, I know he was adamant about keeping the 'five fingers of death' away," Joanne says with a chuckle.

"Wasn't that the beans and franks? Didn't we have about four cases of meals with those in them that Hank adamantly rejected?" John asks as he tries to remember back.

"Yes; Robert took them home, he actually says

he loves them with a warm beer," Joanne says as she squinches her nose and gives a shudder.

"Disgusting, utterly disgusting," John says as his taste buds envision the flavor of congealed pork grease and warm beer.

"He has his quirks, that is for sure; but all in all, he is a pretty decent guy," Joanne defends her commanding officer and friend.

"Yeah, he is. Why don't you bug out, it's my turn to watch the latrine assault," John says as Joanne yawns.

"Okay, I have some errands to run. Oh, Harry approached the gardeners and took a quick jab at Roger; Roger shut him down with a little religious talk," Joanne says as she gets up.

"Jab; about what?" John asks in a worried tone.

"They have little radish seedlings; Harry called him a daddy and Roger said they all were, and then thanked the Lord for them. Oh, and Hank egged them on about being able to survive down there for years; they ran through a bunch of scenarios and actually lived in the end," Joanne says with a chuckle.

"Interesting. I will play back this morning when things get boring. It looks like they are checking out the second section of the garden," John says as he turns his focus to the monitor.

"Okay, have fun and try to stay awake," Joanne says as she heads out the door.

"I will, and be careful please," John says, thinking about the assassin who is still on the loose.

"Yes, sir," Joanne says as the door shuts.

"Please be careful," John says to the closed door.

CHAPTER 22

General Mars is sitting at his desk talking on the phone, "Yes Mr. President, I understand. I will keep you informed of any new developments," General Mars says as he hangs up the phone.

The General sits for a moment contemplating his next move; he picks up the phone and dials the Forensics Division downstairs, "Lieutenant Jamison, General Mars; any new information?" General Mars asks and then listens intensely. "Great, I will be there in five minutes," the General says as he hangs up.

As the General walks into the communications lab of the Forensic Division, Lieutenant Jamison comes over to him and snaps to attention with a salute, "General Mars, sir," she says.

"At ease, Lieutenant Jamison," the General says, returning the salute.

"Sir, we received the phone logs from the phone company concerning Cho Sang's phone," Lieutenant Jamison proclaims.

"And? Did you find the magic bullet?" General Mars eagerly asks.

"No, not the actual magic bullet; you might say we found the gun cabinet the rifle was in that fired the bullet," the Lieutenant says and then continues. "I have been able to correlate off of the cell towers used, and I was able to get a general location of our targets whereabouts," Lieutenant Jamison states.

"I see," the General says, "Am I to assume our target hasn't used her phone since?"

"No sir, she hasn't. The last we have her using her phone is about an hour after she left the facility. I believe she used the GPS on it to get to her final location," the Lieutenant pauses for a moment, and then continues, "She was using some type of software that erased her final destination," Lieutenant Jamison says with a disgusted look on her face.

"So, tell me where this gun cabinet is," the General says, trying to get the Lieutenant back on point by using her own metaphors.

"Woodland Heights, Signal Mountain area; we have it down to about three square miles," the Lieutenant declares.

"That is a big area, but at least it is not all of Chattanooga," the General says as he tries to picture the location.

"I have given this information to Captain Mott in the forensics lab; he is using it to come up with a list of suitable buildings that could house 'The Package,'" the Lieutenant explains.

"Not much space is needed; a garage, warehouse, even a tractor-trailer rig could work for all they need to do," General Mars says as he pictures how small the warhead actually is.

"Sir, may I suggest you check with him? Captain Mott has some ideas; he is in the next office over," Lieutenant Jamison suggests.

"I will; thank you, Lieutenant Jamison," General Mars says as he starts for the door.

"Yes sir, you are welcome sir," the Lieutenant says as she snaps to attention as the General walks out.

As General Mars goes into the main forensic lab, he is met with a technician snapping to attention and saying,

"Officer on deck!" As the other two technicians snap to attention, General Mars says as he returns their salutes, "At ease, soldiers, at ease; and we are on shore now son. Which one of you is Captain Mott?"

"Sir, I am, sir. How can I help you, General Mars, sir?" A tall, brassy-headed, late-20's, lab-coated technician excitedly asks as he comes over to the General.

"You can tell me you know where 'The Package' is," General Mars says, using the code word Lieutenant Jamison coined for the warhead.

"Sir, please come over here, and I will show you what I have come up with," Captain Mott says as he scurries over to his computer station.

Once at his computer, Captain Mott pulls up a satellite map of the eastern half of Tennessee and begins talking while working the keyboard and mouse, "With the information Lieutenant Jamison gave me, I have a ballpark of the phone's last location. We know the phone was being used to find an address, but we do not know what that address was. When we use simple deduction, we can reasonably assume the person using the phone to find the address kept the phone on until the address was found. With this information, I can say with fair certainty that we are in the right ballpark for where the phone was directed."

"Show me the field, Captain," General Mars says as he continues with the baseball analogies as he stares at the computer monitor.

Captain Mott zooms in on a highlighted section of the map on the monitor, "Right here sir, this is the ballpark," Captain Mott says as he points to the highlighted section.

"How can we make that area smaller?" The General asks as he tries to get his bearings on the highlighted location.

"Well, knowing that they will need room to work on

'The Package,' park vehicles, and not draw attention to themselves by coming and going; I figure they need a warehouse type building. Because of this, I have been trying to identify those types of places in our ballpark. And I have been trying to figure out how they would get 'The Package' to ground zero," the Captain says as he stares at the General.

"Well, how do you think they will deliver it?" The General inquires of the Captain who appears to have figured everything out.

"Tractor trailer rig, sir; big enough to carry The Package and any shielding, yet not big enough to throw off any flags," the Captain says while smiling.

"Big rig is possible, but what about a cargo van?" The General asks as he ponders the thought of a tractor-trailer driving into the heart of Chattanooga or Atlanta.

"I don't think so, sir. A cargo van loaded down with The Package and shielding would be pushing a ton of weight and would be unwieldy to drive," the Captain states.

"More unyielding than a semi?" General Mars asks with a raised brow.

"Yes, sir, I believe so. My money is on a semi and trailer; even a cargo container," the Captain states adamantly.

"Well Captain, how many places have you found in the ballpark that can park a big rig inside?" General Mars asks as he understands the Captain's reasoning.

"Thirty-three; I was just getting ready to print the list for you," the Captain says with a smile.

"Thirty-three? That will take some coordination to determine which ones to raid," General Mars ponders as his hopes drop. "Captain, please print me that list and also send it to me electronically with the map. And Captain, continue to scour your ballpark; we can't leave any stones unturned. Don't rule anything out."

"Yes, sir," Captain Mott says, "Here you go, sir," Captain Mott says as he hands General Mars the list off of the printer.

"Thank you, Captain Mott; let me know if you find out any new information," General Mars says as he takes the list.

"Yes sir, General Mars," Captain Mott says as he salutes the General and snaps to attention.

"At ease, son," General Mars says as he returns the salute and walks out the door and back to his office.

Once General Mars is back at his desk, he picks up his phone and dials a number, "Colonel Miller, this is General Mars. Colonel, I need surveillance on thirty-three locations," Frank says and pauses as he listens to Colonel Nick Miller. "I know, Nick, that is a lot; one thing will make it easier, we are only looking for North Korean's," the General says as he sits down in his chair.

"You only have five units available? Well, we will just have to break up the areas. Survey until identified occupancy is fully verified; move on to next as fast as possible, but without losing efficiency, you know the drill, Nick," General Mars instructs. After listening for a moment, the General says, "Thanks, Nick, this is the biggest of big; I will send over names and pictures. And Nick, this is way beyond need to know."

As General Mars hangs up, he pulls up Frank Jones file on his computer and assembles a secure package to send to Colonel Miller. After General Mars clicks the send button, he opens the email from Captain Mott that contains the list of locations, and the map of the area. As the General looks at the list, he realizes he has been around some of these addresses very recently.

With trepidation, the General opens the map file and stares at it; he knows this area. As the General stares at the map, he opens his web browser and goes to the search page where he enters the address for the Harrison Research and Analytical Facility. When the results come up, the General clicks on the map tab of the search engine. As the General stares at his monitor, he zooms slightly out to see the overall area, and sees a location on the map marked, Woodland Height. The General looks at the map scale and then opens his desk drawer and pulls out a ruler which he matches to the scale on the map. The General takes the ruler and places it on his monitor and measures the distance from the center of Woodland Height, to the Facility, "One mile," the General quietly says as he feels a knot form in his stomach, "My baby is at ground zero."

CHAPTER 23

❧ ❧

As Anthony lies on his bunk, he keeps replaying Roger's sermon; he can't seem to shake it, he is a good guy, God will let him into heaven.

Anthony thinks back to when Roger said he was from the Southside, "If he is from the Southside, he must have been from one of the better spots. That boy has silver spoon written all over him," Anthony says aloud as he sits up on the side of the bed.

"Ugh, I hate it when I can't sleep," Anthony says as he finds his coveralls and puts them on. As Anthony fumbles his way to the door, he makes his way out into the courtyard where there is a hint of light coming down the tubes. As Anthony's eyes adjust to the moonlit courtyard, he sees the shape of someone sitting at the tables. Anthony slowly heads over to the tables while trying to figure out who it is.

"Good evening, sir," Roger says to Anthony as he comes to the table.

"Good evening, Roger; you can't sleep either?" Anthony says while thinking, *I can't get away from Silver-Spoon.*

"Not really, I have gotten used to saying goodnight to Rachel and then reading the Gospel until I get tired," Roger says as Anthony sits down.

"How long have you and Rachel been together?" Anthony asks as he tries to make small talk.

"A little over two years," Roger says with a smile.

"Two years? Man, I have never been with somebody that long," Anthony says with a little chuckle.

"Me neither, but when she came in my life, I knew she was the forever and ever one," Roger said, then adds, "I pretty much proposed on the third date. I asked her if I could court her then, but I knew I wanted to marry her after just the first five minutes with her."

"Court? Dude, you are old-fashioned," Anthony says, shaking his head. "What are you, some type of blue-blood that got stuck down on the Southside?" Anthony asks, trying to see what Roger really is about.

"Blue-blood? Far from it. You know how people say they either come from the right or the wrong side of the tracks?" Roger asks as he looks over at Anthony in the dark.

"Yeah," Anthony responds.

"My family thought the wrong side of the tracks was uptown good," Roger says with his head held down.

"Are you saying that you had it bad?" Anthony says doubtfully as he tries to make out Roger's face in the moonlight.

"I saw so much death, drugs, evil; I literally had to die to be saved," Roger volunteers.

"Die; what, like spiritually?" Anthony asks, not understanding and thinking Roger was segueing into a preaching session.

"No, I really died. I took a 38-slug right to the heart; shot trying to steal a purse for drug money," Roger says as he remembers his old self.

"So, you died? Why ain't you still dead; what are you, a zombie?" Anthony mockingly asks, not believing Roger.

"No zombie, I joke and say it was because my heart had been so hardened not even a bullet could penetrate it; but I think it was because God has plans for me, I just don't know what they are yet," Roger says as the thoughts of his earlier life dance in his head.

"So, you are a druggie and a thief," Anthony declares as he really starts to dislike Roger.

"I was a thief, but not a druggie," Roger corrects.

"You just said you were snatching the purse for drug money," Anthony says, thinking he just caught Roger in a lie.

"I was. You see, I grew up around drugs; I saw the death they caused. Drugs took my mom, my sister, and my friends. I decided that morning I was going to let drugs take me. It was the anniversary of my mom's death," Roger slowly says as he stares at Anthony. "I'd given up; I was a two-bit hoodlum staying alive by stealing and running, I figured I had no life ahead of me. Every day I would hear Satan telling me how worthless I was, how nobody would ever care for me, how my life was a worthless waste, how I was better off dead.So I decided he was right and figured I would just go and O.D. and get it over with," Roger says as remembers the pain.

"Let me get this straight, you got killed stealing the purse for the drug money you were going to use to kill yourself? How stinking ironic," Anthony says with a light laugh.

"No doubt. I lived, but by no account of mine. If Momma Betty hadn't prayed for me, hadn't led me to Christ as I lay on the park path with my life slipping away; I know the devil would have won," Roger says as he remembers the love.

"Momma Betty?" Anthony says, confused.

"Yeah, Momma Betty," Roger says with a smile. "You see, the woman whose purse I was stealing, the one who shot me; she not only prayed over me right there, she adopted me after I was released," Roger says with a lump forming in his throat.

"In other words, your momma put your lights out?" Anthony asks, totally dumbfounded at what he was hearing.

"Yep, Momma, turned off my lights so that the Light could shine in; so to speak," Roger says. "I always figured God didn't want me, I was too bad of a kid, a throwaway, worthless; but I was wrong, God wants all of us," Roger says as he stares towards Harry's pod.

"God doesn't want me, that is for sure," Anthony says as he thinks on his life.

"That is where you are wrong, Anthony. God wants us all to be saved, He says so all throughout the Scriptures," Roger says. "All He asks is that you accept the Son on His terms, that you believe in Him with all of your heart," Roger says, then continues, "Have you heard of the Apostle Paul?"

"Yeah, he was one of the dudes who knew Jesus, wasn't he?" Anthony asks as he sees how Roger was swinging this into a sermon.

"Yes, he was. Do you know the story behind Paul?" Roger inquires.

"Wasn't he a fisherman?" Anthony volunteers.

"No, that was Peter and Andrew; Paul was a Christian hunter," Roger corrects and declares.

"A Christian hunter? Wait a minute, I've never heard that one," Anthony says as he stares at Roger.

"Well, most theologians wouldn't word it that way, but he was. Paul, whose Jewish name was Saul of Tarsus and his Roman name was Paul, was a devout Jew, a Pharisee, who had permission from the Jewish High Priest to destroy the Christian church and all who followed Christ," Roger states.

"Wait a minute, his job was to actually kill Christians, yet he was a Christian?" Anthony asks, confused.

"He wasn't a Christian, yet. You see, Paul was doing as

he was taught; destroy all who blasphemed God, and that is what he thought Christians were doing by declaring Jesus as God. You see, Saul Paul did not understand that Jesus was the Messiah spoken of in the Old Testament; the Messiah who is the Son of the Father and came to save us all. Saul Paul knew the Old Testament backward's, and forward, he was extremely well educated; but he was blind to the truth that Jesus was the Messiah as foretold by Scriptures. Only after the Lord came to Saul Paul on the road to Damascus, did Saul Paul realize what was true; the Lord blinded Saul Paul so that he could see," Roger explains.

"So Saul Paul was a murderer, yet God forgave him?" Anthony asks as he tries to take the lesson in.

"Not a murderer, a soldier doing what he thought was right. He was a murderer in the Christians eyes, but a great soldier in the Jewish and Roman eyes; it is all in the perspective of who is looking. That is why we must always remember that God forgives all who come to Him and asks for Salvation; God wants to save us all; even the Saul Paul's out there," Roger adamantly explains.

"And that's all in the Bible; info on Saul Paul?" Anthony asks in disbelief.

"Yep, everything you need to know is in the Scriptures," Roger tells Anthony.

"More to think on, Preacher, more to think on," Anthony says as he realizes his anger towards Roger has gone away.

"Yes, there is; and I am not a preacher," Roger says weakly.

"What is the definition of a preacher?" Anthony bluntly asks.

"I guess one who teaches the Gospel with authority," Roger answers.

"Let's go back to sleep, 'one who teaches the Gospel

with authority'; the lights will be coming on soon," Anthony jabs as he gets up.

"Yeah, I guess you are right, and I am tired now," Roger says as they get up and head back to their pods.

"Lots to think about. Goodnight, Preacher," Anthony says as he retires to his pod.

"Goodnight, Anthony," Roger says as he goes into his pod.

Over by the corner of the latrine, Harry sits staring towards the pods; thinking on all he had just heard. Harry slowly gets up and walks back to his pod, thinking.

CHAPTER 24

As Joanne watches the thermal images on the monitors, as she listens to Roger and Anthony's talk, she feels a tug on her heart that she has not felt for many years. Joanne grabs her notebook and writes a few things down; she knows she needs to look up some stuff later and she knows she will forget. As Joanne watches Roger and Anthony go back into their pods and lay down in their cots, she can't help but wonder what was going through Harry's mind; Joanne knows he could hear everything said by Anthony and Roger.

As Joanne watches Harry go back into his pod, she sees him start slamming his fist on his bed, pummeling it while saying through sobs, "Lies, lies, lies! All a bunch of murderous lies!" After a few moments, Harry stops and sits on the edge of his bed and calmly says, "Time for you and me to have a talk, preacher boy," and Harry gets up and heads out of his pod towards Roger.

"Hank, Hank! Wake up, we have trouble," Joanne yells at Hank through his intercom.

"Good morning to you too, Jo; what is going on?" Hank says as he jumps out of bed and grabs his coveralls; the light is just starting to come through the tubes.

"Harry has snapped and is heading over to Roger's pod; he overheard Roger and Anthony talking about the Lord, and it triggered something in him," Joanne excitedly says.

"Can you patch Roger's intercom over so I can listen

in?" Hank asks Joanne as he begins putting his coveralls on.

"Yes, but shouldn't you get over there before Harry kills Roger?" Joanne asks insistently.

"Not yet. First, Roger has to let him in, and I don't think he is that stupid; second, Harry needs to blow; third, if I say so, hit the gas and come down and take Harry away," Hank says. "What do you see? Has Roger opened up yet? And I need audio, please," Hank insists as he speed laces his boots.

"Here is your audio, and the genius is opening the door," Joanne exclaims.

"Hey, Harry, what can I do for you?" Roger says to Harry as Joanne and Hank listen in. Suddenly, Harry throws a punch at Roger and Roger bobs to the side while jerking Harry into the pod where he crashes into the bookcase against the far wall; Roger slams the door shut and drops the locking bar across. "Hey, Harry, what can I do for you?" Roger asks Harry again, this time with a little more insistence in his voice.

"Jo, what just happened?" Hank questions Joanne.

"I think Roger just neutralized the situation; it was pretty quick, but Harry is on the ground, and Roger has locked themselves in and is cranking up his light," Joanne says, surprised and bewildered.

"What? Oh boy, preacher boy snapped, I didn't see that coming," Hank says as he stands up and moves closer to the intercom.

"Here, sit in the chair and let's talk," Roger says as he moves the chair for Harry to get into and extends his hand to help him up.

Harry grabs Roger's arm and tries to pull Roger down as Harry throws a punch-up at Roger; Roger dodges the punch and holds his ground as he backhands Harry across his cheek.

"Sit in the chair and let's talk," Roger says as he jerks Harry up and swings him into the chair, "We talk my way now, and if you still want to talk your way later; fine, we will," Roger says stubbornly.

"Wow, I would never have suspected Roger would best Harry so quickly," Joanne says as she watches on.

"You better be recording this, I want to watch this later," Hank says as he forces himself not to run over to Roger's pod.

"I am," Joanne says as she notes the time in her notebook.

"You hit me," Harry says to Roger as he rubs his cheek.

"Of course I did, you swung on me," Roger says as he cranks his light a few more times.

"What about turning the other cheek?" Harry asks, still shocked.

"You weren't trying to slap my cheek, you were out for blood; Jesus tells us to defend ourselves with like force," Roger says as he studies Harry.

"Whatever," Harry says as he rubs the sting out of his jaw.

"Now; Harry, why are you all fired up at me?" Roger asks as he leans against the locked door.

"Because of your kind. You all speak about how God is love, and God wants to save us all, but then He takes the ones who trust Him the most!" Harry yells at Roger.

"Go on," Roger says quietly as he feels Harry is going to let him into his world, to see his pain.

"You aren't going to defend your God?" Harry asks, shocked.

"First, He doesn't need me to defend Him. Second, you have stuff you need to say. Third, I will answer your questions after you get everything off your chest," Roger states as he calmly stares at Harry.

"Hey, the kid is good; he could be a negotiator," Hank says as he relaxes a little and raises Roger a couple of notches higher on his respect bar.

"Shhh," Joanne hushes Hank.

"Okay. Yeah, I have stuff I need to say. My parents were devout churchgoers, every Wednesday and Sunday we were at church. We did all the socials, all that church stuff. No cussing, no racy TV, and dad read the Bible to mom every night before bed. But what good did it do for them? They got T-boned on the way to Wednesday night Bible study by a crackhead running from the cops; killed them both instantly. Wednesday night Bible study! Where was God then?" Harry asks, half in tears.

"Where was God then? God was with them. But you don't want to hear that, you want to hear how God saved a young family down the road from getting hit by that crackhead by sacrificing your mom and dad, but I can't tell you that because I don't know that, nobody does. I won't sugar coat an explanation of something I do not know, only God knows; nobody knows why God does what He does, except God. We do not have His wisdom or knowledge, only He does. All things are done according to His will, for the better good that only He can see and know.

What I can tell you is this; if your parents were saved, if they were true believers and had accepted Jesus Christ as their Lord and Saviour, then they live on eternally in heaven with God; no pain, no suffering, pure joy, and pure love.

Until Jesus comes back to earth and locks Satan up for a thousand years; the evils of this world will continue to attack and destroy our physical bodies. Satan is the prince of this world, and he will continue to attack God's children to get them to throw away their godly inheritance. Satan knows he loses in the end, he just wants to take all he can with him. Do not worry about your physical body, worry about your eternal soul. That is what your parents were doing by being devout and following the word of God; they were protecting their souls from eternal damnation, that is what they tried to teach you. If they had Jesus then, then they have Jesus now," Roger says as Harry stares at him through tearing eyes.

"Do you know Jesus, Harry? Have you given your life to Him like your parents did?" Roger pleadingly asks.

"I used to know Him, till they died. I was supposed to go to study with them that night, but a bad stomach bug hit me and kept me home with my older sister who had to watch me," Harry says with his head held low and a lump in his throat as his childhood races through his mind.

As Roger thinks on what Harry says, he says, "Jesus is still there, He has not left you, He has not forsaken you, or your sister; He waits for you to come back to him." Roger then pleads, "Jesus loves you and wants you in heaven with Him and your parents."

"I don't know, I have cussed Him aplenty," Harry says, feeling he is unworthy.

"He knows, but He also knows your heart. He loves you and will forgive you for anything, as long as you ask," Roger states.

"I don't know, I have to think," Harry says, confused.

"Think about it, talk to the Lord and tell Him your pain," Roger says and then asks, "Are we good, or do we do we talk your way?"

"We good for now, I have to think," Harry says as he gets up.

"Go rest and think. Remember, Jesus loves you, and I do too," Roger says as he unlocks the door and opens it.

"Yeah, I gotta think," Harry says as he walks out and

heads back to his pod.

"Amazing, simply amazing," Hank says, "You have all that on tape, right?"

"Yes, I do," Joanne says as the tears begin to fill her eyes.

"Hey, Jo?" Hank says quietly.

"Yes, Hank," Jo responds.

"Can you kill my system for awhile, I think I need some alone time," Hank requests.

"Sure thing cowboy, I can do that," Joanne says, wanting her own alone time.

"Thanks, doll," Hank says as he shuts his light tube shutter and lays back on his bed.

"Goodnight, son," Joanne says as she kills his system and goes back to quietly watching the Bunker.

As Hank lays on his cot, he prays a little prayer, "Am I savable, God? Am I?" Hank drifts off to sleep.

CHAPTER 25

❧

"Good morning Roger," Karen says as Roger comes over to the breakfast table where Karen and Max have been sitting and talking.

"Good morning," Roger says with a yawn.

"No yawning aloud; it seems like most of us slept in this morning," Max says as he glances around to the emptiness.

"Oh, yeah; who is still in bed?" Roger asks, wondering about Harry.

"Anthony just headed to the bathroom, so everyone but us," Karen says.

"I guess bunker life is harder to get used to then I would have thought," Roger says with another yawn.

"It is. It is so boring, nothing really to do; especially without my phone," Karen says as she tries to remember the last update she posted.

"I know, right! By the third day I was ready to snap," Max says as he stares at Karen, " But now, I think I am getting used to not having to check it every five minutes; I have better things to check out now," Max says with a veiled smile.

"This is why I grabbed my Bible," Roger says as he tries to change the subject before Max gets in trouble.

"Better things?" Karen asks Max as a small smile starts to form on her lips, and then quickly she says to Roger, "Yeah, but how many times can you read it before you get bored?"

"I will never get bored with the word of God. The Bible is full of every genre of writing out there; romance, mystery, comedy, drama, action, tragedy, adventure, self-help, and apocalyptic. Each time I read the Bible, I learn something new; as I grow through the Spirit, I peel away another layer and am led to another lesson to be learned," Roger says as he shakes his sleep off. "I remember when I first read in Luke where Jesus was to be counted among the criminals; man, that blew my mind. I mean, the Bible told me that Jesus was considered an outlaw; when I read that, I knew I had to dig deeper," Roger says as his excitement gains.

"Why was Jesus considered an outlaw?" Karen asks, shocked in hearing that God was an outlaw.

"Good morning, Hank," Roger says as Hank come over to the table. Hank does a quick scan of Roger to see if he has any marks on him from last night's activity; none showing.

"Morning all," Hank says through his own yawn.

"Good morning, Hank; Roger was just telling us about the Outlaw Jesus," Max says as he looks up at Hank.

"Outlaw Jesus, eh? Nice, let me grab some coffee first," Hank says as he starts towards the shower.

"You know, coffee sounds good; be right back," Roger says as he hops up and joins Hank as he walks over to the shower.

"You look as tired as I feel," Roger says to Hank as he comes alongside him.

"Yeah, sleep didn't want to come last night. What about you?" Hank probes.

"Hard to sleep without being able to tell my girl goodnight," Roger says.

"Yeah, I bet it is. I will pedal if you want to fill the canteens," Hank says as they arrive at the shower as Anthony comes over to them from the latrine.

"Morning guys," Anthony says with a yawn.

"Morning; did you bring your canteen?" Hank asks as he gets on the bike.

"Nope, be right back," Anthony says as he runs over to his pod.

As Anthony, Hank, and Roger come back to the group with their canteens full of liquid wake-up, Karen greets them, "Well, it is about time boys, I was just getting ready to send Max to come get you."

"Haven't you ever watched horror movies? You never send one to find the rest, never," Max declares as he shakes his head.

"Gotcha; you like horror movies?" Karen probes.

"Not really, I prefer comedies," Max says with a smile which Karen returns.

"So, Outlaw Jesus; spill it, Preacher," Karen says as she turns to Roger.

"Outlaw Jesus. Well, let me grab my Bible," Roger says as he runs over to his pod to retrieve the lone camps Bible.

"Okay, group, let's get this Rebel study going," Roger says as he returns.

As Roger cracks his knuckles and stares at the group, he opens the cover of his Bible and takes a quick glance at a piece of paper he has taped to the cover. "Let me see, for my outlaw study, we need to go to Luke, which is the third book of the New Testament," Roger mumbles as he flips through the pages of his Bible until he gets to Luke, and there he takes out a small sheet of paper with verse numbers written on it and sets it on the table before him. As Roger looks at his group and smiles, he says, "We need to look at **Luke 22:37**, which is right here. In **Luke 22:37**, Jesus says, **"For I tell you, what is written must be fulfilled in Me: And He was counted among the outlaws. Yes, what is written about Me is**

coming to its fulfillment." You see here where Jesus is quoting **Isaiah 53** where Isaiah is speaking of the coming Messiah, Jesus. Here, let me turn to **Isaiah 53**," Roger says as he turns the pages back to the Old Testament after putting his note paper back in Luke 22. "In **Isaiah 53:12**, it says, '**Therefore I will give Him the many as a portion, and He will receive the mighty as spoil, because He submitted Himself to death, and was counted among the rebels; yet He bore the sin of many and interceded for the rebels.**' You see, Jesus was a rebel; He bucked the system, but He did it by being perfect to the word of God. You see, Jesus fulfilled all of the Scripture prophecies. Jesus was considered an outlaw to such an extent, that He was crucified between two criminals," Roger says to his group.

"I remember you telling us about Jesus and the two thieves; one accepted Jesus, and the other didn't," Karen says, excited that she remembered the earlier lesson.

"Yeah, that's right!" Max exclaims.

"Yep, all they had to do was accept that Jesus is the Lord, and they would have both lived in heaven with Jesus," Hank says in total astonishment at himself for not only knowing that fact but voicing it.

"Very true, Hank. That is the lesson we should all know: accept Jesus is the Lord God, and you will live; don't accept, and you will die." Roger says, then continues, "This, and other passages, tell us that Christians will be attacked and persecuted for their faith in Christ; it doesn't say if, it says will. We will be counted among the rebels because we are not to conform to the ways of the world, we are to follow the ways of God. This is not saying we are to attack the system; we are to never attack, we are just to defend ourselves and families. But that is another lesson; for now, garden time," Roger says as he finishes his coffee and gets up.

"Yes, Preacher, leave us in suspense," Hank says as he actually wants to hear this study.

"I will," Roger says with a smile as he and the group head over to the garden.

CHAPTER 26

CB EO

Jung sits at his desk staring at his computer monitor; only eleven days to go before his mission will be completed, a mission that has been decades in the making, and Jung is the finisher.

Jung navigates to a hidden file on his computer and opens it; in the file is just one item, a picture of his wife and son. Oh, how he misses them, "Soon, my love; soon I will be coming home to my family, soon America will pay for what they have done to our people," Jung says aloud. "Soon I will have my family back in my arms," Jung says as he thinks back to when he said goodbye to them, over four years ago at the little North Korean border town of Namyang.

Soon, how Jung hates that word; soon is never soon, soon always seems to be forever. However, now soon means eleven days; eleven days to remove all nerves and prepare for a perfect delivery.

"Kim, Daniel, Cho; office!" Jung yells out into the quietness of the warehouse.

"Yes, sir?" Daniel asks as he comes running into the office ready to battle an unseen, unknown force.

"Yes, sir!" Kim exclaims as he and Cho come bursting into the office behind Daniel.

"It is time for us to begin preparing for the mission. We only have eleven days, and we must pull this off without any issues," Jung commands as he stares at his crew; the hopes of his people rest on this mission, on these three standing before him.

"Yes, sir; what are the plans?" Cho eagerly asks.

"Sit," Jung commands. As everyone sits down, Jung begins, "On the morning of the Day of Songun, Kim will prepare the Supreme Leaders Fist for travel; Kim, what is needed?" Jung asks as he stares at his little genius.

"I will attach the key and start the program. Then we just turn the key and push detonator button when ready," Kim says in his broken English with a smile.

"How much time will we have before detonation?" Cho asks as she tries to picture the explosion to come.

"No time, the blast will be instant," Daniel quietly says as he sits up perfectly straight, knowing that this will be his last mission.

"Oh, very good," Cho says as the realization begins to set in.

"Yes, very good; we will be remembered as the ones who destroyed the imperialist dogs of America; we will be the actual shot heard around the world," Jung says; smiling, and thinking. "The Supreme Leader has told me that we will forever be the faces of the Day of Songun," Jung tells everyone as he holds his head higher and puffs out his chest.

"After Kim prepares the Fist, I will take the car and set up the video cameras and transmitters," Jung says as he continues explaining the coming day's events.

"Video cameras?" Cho asks as she looks at the others.

"Yes, I will transmit the blast to the Supreme Leader and our countrymen. I will set up one hardened camera and transmitter on Signal Mountain; this will be a live feed to the people of the Democratic People's Republic of Korea to watch as we take the war to America. Once I set up that system, I will head to ground zero and begin transmitting as Daniel drives up; this will go straight to the Supreme Leader himself," Jung says with a smile, and a lie.

"When will we set off the bomb?" Cho asks as she feels her hands begin to sweat.

"Daniel needs to be at the intersection of Central Avenue and McCallie Avenue at precisely noon, that is when Kim will detonate," Jung says.

"That is the best area, many enemies' dead," Kim says with a smile and a nod of his head.

"And we do it at noon when everyone is in town," Daniel adds.

"So, Daniel drives, Kim takes care of the bomb, you film; what do I do?" Cho asks as she begins to feel left out.

"You will be the navigator in case of traffic issues, and you will take over where needed if anything happens; you are very needed, as this mission cannot fail, and we only have one shot at it," Jung says with a serious tone.

"Yes, sir!" Cho says excitedly, "I must avenge Park," Cho says as sadness comes over her.

"You will do not worry," Jung says. "The Supreme Leader has told me part of the plan on the destruction of America," Jung says with a smile.

"He has? Please tell us, sir!" Kim pleads as he slides forward in his chair.

"When our people see the blast on TV, that will be the signal to our military to launch our nukes at Seoul, Daegu, and Tokyo, along with the two nukes we have in satellite orbit being detonated over the center of the imperialist United States. Once they launch, our military will cross the DMZ and head straight into battle. The devastation will be unreal," Jung says with a Cheshire grin.

"What will keep the American's from firing back upon our homeland?" Cho asks.

"They won't know how to respond at first; then it

will be too late. Once the high-altitude nukes go off, the Americans will lose all electronics forever due to the EMP effect. The people of America will be in the dark ages instantly and in total chaos," Daniel says as he thinks of how indecisive the American government has been since the Reagan years.

"Correct. Once we push into South Korea, they will not be able to attack without running the risk of killing their own forces. We will overtake the traitorous South Korean's and make our country complete again. Then we will attack Japan with the very weapons America has kept in South Korea to use against us. At that time, China will attack America and Russia will attack Europe. The Supreme Leader has planned this all out; he will rule a third of the world," Jung says as he stands. "We cannot fail, we are the beginning of the rebirth of our nation, of the world; a rebirth from the oppressive Americans," Jung says with a tear in his eye.

"We will not fail!" Kim says as they all stand.

CHAPTER 27

As the light begins to shine down on Harry's face, he pulls the blanket up over his head; sleep has been fleeting these last few days.

Every night since his tussle with Roger, Harry has been replaying not only what Roger had said to him, but also what his own parents had drilled into his head all throughout his life. Harry knew that Roger was right, Harry knew that he needed to change; Harry knew he needed to talk to Roger again.

As Harry walks out of his pod, his canteen and coffee packets in hand, he scans the area to see who is up; Harry sees Frederick sitting alone at the table with his crank light going, drinking his coffee, and reading a very large book.

"Good morning Frederick," Harry says as he walks by heading to the shower for his coffee water.

"Good morning Mr. Harry, I hope you slumbered well. The water ought to be still hot; I just heated it to make myself a stimulating cup of coffee this beautiful morning. Go and draw yourself a cup and come and sit with me for breakfast," Frederick says to Harry in response to his greeting.

"Sure thing Professor," Harry says with a smile as he heads over to the shower.

As Harry comes back to the table, he says, "You were right; the water is still hot. You know that is a pretty nifty contraption; I bet it would be welcomed in the backwoods around here."

"Most unquestionably it would be appreciated," Frederick says as he sets his book down. "Not only here, but in any area that does not have a viable way to heat water. In the right hands, this would be an excellent and valuable commodity; strange we have not heard of it in use," Frederick says to Harry.

"Well, maybe they are working the bugs out of it; or, maybe they are afraid of what people might use it for," Harry says as he thinks of drug lords and cartels using it.

"Afraid of use; do you think it could be used nefariously?" Frederick asks in shock.

"Oh yeah, I could definitely see that; things you shouldn't think about, Professor," Harry says as he looks over at the shower area.

"It is sad that people pervert the correct usage of technology," Frederick says as he hangs his head. "Enough of those thoughts this morning, let us have some breakfast," Frederick says to Harry in an attempt to change the subject.

"Sounds good. How is the food sitting with you?" Harry asks as he remembers the bathroom rush of a few days ago.

"To be forthright, I believe I have shed about ten pounds in the last eight days, but my body is accepting these victuals now," Frederick says, before adding, "Chung-Hee and Kevin are also recovering, but I do not anticipate seeing them until later, their bodies are not as resilient as mine; they are exhausted."

"Yeah, they have been camped at the latrine for days. No need for them to do anything though, all we have to do is survive six more days and make sure the garden stays alive," Harry says.

"You are correct, sir; survive and garden," Frederick says as he prepares his MRE package.

"I guess it is a good thing we have Roger down here with us; he worked that garden into shape pretty quick," Harry says as he begins eating his MRE.

"Yes, in that aspect it is a good thing they chose him," Frederick states.

"In that aspect? Do you feel Roger is a bad thing?" Harry asks as he clues in on a strange tone in Frederick's voice.

"I have observed your interactions with him, and I am under the assumption you and I see things the same way. With that said, I most definitely believe Roger is a bad thing; we have been in a battle with his kind for several thousands of years. His postulations about a fairy-tale God is not welcome to me; his fables are for the ignorant heathens and have no place in an educated and enlightened world," Frederick declares. "Now, do not get me wrong; we need his kind to perform the unskilled and tedious labor tasks such as agricultural and construction, but we must keep them in their place. I, and others, fear that they will someday try and seize high positions of power, and in turn upset the balance of enlightened rule that we have strived for since the great Roman times," Frederick says as his brow furrows.

As Harry realizes where Frederick's mindset is, Harry decides to play along with Frederick, "Ah, yes, we must not let their kind get too big for their britches; we must keep them in their place."

"I see you have chosen not to drink the proverbial Kool-Aid he pours out to his zealots in training," Frederick says with a disgusted look on his face as Harry holds back on the answer he wants to give.

"Speaking of the ascetic zealots, I see they have awakened," Frederick says as Roger and Anthony both exits their pods at the same time.

"Good morning guys; coffee water might still be hot

if you hurry," Harry says to the twin yawners as he tries to figure out what Frederick had just said.

"Thank you, Harry; and good morning to the both of you," Roger says as he and Anthony head to the shower to get their coffee water.

"Morning," Anthony is able to squeeze out between yawns.

"Good morning, gentlemen," Frederick says as he hides his disdain.

Once Roger and Anthony are out of earshot, Frederick says, "I do trust you will keep our conversation quiet. Once Chung-Hee is up, we can speak more."

"Chung-Hee; does he follow our same philosophy?" Harry asks between bites.

"Oh yes, very much so; we cannot wait to leave here," Frederick says with a huff.

"You know what, I think I will buddy up to the group and try to find out what their actual plans may be," Harry says as he decides the path he will take.

"You would do that? Oh, that would be exquisite indeed," Frederick says excitedly.

"No problem; anything to destroy their destructive ways," Harry says with a glare; a glare that is really meant for Frederick.

As Roger and Anthony come back to the table with their coffee, Harry asks, "How is the garden doing, Green Jeans?"

"Not bad so far, the radishes, cucumbers, melons, and lettuce have come up, and I thought I saw a hint of the ground pushing up around the beans and peas yesterday," Roger answers.

"Really? I would never have thought stuff would grow down here," Harry says, impressed.

"Enough light, good soil, almost perfect temperature, and plenty of water; almost a perfect situation," Roger says, happy to see Harry doesn't appear to be harboring any ill feelings; Roger feels a new calm coming from Harry.

"Yeah, I guess so," Harry says as Roger and Anthony open their breakfast.

"You know what? I am starting to like this stuff," Anthony says as he takes a bite.

"You are one sick individual," Harry says as he gets up and walks towards the garden.

"I concur with young Harry," Frederick says with a disgusted look on his face.

"Yeah, me too," Roger says as he finishes his pouch and takes it to the trash can by the elevator.

"Not sick, adaptable," Anthony smiles as he gets up and throws away his empty pouch.

As Harry is surveying the garden, Roger and Anthony come up to him, "You have done well, Preacher," Harry says to Roger.

"Not me, everyone. By the grace of God and the sweat of our backs, we put this garden in, and God has made it grow; all the glory to Him," Roger says as he expects Harry to leave with the mention of God.

"Yeah, I agree," Harry says in a low voice so that it does not carry to Frederick.

As Anthony and Roger catch eyes with Harry, Harry gives a slight shake of his head and shoots a glance towards Frederick to warn them. "What are those popping up there?" Harry asks loudly.

"Bush beans there; peas, radishes, lettuce, cucumbers, watermelon, and zucchini squash there," Roger says while pointing out each type of seedling, his mind trying to figure out what is going on between Harry and Frederick.

"Wow, I am impressed. Could you imagine living like this for the rest of your life? I mean, in a group that is dependent on each other; weak links and all?" Harry asks without even knowing why.

"In a Utopian world, this is a decent setup; the only things missing are ways of making clothing and tools," Anthony says as he heads for the study table and a chair.

"Utopian world? Isn't that a fancy way of saying a world that cannot exist; it only exists on paper?" Harry asks as he joins Anthony at the table.

"Yes, it is; like pure communism," Anthony says as his thoughts begin to form.

"You equate communism to utopia?" Roger questions as he sits down.

"In essence, yes. You see, communism in its purest form is the closest thing to utopia. Let me elaborate," Anthony says as he gets into his psychology groove. "Pure communism is basically where everyone owns everything, and everyone works for everyone's benefit; those who work prosper, and those who don't fail. Everyone pulls their own weight, and those that are too old or feeble, the others carry; but all who are able-bodied work in one fashion or another."

"You are describing a genuinely Christian society; are you saying that the ideal Christian society is communist?" Roger asks with a confused look as he wonders where this conversation is going.

"If you conclude my definition of the perfect communist society to an ideal Christian society, then yes," Anthony says with a cock to his head as he thinks about the question.

"I can't see that working; slackers are all around us," Harry says as he glances towards Frederick.

"In a pure communist state, it would work; however, you are right, it would crumble because nothing stays pure; you have the power hungry, the snivelers, and the lazy ones with their hands out," Anthony says and continues. "There is always somebody out there wanting to have power over others; and in a communist state where work equality is the rule, a shrewd person who is power hungry will place themselves over everyone else before anyone even knows it. This is where communism gets twisted into a dictatorship, usually very quickly."

"So communist countries become dictatorship countries, I can see that; then what?" Roger asks as he sees where communist countries start with a leaderless vacuum that begs for a leader, any leader; yet a Christian community begins with God as the real and Eternal Leader.

"From what I have observed in my studies and readings, is that governments usually run the gamut from monarchy to republic, to socialist, to communist, to dictatorship, to totalitarianism, and then finally, total anarchy," Anthony says as he checks off his mental list.

"Well, where does the U.S. stand?" Harry cautiously asks.

"I would say we are in the final process of becoming a socialist country," Anthony says with a sad look on his face.

"I agree," Roger says without hesitation.

"Yeah, I can see that," Harry agrees.

"So, what do we do, oh wise one?" Roger asks with a smile.

"There is nothing that we can do, history will run its course; that is unless war breaks out, then all bets are off," Anthony states as he looks at the coffee cup in his hand.

"Yeah, I guess war would change things. But who in their right mind would attack us?" Harry asks Anthony.

"Russia, China, North Korea, Iran, terrorist; you name it, somebody always wants a piece of us," Hank says as he comes up to the surprise of the group. "Oh, look at the little baby-waby plants," Hank says as he wiggles his fingers in a wave to the seedlings.

"Howdy, Hank," Roger says as he shakes his head.

"Howdy kids," Hank says as he glances at Harry and notices that Harry doesn't have the hatred in his eyes anymore.

"Howdy," Harry and Anthony say back in unison.

"Anthony was just teaching us about the progression of governments from monarchy to anarchy, with all the malarkey in-between," Harry calmly says to Hank.

"Ugh, I hated government in school. Okay, teacher, what type of government do we have now?" Hank asks Anthony.

"I would say pre-socialist," Anthony states.

"Very little pre, I would say," Hank says disheteningly.

"You think another country would attack us?" Harry asks Hank.

"Look around you; we are in a nuclear bunker, one-hundred feet underground. We have been placed down here to see how we would survive a nuclear war. I have a feeling a lot smarter people than us figure we will be going to war sometime in the near future," Hank says rationally.

"But nobody would survive an all-out nuclear war. What do they call that? MAD; mutually assured destruction?" Roger asks with a shudder.

"Yep. 'Shall we play a game?'" Anthony says in his best rendition of Joshua from the movie *War Games*.

"Exactly; however, I feel a nuclear attack would most likely come from terrorists. There are enough rogue countries out there that wouldn't have a problem selling a nuke to anyone with enough money," Hank says as he remembers his last Middle East mission; the mission that wakes him nightly. "And once a nuke goes off, all major countries go to DEFCON one status, and itchy-finger level goes off the charts."

"DEFCON one? What is that?" Harry asks as he tries to think of where he has heard that term before.

"DEFCON stands for 'DEFense readiness CONdition' of the U.S. military. It is a five-level system that ranges from DEFCON five, no hazard, to DEFCON one, nuclear war imminent," Hank explains.

"Have we ever been at DEFCON one?" Harry quietly asks.

"Not yet, but we have gone to three and two," Karen says as she and Max walk up to the group.

"How close have we come to World War Three?" Max asks as he looks at Karen with his mouth dropping open slightly.

"Closer than any of us will ever know," Hank says, even though he knows of a few times more than these people will ever know. "I believe we went to DEFCON 2 at the start of the Gulf War, and DEFCON 3 during the 9/11 attacks."

Harry interrupts, "Just to catch you guys up; Anthony was explaining that we have progressed to the start of a socialist country. I asked how to stop becoming a socialist country, and Anthony said we really can't since that is the way things work; unless war breaks out, then all bets are off. I asked who would dare attack us, and Hank was explaining that it could be anyone, even terrorists. Then we started talking about the DEFCON thing," Harry says to Karen and Max.

"Gotcha. My bet is either a terrorist organization or North Korea will use a nuke in the next five years, maybe even Iran," Karen says.

"Man, that is a scary thought," Max says as he continues to stare at Karen.

"But Karen is right; war is inevitable; it is human

nature. Think about it, we are in a multi-million-dollar nuclear bunker one-hundred feet underground, somebody important must feel that war is coming to America," Hank states again, feeding more fear into the group.

"Bad things happen, that is fer'sure," Harry says, thinking back to his parents.

"So, Preacher, why do bad things happen?" Kevin asks as he, Jack, and Alfonso come over.

"Bad things happen because the world was given over to Satan after the fall in the garden; because of the fall, we are all sinners. Jesus Himself tells us that we will have suffering in this world, but we are to be courageous because He has conquered the world. You see, no matter what bad things happen in this world, the glory of eternal life will erase all of it for the children of God; this world is fleeting, eternity is forever," Roger declares.

"But if God is all awesome, why can't He just make all pain and suffering go away?" Kevin questions.

"You mean paradise on earth? We had that, and Adam gave it away in the blink of an eye, but it is coming back to the children of God soon," Roger says with a smile.

"That was Adam's mistake, not mine," Kevin says forcefully.

"We all have sin; we all fall short of the glory of God. Look at it this way, if you were a parent and let your kid get away with whatever they wanted no matter the consequences, would you be a good parent or a bad parent?" Roger asks.

"Well, a bad parent; but I wouldn't make them suffer," Kevin says.

"If you tell your child, if you do this, I will punish you, and then not follow through on the consequences, what type of parent does that make you; good or bad?" Roger asks his question differently.

"A bad parent I guess; but I still wouldn't make them

suffer," Kevin again states.

"God doesn't want His children to suffer; this is why He sent His Son, Jesus, to save us. Through the sufferings of the Lord, Jesus paid for our sins, Jesus made us right before the Father so that we could enter into the Kingdom of Heaven; all God asks is that we truly acknowledge who Jesus is, and the price He paid," Roger explains to the group. "The Devil wants us all to believe that God causes suffering; but you must remember, only good comes from God, evil from the Devil. God allows bad things to happen, but He has His reasons that we cannot comprehend."

"Yeah, ask Job," Jack says with a little huff.

"Exactly. You see, I have suffered greatly in this life, and I will suffer more, yet I know my award greatly outweighs all the sufferings of this world," Roger tells them.

"I don't get it Preacher sounds like a fairy tale to me. I will take my chances and live life the way I want to, by my rules," Kevin says.

"Kevin, I wish you would think of the Gift God is offering to you. Think about if there is just a one-tenth of one percent chance that all of this is true, think about your fate if you throw it all away for the fleeting and unfulfilling ways of this world," Roger pleads.

"No thanks, Preacher; those are bad odds to stifle my life for. Keep your creationism, salvation, religion, and mythology, I will stick to science and facts," Kevin says as he walks away and heads over to the table where Frederick is sitting.

"Whose science; whose facts? Science is but a religion upon itself," Roger says as he hangs his head.

"Let him be, he is following a different drummer," Hank consoles Roger, not knowing which drummer he himself is following.

"A drummer who dances each time he entices a child away from God; Satan, the ultimate author of confusion, chaos, and lies," Roger says as sadness floods over him.

"Come on Preacher, let's go back and relax for a bit," Anthony suggests.

"Yeah, I guess so," Roger says as they all walk back to their pods.

CHAPTER 28

CB EO

"**G**ood morning Joanne, how have things been this morning?" John asks as he comes into the monitor room with two cups of coffee.

"Good; a lot of interesting stuff has been going on so far," Joanne, says, peaking John's curiosity.

"Really? Do tell how are little soap opera is playing out," John, says as he sits down in front of the monitors.

"Well, in last night's episode of 'As The Bunker Screams,' it looks like the talk Roger and Harry had was beneficial, Harry has lightened up.

Frederick has shown his true colors; he hates Roger and the bunch because they are Neanderthals, but he knows that his 'elitist' type needs them around to clean toilets and fetch his slippers. Frederick has brought Chung-Hee into his way of thinking, and has offered to bring Harry into his group; but I think Harry is playing the double-agent type and is actually on Team Roger, not Team Frederick.

Anthony gave a lesson on communism and the fate of America, and Hank grabbed ahold of that and planted more seeds of nuclear war into the group.

Kevin told Roger to take his religion and keep it to himself; he will follow his own drummer. I am pretty sure Kevin went over to Team Freddy," Joanne says to John.

"Wow, it has been a busy morning," John says as he stares into his coffee. "So, we have divisions setting up."

John finally states.

"Looks like it. I see Frederick, Chung-Hee, and Kevin on one side, Alfonso and Jack in the middle, and everyone else on the other side; Team Frederick, Team Roger," Joanne says.

"You like saying that, don't you? Team Frederick, Team Roger," John teases Joanne.

"Yep, and it should get real interesting come blast day," Joanne says, referring to the coming faked nuclear war.

"That will be an interesting day; and the days to follow," John says as his palms begin to sweat.

"I can't wait till you bring them out and tell them everything was faked; I will be videotaping that moment," Joanne says with a chuckle.

"You are evil, my dear," John says; he is dreading that day also.

"Attention!" Robert yells as he swings the door open. Joanne jumps up and snaps to attention while John is startled so bad he spills his coffee on his lap.

"What the...! John yells as he tries to get the coffee off his lap before the burns go beyond first-degree.

"Oops, sorry John," General Mars says as he comes in, "Get to the bathroom and clean yourself up, soldier," the General says as he tries to hold back his laughter.

"Frank, you know I hate it when you do that," John says as he heads down the hall shaking his head while mumbling to himself.

"I know, but that is why I have to do it," the General says with a chuckle.

"General Mars, sir, what brings you here today? If I knew you were coming, I would have had some lemon cookies handy. Any word on the events of the other day?" Joanne asks as she tries to regain her composure.

"No more cookies for me, I have been reminded of

my diet. But, I do have some suspicions about the other day, and that is why I am here; let's wait till fumble-fingers gets back," General Mars says with a half-laugh. "How are the recruits doing?"

"Good so far, but the real test will be when we fake the blast," Joanne says.

"I can't believe you were able to recruit my daughter; no matter how much I tried to get her to join, she wouldn't. How did you do it, Major; what is your secret?" General Mars asks Joanne.

"Simple, I tricked her and all the rest. You see, they don't even know they are recruits," Joanne says as she glances away.

"Is that legal?" General Mars asks in his sternest tone.

"Probably not, but our legal team said it was, and that they couldn't find any issues with it. However, that was our legal team," Joanne says with a weak smile.

"I see. Well, if it works, go with it," the General says as John walks back in with a dry pair of pants on. "How are you feeling John, would you like a cup of coffee?"

"No thank you, funnyman," John says as he grabs his seat.

"Everyone, take a seat please," the General says in a serious tone.

"What is it, sir?" Robert asks as he takes sits down.

"What I am about to say is for our ears only and cannot leave this room," the General declares.

"Of course, Frank, go on," John says in scorched agreement.

"From what I have been able to find out, Frank Jones was killed by a North Korean assassin; one of their best. From the looks of it, the assassin, Cho, and two other North Koreans have possession of the warhead," General Mars says as he judges the reaction of the group.

"Do you know where they are, sir?" Joanne asks after

a silent moment.

"The last phone triangulation we have places Cho within three miles of here in the Woodland Height's area, and that was over an hour after Frank was shot; her phone has been dead since," General Mars says, gravely.

"So, you figure she met up with the group after the shooting. Do you think she was with them all along?" Joanne asks as she runs scenarios through her mind.

"Possible, Cho's brother was the connection between North Korea and Jones," the General says.

"Do you think they are in the Woodland Height's area, or that is just where she met up with the group?" John asks in a hopeful tone.

"The assumption is that they are in the Woodland Height's area," the General says as he quashes John's hopes that they were in the clear.

"What do you want from us, sir?" Robert interjects.

"When do plan on being done here?" The General asks flatly.

"The study? Well, we started on August seventh; today is August fifteenth, the faked blast is scheduled for August nineteenth; extraction on September second," John says as he pictures his schedule.

"I have a feeling they will be aiming for Labor Day; we have to have this area cleared by then just in case everything goes south," General Mars says earnestly.

"We will be done and back at the base by then, sir; don't worry about that," Robert says as he tries to alleviate the General's fears.

"Thank you; the least to worry about, the better," General Mars says as he gets up.

"General, are you talking mass evacuation?" Joanne asks the General as she pictures the chaos that would ensue.

"No, just essential personnel in the possible zone. If

we attempt an evacuation of a hundred-thousand people, that plays our hand; and if nothing happens, that makes it all the worse actually," General Mars says with a hang of his head. After a moment of awkward silence, General Mars starts for the door while saying, "Now John, please try not to embarrass yourself anymore."

"Yes, sir; now go catch some bad guys," John says as he tries to shoo the General out.

"Sir, thank you for the update; if you hear any more, please let us know," Robert says as he shakes the General's hand.

"I will keep you updated; but remember, strictest secrecy must be maintained," the General says.

"Be careful, sir," Joanne says as the General walks out the door.

"I will, I have only six months to go until retirement," General Mars says as he heads out the door.

"Well, this has been a heck of a morning. Boys, I am going to bed now, please don't wake me till it is my time. Oh, unless something juicy happens on our soap," Joanne says as she gets up and heads out the door for her bunk.

"Night Jo," John and Robert say in unison as Joanne disappears into her room.

"Well, Robert, what do you think of that?" John asks.

"The General will find them; I have faith in him. You know, I read a report once that, on average, one nuclear device a year is lost or stolen in the U.S. alone; one a year, can you believe that? And you know what; they find them all without us even knowing anything about it," Robert says.

"I believe it. Remember Hank's last mission? He said they dealt with a suitcase nuke that the terrorist had which didn't go off," John says.

"I remember him talking about it. He said once they figured out what they had, that it wasn't a conventional

IUD, they all about lost it; especially when they realized it contained American parts," Robert says. "I have to run to Knoxville, so I might be a little bit late for my shift."

"That is okay; I will put overtime on your bill," John says as Robert heads out the door.

"Go for it; I will put a fresh pot of coffee on for you on the way out," Robert says as he ducks out the door.

"Thanks, I have a feeling I will need it. Drive safe, Colonel," John says as he turns back to the monitors.

CHAPTER 29

As Roger lies in his bunk, he hears a light tap on his door. As Roger gets up and reaches for the handle, he is a little hesitant after the last time somebody knocked on his door; Roger opens the door, and Harry comes in quickly.

"I come in peace, Preacher," Harry says lightly, "Shut the door, quick."

"What's up?" Roger asks as he shuts the door and latches it.

"First, I have done a lot of thinking these last five days, and you were right. I blamed God for stuff I have no clue of; I can't try to outthink Him," Harry acknowledges.

"I am glad you have had that revelation, Harry," Roger says as he motions Harry to the chair.

"Oh, me and the Lord have had a few long talks these last few days, trust me," Harry says with his head held down.

"The Lord forgives the one who seeks Him honestly," Roger says with a smile.

"I know, and I do now; seek Him, that is. Now for the second thing; remember this morning when I was talking to Frederick? Well, Frederick was trying to recruit me into his group. Frederick considers himself a member of some higher-power elitist group that considers the rest of us as necessary scum to do all the slave labor. He mentioned that he and others were part of some group that has been in an enlightened place since the time of the Romans," Harry says, and then he adds, "He also said Chung-Hee is part of his click."

"Interesting; do you think they will get violent?" Roger asks as he wonders how big this group is.

"I don't know," Harry says just as another knock on the door comes.

"Step to the side," Roger instructs Harry.

Roger opens the door expecting Chung-Hee or Frederick to come bursting in, but Anthony and Hank are standing in the doorway, "Get in here," Roger says as he pulls Anthony in with Hank in tow.

"Howdy," Harry says as Anthony and Hank look around the pod and focus their eyes on Harry, "No worries, we are it so far."

"What's up?" Roger asks.

"I don't really know, we just had a feeling we should be here," Anthony says as he stares at Harry.

"Don't worry about Harry, he was just telling me some good news, and some not so good news," Roger says.

"Yeah, don't worry about me; I got me some good old-fashioned rebuking and conviction," Harry says as he rubs his jaw.

"Let me guess, that is the good news. What is the not so good news?" Hank asks as he continues to stare at Harry.

"Find a seat, guys, this room is getting mighty cozy," Roger directs everyone.

"Frederick and Chung-Hee see themselves as a chosen group of elitists who want to keep us around for slave labor for the next five days," Harry says as he grabs his chair.

"I figured Frederick was too good for us. Chung-Hee, I can see that also. I will almost guarantee that you won't be seeing Kevin around the garden after today's fiery bow out," Anthony says. "Five more days is all, might be best to wait it out," Anthony adds.

"True, it is not like we are really stuck down here," Harry admits.

"Yeah, that would change up the thought process," Hank says as he cranks Roger's dimming light back up.

"You know, a little solar light in the tube would have been nice," Anthony says as Hank cranks away.

"Well, when they debrief us we can tell them that," Roger says with a chuckle. "Since I have you guys here, is there anything else you have wanted to talk about? Anything weighing on you?"

"Like what, Karen and Max googly-eyeing each other?" Hank says with a wry laugh.

"No, let's leave Bunker romance out of this please," Roger says as he shakes his head.

"I think he is meaning Bible questions. I got one for you, Preacher. What about all the inconsistencies people say the Bible has?" Anthony asks.

"That is a good one, Anthony. When people say that the Bible has inconsistencies, they are not taking into account different people writing about a subject which they do not have the same training in or different views of the same event," Roger says as Anthony looks at him bewildered.

"Don't lose me, Preacher," Anthony says.

Roger continues, "Let me explain it this way: let's say that you ask a seasoned surgeon and a plumber to each document a recent appendectomy surgery they observed together, from start to finish. The plumber, with no assistance, documents what he saw; the surgeon, with no assistance, documents what he saw. Once they have finished, they give both reports to Harry, a layman in the medical field, to read. When Harry reads the reports, he sees differences between the two; different terms, different descriptions. To Harry, he believes he is reading about two different surgeries; however, it is the same surgery. Why did Harry think this was two separate surgeries?" Roger asks Anthony.

"The plumber saw it one way, and the surgeon saw it differently?" Anthony answers with a question.

"Or, maybe the surgeon knows all of the terms, the plumber doesn't," Hank volunteers.

"Or I have no clue what I am reading," Harry says.

"Correct gentlemen; different views, different knowledge base, and knowledge of what you are reading. If I read a book about investing in the stock market, I would be lost, but Harry wouldn't be. If I read a book about psychology, I am lost, but Anthony isn't. If someone doesn't have the Holy Spirit to guide them in their Bible study, they are lost," Roger says to his little group. "Remember that the Apostles wrote most of the new testament, and the Apostles were composed of a surgeon, a tax-collector, a fisherman, and a laymen; all different perspectives, all seeing from divergent views."

"Why do some people say that the Bible says one thing, but others say different?" Hank find himself asking.

"One reason is that they are not reading in context. Most of the Bible was not meant to be read only one verse here or one sentence there; the Bible was meant to be read in the context of the whole subject." Roger says, then continues, "Another reason is that the Bible has many layers of meanings; it is like an onion, and some readers are not ready for the next layer."

"Hey, my dad used to say that to me, 'Harry, the Bible is an onion; start peeling that onion,'" Harry says with a smile as he finally is able to remember his parents without anger flooding over him.

"Your father was a smart man, he knew the Bible has

many layers of meanings. The Bible tells us that we start as children in learning the Scriptures, but we grow to adults; we start on milk, and finish on meat," Roger says.

"Give an example, please," Hank says as his curiosity peaks.

"Sure, let me think," Roger says as he grabs his Bible and opens it to Genesis after a moment of thinking. "In **Genesis 2:14-15**, God tells the serpent right after Adam and Eve had eaten of the forbidden fruit, **'Because you have done this, you are cursed more than any livestock and more than any wild animal. You will move on your belly and eat dust all the days of your life. I will put hostility between you and the woman, and between your seed and her seed. He will strike your head, and you will strike his heel.'** When a new believer, or non-believer, read this, they don't really understand it beyond 'women will hate snakes and try and kill them.' However, when somebody who has wisdom and guidance reads this, they see where it is speaking of Jesus destroying Satan and his minions in the end; they see the Seed of Man destroying the seed of the devil; they see where the Light overtakes the darkness," Roger explains.

"So how is someone to know what the Bible is supposed to mean? Doesn't this leave everything open to man's interpretation?" Anthony asks with attitude.

"This is where you must have the Holy Spirit to guide you. Without the Holy Spirit, you are interpreting with a human mind; with the Holy Spirit, your understanding is being guided by God," Roger says calmly.

"How do we get the Holy Spirit to guide us, we aren't priest," Harry pipes up and asks.

"In essence, if you accept Jesus Christ as your Lord and Saviour, you are a child of God and have the Holy Spirit as your priest, pastor, minister, what-not. Jesus does not say, 'have this man interpret God's word for you,' Jesus says, 'the Father sends you the Counselor, the Holy Spirit, in My name to teach you all things.' Do not get me wrong, when we are a new child of God, we need the milk, not the meat, of Scriptures, because we will become frustrated, and walk away; therefore, we need wise counsel to aid us on our journey. But, and this is a big but, we should never rely on mankind to tell us what God is saying in the Scriptures. Black is black, white is white; those who mix the black and white and say God meant gray, is adding to and taking away from the word of God," Roger tells them.

"Example of a gray area," Anthony asks with a cocked head.

Roger thinks for a second, and says, "Sexual immorality, one of the big hot-button issues. You will hear some Christians say that homosexuals are damned to fire and brimstone because they are abominations, yet these hypocritical Christians are living with someone out of wedlock, or watching porn, or checking out a coworker in a lustful way. These are hypocritical Christians who see their perverse ways as acceptable, but the ways of a homosexual as an abomination, yet they both are sexually immoral and bring the sting of eternal death. They believe their gray interpretation is acceptable while proclaiming black and white on others."

"Isn't that the Old Testament way of thinking?" Harry asks, trying to grasp what he is hearing.

"Old and New. Sexual immorality is a big sin with God. God knows that sex is the weak link we mortals have; Satan knows it too, that is why Satan uses it against us every chance he gets. So much sin comes from sex, the allusion of sex, the allure of sex; it is mind-blowing," Roger says as he hangs his head.

"You are a man of God, are you tempted by sex?" Harry asks as Hank gives him a smirk.

"Of course I am; I am engaged to a very beautiful and enticing woman. However, I know that I must obey God's commands. In other words, a lot of prayers and cold showers," Roger says with a light laugh.

"So, you never want to just give in?" Harry asks with a smile.

"The urge is there, but I know that whatever would happen in that twenty-two seconds of passion, is not worth it; once married, I have eternity, not twenty-two seconds. God gave us a great gift in sex, He just wants us to keep it between husband and wife."

"Man, at least he is honest," Hank says with a laugh.

"Guys, we are in a battle, a battle most of us do not know about or understand; a battle for our eternal lives. The enemy is the most cunning and sadistic of them all; he knows he will lose in the end, but he doesn't care, all he cares about is how many he can take with him in the end. This battle is not fought hand to hand, it is fought through the word of God. Those who accept Jesus Christ as their Lord and Saviour not only become children of God, but they become warriors in God's holy army. They have the best armor to wear, they have weapons that cannot be blocked, they have the greatest General of all times leading them; all they have to do is ask, and read the Playbook. Gentlemen, I ask you, with all of my heart I ask you, accept Jesus Christ as your Lord and Saviour and put on the Armour of God, give yourself and your worries to Him, let Him carry your burdens as you go to battle for Him; accept Him, lock, stock, and barrel so that you may live for eternity in heaven," Roger pleads with the three.

As Anthony, Hank, and Harry look at each other and then at their feet, Harry pipes up and says, "I thought I had accepted the Lord when I was young, but I ran from Him when my parents died; I blamed God for their deaths. I have held a hatred against God since that day, but I also held an emptiness that could not be filled. I have always said, everything happens for a reason, well, I am here for a reason, and that reason is not to beat up on Preacher Green Jeans, that reason is to come home to my true family. Jesus, Father, I am sorry for the sins I have committed against You; I am sorry for being an idiot and lashing out against You; I am sorry for rejecting Your Gift; I am sorry. Father, please forgive me and accept me back as Your child."

As Harry says this as the tears form, Roger reaches over and squeezes his shoulder while saying, "You have always been His child, you are one of the prodigals who has come back." Roger looks at Hank and Anthony, "No pressure guys, just think about it. If you think you are too far gone, let me remind you of Saul Paul, the Christian hunter. God wants to save us all; we are all redeemable," with this said, Hank and Anthony give Roger a wry smile, and Hank says, "Cold showers, eh?" And they all burst into laughter.

CHAPTER 30

CB EO

"So, tomorrow we rock their world; who is your money on to completely lose it and start crying like a baby?" Major Camron asks Colonel Johnson concerning their planned faked nuclear blast.

"Jo, that isn't nice; but, if I was a betting man and it was legal, I would bet you a sawbuck Frederick loses it," the Colonel says to Joanne with a wry smile.

"The Professor? My money is on Max," Joanne says to Robert.

"Mine is on Anthony, Kevin, and Harry," John says as he comes into the room.

"A sawbuck on each? I will take that bet," Robert says as he grabs a sheet of paper to write down the bets.

"Betting, Colonel? You know that is against the rules; but if you are condoning it, I'm in," Joanne says with a smirk.

"Okay; I have Frederick, Jo has Max, and Mr. Confident has Anthony, Kevin, and Harry for ten a piece," Robert says as he finishes writing it all down.

"How will tomorrow go down?" Joanne asks.

"Tomorrow at twenty-two hundred hours, while everyone is back in their pods sound asleep, we unleash the nightmare upon them," John says in a detached voice.

"Come on Doc, it won't be so terrible," Robert says with a mild sternness.

"I hope not, but this is uncharted waters. I mean, maybe back during all the secret tests the government conducted in the forties or fifties we did something like this, but I have no way of knowing nowadays; I even tried searching the Russian database before undertaking this study."

"The Russians; you can see their stuff?" Jo asks John in a confused tone.

"Some of it, we share a lot of information nowadays; remember, the wall came down and we are all friends," John says while rolling his eyes.

"Yeah, right," Robert pipes in.

"So, at twenty-two hundred hours we shake things up; does Hank know the actual when?" Joanne asks as she tries to get everyone back on track.

"No, he only knows it will be tomorrow. If Hank has planted enough seeds of foreboding, his work will be cut out for him," John says as he looks at Robert.

"He has planted some doozies, that is for sure; I do not envy him for the next ten days," Robert says with a shake of his head.

"So, you finally admit you have envied the Captain in the past, just not now; this is a good first step to recovery, sir," Jo says while trying to hold back a laugh.

"Ha, ha, Groucho. On a different note, I wonder how General Mars is doing," Robert says, as he starts thinking that being in the Bunker right now might be the safest place around.

"I don't know, but I have faith in him. What drives people to the point they want to lash out and kill anything and everything; and to kill on such a grand scale?" Jo asks, not really wanting to know the answer.

"The specific reasons are numerous, but they can be boiled down to about three main categorical reasons: First, outright clinical insanity; a genuine mental illness where the individual is possibly a homicidal schizophrenic. Second, a mental illness where they believe they can affect a positive change using negative actions; the greater the adverse action, the more positive change they expect in return. You can see this form of mental illness in most totalitarian dictators, such as Stalin, Mussolini, and Pol Pot to name a few. And third, a lone person who despises a particular group to the point that he, or she, fully believe they must entirely eradicate that group for the good of mankind; think of Hitler and his actions against the Jewish people. Now, when you have a combination of these mental illnesses wrapped up in one person, and this individual is charismatic, like Hitler, that person is beyond dangerous, that person is the devil in human form," John answers.

"Could you imagine if Hitler had a nuke?" Robert asks with a shudder.

"The current school of thought is that he was close, maybe a year or two away from having one. He would have used it if he had it," John says as he thinks of which way the war might have gone had Hitler been able to drop a nuclear bomb on the United States or England.

"Pandora's Box; by sheer faith, we are not living as a part of the Third Reich," Joanne says while looking up, beyond the ceiling.

"Exactly; one different decision here, one there, and history would have been different. Life is made up of one decision after another; forks in the road, so to speak; each fork leads to other forks, and we cross many paths in our journeys, crosses that might change the path of another," John says in an eerily calm tone.

"Okay Confucius, this is getting too deep for me. If everything is ready for tomorrow, I am going to grab supper and hit the bunks," Robert says as he gets up.

"Yeah, that sounds like a good plan," Joanne says as she gets up, she knows that she doesn't want to get into an in-depth conversation between these two.

"Okay guys, but to answer the question, you are not asking; my thoughts are it is a person with the second illness I mentioned, positive reaction through negative actions. I would bet you a dollar to a doughnut that the one calling the shots is Kim Jong-un," John says as he stares at the two in the doorway.

"Yeah, that is my thoughts also," Robert says quietly.

"And if it is him, we are talking a much bigger possibility; all-out war," Joanne says as she stares at John.

"A war no one would win; a war with many deaths," Robert says as he fixes his eyes on John's.

"Try not to think of it, General Mars is on the case; go get your rest, and I will see you guys later," John says as he turns back to the monitor. "Oh, Jo; if you run to town later, can you pick up some popcorn for the show tomorrow?"

"Yes, I can do that; light butter," the major says as she walks out.

"Extra butter, please!" John yells even though he knows it will do no good; Jo never gets the extra-butter popcorn.

CHAPTER 31

☙ ❧

"Two more days and we will be leaving this tedious drivel place," Frederick says to Harry as they finish their morning meal together.

"I can't wait to get out of here; my nerves can't take much more of them," Harry says as he continues his act.

"You know, I almost wish that we were imprisoned down here forever; it would be quite gratifying to take rule over these barbarians," Frederick says with a sinister snicker that makes Harry wonder about Frederick's sanity.

"Well, all the plants are up, second mini-block planted, second main block furrowed up, and over two and a half more months of food left; too bad the elevator will be coming down in two days. Tell me, what is the plan after we leave here?" Harry probes Frederick; for some innate reason, Harry feels he needs to know what Frederick has planned.

Frederick leans towards Harry and quietly says, "I will be bringing Chung-Hee and Kevin to meet my associates; and if they pass the interview and are accepted, they will be invited to join in our cause. I have meant to ask you if you would like to be invited; would you?" Frederick asks Harry quietly.

"The cause? Are you talking about the group you spoke of before; the ones since the Roman times?" Harry asks in an intense tone.

"Yes. One must pass the interview process before

being accepted; once accepted, you are committed for life," Frederick says as his eyes burn into Harry's.

"What does the interview consist of? This isn't some type of hazing ritual, is it?" Harry asks, leery of the answer.

"No hazing, you can be most assured of that; we are not Toga wearing Neanderthals who live only for personal gratification; we are the elite. The interview consists of a series of questions that determine if you are worthy of being called an elect."

"Yes, I believe that sounds most agreeable to me; I am tired of these types," Harry says as he plays along, almost too well.

"Good; I will inform the others that you will join in the interview process. I will warn you, the interview process is very intense, and only a few make it; however, I have had good luck with my choices of candidates," Frederick says with a smile.

"Tell me, how many members are in the Cause; and does the Cause have an official name?" Harry asks.

"Upon acceptance, you will know the official name, and only then; it is one of our most guarded secrets. And I cannot give you a total number of colleagues since nobody truly knows, but my estimate would be around fifty-thousand worldwide with twenty colleagues in the Chattanooga area," Frederick says in a quieter tone.

"Fifty-thousand? I would not have thought that high," Harry says as he tries to contain his shock.

"For almost two-thousand years we have been growing, and we have filled most of the political offices around the world. I believe in our lifetime, the Cause will enact its coup de grace and bring the world under one government; and when that happens, we will rule uninhibited. The world will be our oyster, as they say," Frederick says as a wild gleam comes into his eyes.

"Shhh, the heathens arise," Harry says as Roger's pod door opens.

"Yes, we must never let them know," Frederick says as his possessed look fades.

"Good morning, Roger, did you sleep well?" Frederick asks with a smile.

"Good morning, gentlemen; not too bad, and yourselves?" Roger answers back.

"Quite well, myself," Frederick responds with a smile.

"Not too shabby, but I can't wait to get back to my own bed," Harry says as he sincerely wishes he was back above.

"Soon, two more days," Roger says as he walks over to the latrine.

"Yes, two more days," Frederick says with his smirk.

"I guess it is show time for me; we will speak more later," Harry utters under his breath as he gets up and begins walking over to the garden.

"Yes, good luck," Frederick says quietly as Harry walks away.

CHAPTER 32

ଓଃ ৪ଠ

"**P**opcorn is ready, Doc," Joanne says to John as she brings in two large bowls of popcorn; one bowl of plain white popcorn, and the other glistening with a beautiful golden hue of indulgence.

"Jo, is that extra butter?" John asks in amazement.

"Yes, John; I figured you deserved it," Joanne says as she offers him the bowl with a smile.

"Am I dying? What have you heard? Wait, are you really Joanne Suzanne Camron, or are you a North Korean spy?" John fearfully rambles as he takes the bowl of popcorn from Jo.

"First, my middle name is not Suzanne, it is Suzy; second, don't make me hurt you; and third, I will take your popcorn away just as easy as I gave it," Joanne says in her scariest tone.

"Yes, ma'am; I had to check," John says just as Robert comes in.

"Here Robert, have some popcorn; if you want extra butter, you can take John's," Joanne offers Robert.

"Oh, thank you Jo; no butter for me, I prefer the taste of the popcorn, not the grease," Robert says as he sits down and gives Jo a smile, then gives John a questioning look which John returns with his own scared look.

"Okay, T-minus fifteen minutes; is everything ready, John?" Robert asks as he stares into the darkness of the cameras.

"Shaker ready and set to go off one second after lights

flash, and lights are ready and set for a three-second intense light-on followed by a two-second dim-down," John says through a mouthful of popcorn as he goes down his checklist.

"All cameras recording? Audio all checked?" Robert asks as he reviews the list.

"Yep, we are as ready as we will ever be," John says as he watches another minute click off the clock.

"Things will get interesting; Freddy was talking to Harry this morning about his elitist group and how he wants Harry to interview for it. Freddy says he thinks there are fifty-thousand members in it worldwide," Joanne fills in John and Robert on the morning's events.

"Really; did he say what they call themselves?" Robert asks as he wonders if he has heard of them.

"Nope, he just mentioned them as the Cause; Harry actually asked what they called themselves and Freddy shot him down," Joanne says as she pops a piece of popcorn in her mouth.

"I hate cliques," John says as he watches another minute go by as he slowly takes in another handful of his grease-ladened morsels.

"Me too. My concern is if this is real or made up. Freddy says he thinks fifty-thousand worldwide, and twenty in Chattanooga; and they are in every political position. If this is true, all of the conspiracy theories have some weight; if false, we have twenty whacked out people in Chattanooga that think they will be part of ruling the world," Joanne says with a shake of her head.

"I am thinking the latter; look at who he wishes to recruit from this group; no elitist there, but he has found three he wants. And we have a lot more than twenty whacked out people in Chat-Town," John says as he states the obvious.

"Well, we will see how well Mr. Elite reacts to pure

chaos," Robert says as he looks at the bet sheet.

"Anyone want coffee?" Jo asks as she watches John shovel another handful of popcorn into his mouth.

"If you have time, I could take some, and maybe a towel, please," John says as he licks some salty butter off of his fingers.

"Same here, but only if you have time," Robert says as he watches a minute click off, twelve to go.

"I have time, John is the button pusher, he can wait a minute or two if need be," Jo says with a half-grin, half-disgusted look as she knows John is Mr. Precise in all he does; no variations from the plan allowed, even when licking his fingers.

"Hurry, please," John says as Jo heads out to the kitchen to get the coffee she had already had brewing.

"History will be made in eleven minutes; are you excited, or scared?" Robert asks John.

"Both. This is ten years of work, but it feels like the first day right now," John says as Jo comes back in with the coffee and towel.

"I should have known the Major already had it ready," Robert says with a chuckle as Joanne tosses the towel to John.

"Always prepared," Jo answers back as they each take a cup and sit quietly as the clock counts down.

"At T-minus five minutes, I will let Hank know," John says to the group as he finishes wiping the butter off of his hands.

"Five minutes? He won't be happy with only five minutes," Jo says with a shake of her head as she takes a sip of her coffee.

"Is he alone?" Robert asks.

"Affirmative, they all are alone in their pods; and I believe all are asleep," John says as he reviews the monitors.

"Six minutes," Jo says as John reaches for the mike and makes sure it is set for Hank's pod.

When the timer switches to five minutes remaining, Jo lets out a small gasp as John keys the mike, "Hank, show time in five minutes; are you awake?"

"Five minutes; really? Not cool guys!" Hank says as he starts winding his light up and then putting his coveralls on.

"Try to keep everything real; business as usual, so to speak," Robert cautions.

"I will don't worry; I just don't want to be running around in my skivvies," Hank exclaims as he finishes buttoning up.

"Thank you for the consideration," John says as he puts another piece of popcorn in his mouth.

"Speak for yourself," Jo scolds John as she reaches for his popcorn, which he greedily pulls back.

"Two minutes; do you want in on the pool for who loses it?" John asks Hank as he reaches for the betting sheet.

"Put me down for Al, Jack, and Anthony," Hank says as he stretches his arms over his head and behind him.

"All three?" John asks, surprised.

"Yep, all three; and maybe Roger; yeah, Roger too," Hank says as he switches to stretching his neck.

"T-minus thirty seconds," Jo says as she watches the computer timer slowly count down.

"Lock and load, Captain," Robert commands, "But don't be the first one out of your pod. Remember, you are an actor, and this is your stage."

"Five, four, three, two, one, show time," John says as he clicks on the master button.

Immediately the screens go white from the flash, and then the blinding light slowly dims down, followed by the walls shaking, and dust blowing down from the hidden pipes next to the light tubes. Almost immediately, the doors to the pods begin to fly open as the recruits rush out to see what has happened.

"What was that?! Karen, where are you?" Max yells as he comes stumbling out of his pod as he tries to get his boot on.

"Right here, Max," Karen says as she comes over to Max through the dark and dust.

"Did we just have a cave-in; an earthquake?" Alfonso asks as he runs to the elevator doors while cranking his light.

"I don't think so; a cave-in wouldn't have had a flash of light," Harry says as he stands in front of his pod, light in hand and coveralls unbuttoned.

"Was that a bomb?" Hank asks as he comes out of his pod and is almost ran over by Chung-Hee as he runs out of his own pod wild-eyed.

"It happened; that was an explosion, we have been bombed!" Chung-Hee exclaims as he drops to his knees and starts crying; Hank's little seed being watered by Chung-Hee's tears.

"Everyone, please calm down, let's not get hysterical. Is anyone hurt?" Kevin asks in a firm tone as he holds his light up high.

"I'm okay. Max, how are you?" Karen says as she looks Max over.

"I'm good," Max says as he stands in front of Karen as he tries to protect her from some unseen enemy.

"All good here; Chung-Hee, are you hurt?" Harry asks Chung-Hee as he slowly gets up.

"No, not hurt."

"Everyone, we need to grab our lights and come to the tables so we can make sure nobody is injured," Anthony says as he cranks his light up a few more turns.

"Anthony is right; crank your lights up so we can all

see," Alfonso says with a little shake in his voice.

As the lights are retrieved and cranked up, everyone makes their way over to the dining tables as the final dust settles. "Okay everyone, check yourselves out for any injuries, and then check out the person next to you," Anthony commands. "Wait, where is Frederick?" Anthony worriedly asks as he looks around for Frederick.

"I don't think he came out; I will check his pod," Harry says as he jogs over to Frederick's pod and knocks on the door, "Frederick, are you Okay?"

As Frederick slowly opens his door, he peers out and says, "Yes, I was just trying to see up the periscope. I could not see any planes or ships overhead," Frederick says to Harry while staying behind the door, "I will keep observing for a while."

"Okay, good idea, but let me first check to see if you have any injuries," Harry says as he tries to evaluate Frederick's mental state.

"Soldier, I do not believe I have been injured, but check if you must," Frederick says as he opens the door a little more and raises his arms while turning around.

"No injuries, all looks well. Would you like to come out with us as we try to figure out what just happened?" Harry asks as Frederick looks up the light tube.

"No, it is best I stay at the helm and maintain attentiveness on the periscope," Frederick says as he begins to stare intently up the light tube. "You need to check the engine room, it might have sustained damage, and shut the door as you depart, I do not wish to be disturbed."

"Okay, I will tell the others you are on watch; and I will inspect the engine room, sir," Harry says as he shuts the door and heads back to the group, not knowing really what is going on with Frederick.

"Is Frederick alright?" Hank asks as Harry comes

back to the table.

"Yeah, he appears to be physically Okay; he is keeping an eye on the light tube for any signs from above," Harry says to the group as he gives Anthony a long blink to try and signal him that something was amiss with Frederick.

"Um, good, he is Okay and is being useful; I will check on him in a bit," Anthony says as he catches Harry's hint. "So, any injuries?" Anthony says as he tries to pull the attention away from Frederick.

"No, we all appear to be Okay," Roger says as he wiggles his fingers.

"Good, everybody, please sit down; let's try and figure out what just happened," Anthony says as he sits down while trying to put his mind on the primary task at hand.

"Well, what do we know?" Hank says as he prepares to water the seeds he has so firmly planted.

"Big flash of light and ground shook is what happened," Karen states the obvious in a shaken voice.

"That light lasted a while, too," Max says to Karen as he sits closely beside her.

"And the power went out to the camera lights; no little red eyes staring at us," Kevin says nervously as he looks around the Bunker.

"What would cause a flash of light that intense, and make the ground a hundred feet down shake at the same time?" Hank asks as he hopes somebody states the obvious.

"A bomb; a big bomb," Chung-Hee says through light, seed-watering sobs.

"We are a hundred feet down; the only bomb big enough to shake us would be a nuke," Jack mutters as he stares towards the garden.

"A nuke would account for the magnitude of the light also," Hank says as he continues to tend his sprouting seeds.

"Sequoyah melted down? Terrorist? World War Three?" Karen asks in an apprehensive tone.

"Not Sequoyah, this was a blast, not a meltdown," Anthony says as he thinks about the nuclear power plant just north of them.

"We won't know till we are up above; they should be coming to get us," Kevin manages to squeak out.

"With the camera lights going out, we must assume they are not watching us anymore; or are even above," Alfonso pessimistically suggests as he stares at the elevator doors.

"Do you think somebody blew up Chattanooga?!" Chung-Hee says hysterically as he grasps what Alfonso said.

"Please Chung-Hee, try to calm down. We must not dwell on the unknown; we must move forward with what we actually do know. If a nuclear blast did occur, we must assume we are on our own, for now. We need to take inventory of what we have, and then form a plan for our survival," Roger says to the group as he tries not to think of Rachel and his family above.

"Roger is right, that is all we can do, and I suggest we do it in the morning when we have more light and have rested," Anthony says in his most calming tone as he tries to calm the hysteria that is bordering on erupting.

"Good idea, I think we should all head back to our pods and tackle this first thing in the morning; there is nothing we can do right now, we are actually pretty safe down here," Harry says, wondering if anyone will actually be able to sleep.

"If anybody wants to join me in prayer, you are welcome to come back to my pod," Roger offers as he gets up.

"Yeah, I think I will take you up on that," Harry says quietly.

"No thanks, I think I am going to turn in and try to process all of this. Good night guys," Karen says to the group as she shakily gets up and heads to her pod.

"Same here, night all," Max blurts out as he hops up and hurries after Karen.

"I am going to head in also, but I first need to check on Frederick. See you all in the morning," Anthony says as he gets up and heads for Frederick's pod while cranking his light.

"Same here, night," Alfonso somberly says as he starts for his pod.

Kevin, Jack, and Chung-Hee quietly get up and head to their pods without uttering a sound.

As Karen gets to her pod door, Max comes up and says, "Karen, I know this is horrible timing, but I think it is the only time I have now. I was going to save this till we got topside, but we don't really know when that will be."

"Go ahead, spit it out," Karen says with an exhausted, but coy, smile.

"Well; Karen, I have been wondering, would you like to be a couple?" Max stammers out awkwardly.

"A couple of what?" Karen says as she watches Max squirm as she toys with him like a cat with a mouse.

"A couple, as in boyfriend girlfriend; you and me," Max says flustered as he feels the walls closing in on him.

"Oh, you want to be my boyfriend; gotcha. Well, we have only known each other for twelve days, this is sudden. And with everything going on, I am going to have to think on this," Karen continues to toy with Max as she feels her spirits lifting; she had been hoping he would ask her out once they finished the study.

"I understand, but I am not going anywhere; even if you say no," Max says as he finds a little of his backbone.

"Really? You aren't going anywhere?" Karen says as she puts her hands on her hips, squares her shoulders, and stares at Max; for Karen, this is going to be Max's moment of truth.

"No ma'am, I'm not," Max says as he stands up straight and stares back at Karen with a new found spine of steel.

"Well then, I guess you are my boyfriend; now go to bed, and I will see you in the morning," Karen says as she leans into Max and gives him a light kiss on the cheek before spinning and going into her pod; leaving Max just standing there.

"Hey, Max," Hank calls over to Max.

"Yeah," Max says as he stares at Karen's door.

"Go to bed, lover boy."

"Yeah," Max says as he quietly turns and goes into his pod.

As the remaining group around the table stare quietly over towards the pods, Hank breaks the silence with, "You know, I don't know what the biggest event of today is; the possibilities of Chattanooga being nuked, or that Max actually asked Karen to date, and she said yes," Hank says to Roger and Harry with a light chuckle.

"Sad, but true; and he lived," Harry says as they all laugh at the small moment of levity.

"You want to join us?" Roger asks Hank, referring to the prayer meeting.

"No, I have a feeling I am going to need all the rest I can get. See you guys in the morning," Hank says as he heads back to his pod.

"Night, Hank," Harry and Roger both say to Hank as they head to Roger's pod.

As Hank closes and latches his door, he quietly says, "You guys still awake?"

"We're here. How is it going?" John asks quietly; they

have watched and heard all of the events, but John needs to know how Hank's mind is processing everything from his inside perspective.

"Well, Freddy has locked himself in his pod, Chung-Hee is borderline, Anthony and Harry have actually stepped up, way up, and Max and Karen are engaged," Hank says with a little stretch of the truth.

"They aren't engaged, we can still hear and see all," Joanne corrects Hank.

"I know, Jo, just checking to see if you have been paying attention," Hank says as he unlaces his boots and pulls them off.

"Very much so. Frederick is really out there; I am pretty sure he has snapped. I will need you to speak with him and get a read on his mental status," John says, worried that they will have to scuttle the entire test to extract Frederick.

"Anthony went to check on Freddy, so hopefully he will have some insight into his mental state, and Harry says Freddy is doing okay right now," Hank says as he recalls how Anthony took over the situation of making sure everyone calmed down.

As John stares at Frederick's monitor, he sees Frederick sitting on his bed as Anthony knocks at his door; Frederick lies down on the bed and rolls onto his side, away from the door as Anthony walks away after a few moments of silence. John then asks Hank, "What about Jack and Kevin?"

"Jack is in classic shock; it hasn't sunk in yet with him. Kevin; hard to say right now. Alfonso on the other hand, he is rolling with it."

"Interesting, not how I would have envisioned this playing out," John says as he scribbles down some notes.

"Wait another week, that is when it should get good. Oh, and who is going to tell General Mars that his little girl has a boyfriend?" Hank semi-jokingly asks.

"Jo will. You better catch some shut-eye; we will holler if your assistance is needed," Robert says as Jo shoots him 'the look.'

"Yes, sir, I can do that. Captain Hank McPherson, heavily decorated Green Beret and babysitter extraordinaire, over and out," Hank says as he turns off his light and slides into his bunk, knowing that the nightmares will come full-bore tonight.

CHAPTER 33

೮೮ ೫೦

As Anthony lies silently in his bunk, half wondering if the sun would actually rise today, his mind drifts back to the most plausible, and most terrifying, scenario; at least one nuclear bomb had been detonated above. Anthony had entertained a hundred reasons why, along with speculating on the who, but the only reality he has concluded was that the bomb was real.

With the certainty of assured destruction above, now the main question comes into full play; how does a group of people survive one-hundred feet underground with the barest of essentials, and hopes rested on the unknown? With that question deeply residing in Anthony's mind, he notices the light tube slowly beginning to shine; the sun is coming up, and at least this tube is still working, all is not lost.

As Anthony rises and heads out to the courtyard, he sees that everyone but Frederick is already up and sitting at the table.

"Hey, Anthony, grab some coffee and come sit," Roger says through bloodshot eyes.

"Yeah, I need it; has anyone checked on Frederick?" Anthony inquiries as he looks towards Frederick's pod. Frederick wouldn't answer his door last night when Anthony knocked on it; Anthony hoped he had fallen asleep and not snapped and tried to climb up the light tube.

"No, he is on his own," Chung-Hee quietly says as he

stares into his cup.

"Gotcha," Anthony says through a glare at Chung-Hee, and then heads over to Frederick's pod and knocks on the door, "Frederick, it's Anthony; is everything alright?"

After a moment, Anthony hears the lock on the door slide open; Frederick peers out and says, "All is well, I did not see any hostile forces topside last night. I believe it will be for the best if we descend to the ocean floor and run silently so that the crew can rest."

"Yes, I think that is a very good idea; I will inform the crew. Would you like some breakfast, sir?" Anthony asks as he plays along with Frederick's alternate reality.

"No, I am good; I ate a hearty breakfast a bit ago. Thank you for the offer though, and be sure to have the crew stay quiet as we lie in the depths."

"Of course. Good night Frederick, try to rest," Anthony says as Frederick closes and latches his door.

As Anthony heads to the shower to get his coffee water, Hank comes up alongside him, "How's Freddy?"

"Delicate, to say the least. We need to keep the others away from him; he is not dangerous, just delicate. He thinks we are on a submarine, and I believe he thinks he is the commanding officer," Anthony says as he racks his brain on how to handle PTSD.

"So, he is in the Navy now? Nice. Don't worry, we can keep him isolated; I don't see his posse running to be by his side anytime soon," Hank mutters as he stares over at Chung-Hee and Kevin as they sit staring into their coffee.

"Yeah, great friends," Anthony says under his breath.

"Hey guys," Harry says as he and Roger approach them.

"How is everything?" Hank asks as he still questions Harry's newfound loyalty.

"We are alive. How hard do you think it will be to open the elevator doors and climb the shaft out of here?" Harry asks bluntly.

"Hard, very hard," Hank says as he tries to discourage the destruction of their only way out. "First, to pry the doors open you would need a lot of leverage and strength; second, you would have to climb a hundred feet up with no lifelines; third, you would have to get around the elevator car that is up top; fourth, you would then have to get through the blast doors."

"See, I told you it was doable," Harry says to Roger with a smile.

"Doable as building a rocket ship to the moon," Roger says with a hard stare, "And we still don't know what has happened above. I would hate to be climbing up that shaft when the elevator comes down."

"I agree. I think we need to wait before we attempt an escape," Hank says; glad that Roger is on his side.

"I will wait, but I have a feeling we will be heading up that shaft soon," Harry ardently states as he stares over at the elevator.

"Come on, let's grab our coffee and get back to the group; we need to take inventory," Anthony says as he hops on the bike and starts pedaling.

"Sounds good; pedal man, pedal!" Hank commands as he grabs Anthony's canteen along with his own and heads into the shower stall to fill them.

As Hank's group comes back to the table, Max says, "We started the inventory; and for just us six, we have not been doing well."

"We have all been eating two MRE's a day," Karen says as she hangs her head as she awaits a scolding.

"I must confess, I have been eating two a day also," Roger says as he looks at the group.

"Same here; they might claim to have all the nutrients

for a full day, but they don't fill you up," Anthony fesses up.

"Ditto here, but I told you I was going to pig out," Hank says with a wry smile.

"So, it is best to assume that Frederick ate two a day also; that we all did," Harry says, "And if that is the case, we have lost about a month of our three-month supply of food."

"Safe assumption; and we better stop eating double right now," Karen commands as Max's stomach growls.

"Well Green Jeans, how long before we start eating from the garden?" Hank directly asks Roger.

"A few radish greens tonight, radishes in a couple of weeks, rest of the veggies in about a month and a half," Roger says as he looks at the group.

"A month and a half? Hopefully, we won't be down here that long," Max says, "I am betting that this is just part of the experiment; see if we go cannibal on our last days."

"Yeah, that is probably it; the elevator will be coming down tomorrow afternoon, and we will all have a good laugh; well, except Frederick," Hank declares.

"Should we try and bring him out?" Karen asks Anthony.

"No, it is best that he stays secluded for a little while; at least until we figure out what's going on," Anthony says as he stares at Frederick's pod.

"Well, I am going to check on the garden; that could very well be our lifeblood from here on out," Roger says as he starts towards the garden.

"Very true," Anthony says as he and half the group follow Roger to the garden.

"The radishes are pretty small still," Alfonso says as they all stare at the two-inch-high plants.

"Yes, they are, that is why we will only take out every

other one; that way, the ones we leave will grow much larger. Oh, and we will need to make another planting of them also," Roger says as he looks at the babies coming up in the row they planted last week.

"Hopefully, this will all be for naught, and the elevator will come down tomorrow," Anthony says as he tries to give the others hope.

"Yeah, but we need to be prepared," Max says as he squeezes Karen's hand.

"We will go ahead and gently pull every other seventh one in this row. Brush the dirt off gently and place them in a basket; we will divvy them up back at the table," Roger instructs his crew.

"Why every seventh one; I thought you said we will be taking every other one?" Max asks.

"If we pull every seventh one from this row for seven days while skipping one every subsequent day, I believe it will thin out the row and give us greens every day. Next week we will start on the second row and lay off of this one as the radishes form," Roger says as he tries to picture his idea.

"Aye, aye Captain Green Jeans, I think I understand," Hank says as he crouches down next to the row and gently plucks a radish.

"Heavenly Father, we thank You for this harvest, we thank You for watching over us, we thank You for the guidance only You can give us. Heavenly Father, we ask that You continue to watch over and protect us; but above all, we ask that You let Your will be known to us so that we may be obedient to Your will. Heavenly Father, we pray this in Your Son's name, our Lord, and Saviour, Jesus Christ. Amen," Roger prays as all stop and bow their heads.

"I hope He heard you; we need all the help we can get," Max says as he looks up at the ceiling.

"He heard him; God hears all," Karen says as she squeezes Max's hand and leads him into the radish row.

As they all gather around the table after finishing their first harvest, Roger dumps the basket full of radish greens out, "We will divide them up evenly. There is not very many, but that might be a good thing."

"Two weeks of MRE's, followed by raw veggies; yeah, you don't want to eat very many," Hank says as he looks towards the latrine.

"Karen, can you assist?" Roger asks as he starts making eleven piles of radish plants.

"Of course," Karen says as she goes over and helps Roger divvy up their bounty.

Once all is divided up, Karen looks down at the eleven little green piles, and with a smile says, "Well, a large handful apiece; this is a good harvest."

"You did good, Green Jeans," Harry says as he scoops up his pile.

"We did good, and the Lord smiled upon us," Roger says as he stares at the group; a group of people he didn't expect to see after tomorrow, now it might be forever.

"Yes, He did; who would have expected we could garden a hundred feet underground?" Jack says as he stares over at the garden full of seedlings.

"If it wasn't for the light from the tubes, we couldn't. Whoever designed those things is a genius," Max says as he stares up at the light shining down.

"They are something, pretty impressive," Karen says as they all stare at the tubes as Hank tries his darnedest not to smile.

"Let's eat," Hank says as he finishes basking in his quiet moment.

"Chung-Hee, Kevin, come on over and get some radish greens to go with your dinner. We are going to need to supplement the MRE's with these, and only one

MRE a day or we will run out too soon," Karen shouts over to Chung-Hee and Kevin who are standing over by their pods.

"What do they taste like?" Chung-Hee asks as he follows Kevin over.

"Peppery, but good," Harry says as he slowly chews on a leaf.

"Harry, I am going to take Frederick's over; do you want to come?" Anthony asks Harry.

"Sure, I need to see if he has seen anything yet," Harry lightly jokes as they grab their little delicacies and head over to Frederick's pod.

"You know, these aren't half bad," Harry says as he pops the last little radish seedling into his mouth.

"Anything that doesn't come out of a pouch isn't half bad right now," Anthony says as he finishes his radishes off, "But I have a feeling I will have some indigestion shortly."

"Yeah, a little is going to go a long way," Harry says with a chuckle.

"Frederick, we have brought you some salad," Anthony says as he knocks on Frederick's door.

As they hear the latch open on the door, the door flies open to reveal Frederick standing straight as an arrow, "What is the meaning of this intrusion? Porter, I told you I was not to be disturbed until we reached the station. Have we reached the station?" Frederick demands in a violent tone.

"Uh, no sir, we have not yet reached the station. The chef wanted to send you down a small salad to help tide you over," Anthony says as he attempts to hand Frederick the small bowl of radish greens while trying to read the moment.

"What is this; lawn clippings? Take this away and tell the chef I would like my steak cooked medium tonight, not burnt to the point of being shoe leather as he did last night. Baked potato, and a real salad, not this collection of weeds. Wake me when dinner is ready, not a minute earlier," Frederick demands as he slams the door on them and latches it.

"He lost his last oar," Anthony says as they stand there.

"Huh?"

"Earlier he only had one oar in the water, but I had hopes; now, he lost his last oar, and it is just floating with the current. Freddy has left the building," Anthony says as they turn and start walking back to the group.

As Harry grabs a few leaves out of Frederick's bowl, he says to Anthony, "I think we need to keep this quiet. Frederick is presently on a train to somewhere, and hopefully tomorrow the elevator will come down, and they will get him some help. I don't think the others should know; maybe just Roger and Hank."

"Yeah, that will be for the best," Anthony says as he eats a few of the radishes.

"I am hurt; he didn't want any radishes?" Roger says as Anthony and Harry come back to the table.

"No, he called them weeds and told me to split them up amongst the group," Harry lies as he sets the bowl on the table.

"I thought I heard him yell at you. Well, his loss is our gain," Max says as he grabs a couple of leaves and pops them in his mouth.

"You will eat anything, won't you?" Karen asks with a light laugh.

"Pretty much so; I try not to turn down food, you never know when you won't have any," Max says as he hands a few leaves to Karen.

"True. How is Frederick doing?" Karen asks Anthony as she takes her boyfriend's offering.

"Much better, he is resting now," Anthony lies to the group.

"That is good, rest is good. Do you think the elevator will come down tomorrow?" Karen asks.

"Hard to tell, but I hope so," Roger says as he looks over to the ominous elevator doors.

"The worst part is not knowing what happened above, but we have to keep preparing ourselves for all possibilities," Hank says as he tries to keep his seeds of doubt growing.

"True. Garden is doing good, rationing is going on, water is still flowing; we should be exercising though," Harry says as he continues to process.

"Good idea, I am going for a jog," Hank says as he hops up and starts jogging towards the garden area as if a starter's pistol had gone off.

"Well, when in Rome," Harry says as he takes off jogging after Hank.

"Yeah, when in Rome," Anthony says as he and Roger start jogging also.

"Ugh, I thought I got out of calisthenics when I left home. Come on boys," Karen says as she gets up and grudgingly starts jogging after them with Max and Alfonso in tow.

"What do you think?" Chung-Hee asks Kevin and Jack.

"Nope, saving my calories," Kevin coldly says as he gets up and starts for his pod.

"Not me, I have a feeling those radish greens will be hitting my digestion soon," Jack says as he starts for his pod.

"Yeah, no sense following the leader and getting all sweaty," Chung-Hee says as he also begins heading for his pod. "Hey, should we check on Frederick? If we get above, we will need him to get into the Cause."

"Heck with him, he is not worthy of the Cause, and we won't need him," Kevin says as he closes his pod door.

As Chung-Hee opens his pod door, he looks over at Frederick's pod, "I guess you aren't so special now, are you? More false promises."

As the group finishes their last lap, Hank hollers at them, "Okay, now drop and give me twenty pushups!"

"Drop? I can do that," Anthony says as he grabs a chair at the table and sits down.

"No! Twenty pushups!" Hank bellows at them as they all grab a seat at the table.

"Sorry Hank, I will have to take a rain check on the pushups; but you can go right ahead and show us how they are done," Max teases Hank which elicits a giggle from Karen as she catches her breath.

"Ugh, civilians!" Hank exclaims as he sits down beside them.

"No pushups for you, Hank?" Karen continues the tease.

"I will do mine later when I am surrounded by those who appreciate me; me, myself, and I," Hank says as he takes a drink of water.

"Shower time, then some reading and relaxing," Roger says as he gets up and heads for the shower.

"Sounds good; I'll pedal for you," Anthony volunteers as he gets up.

"Thanks, I will catch you after I get out," Roger says.

"Holler when you guys get almost done, and I will come and take over pedaling so you can all finish up," Max says to the group.

"I will pedal for you Max, as long as you pedal for me," Karen says as she smiles at Max.

"Works for me. Let's relax while they pedal up," Max says as he misses the meaning of the promise Karen gives him; they both get up and head over to her pod.

"Guys, I am going to go stretch out for a bit; let me know when it is my turn to pedal," Alfonso says as he stiffly gets up.

"Will do, old man," Harry says as Alfonso hobbles over to his pod.

As Hank, Harry, Anthony, and Roger assemble by the bike, Anthony says in a low tone, "Frederick has fully snapped."

"He has; how so?" Hank asks, worried now.

"When we went to check on him, he called me the Porter and pretty much said not to bother him until we bring him his steak and potato supper," Anthony recalls to the group.

"Porter? Does he think he is on a train now?" Hank asks, utterly bewildered.

"Yes, a train. First, he thought he was an officer on a submarine, but he at least recognized us. Now, he doesn't even remember us and thinks he is on a train," Harry quietly says.

"Not good. Do you think he is a danger to himself or others?" Hank asks as he thinks back to others he has known that have altered reality to cope.

"Hard to say, really hard to tell; we barely covered PTSD in school. We are aware he is not going to wander off anywhere, but we don't know what he might do. I think we should quietly guard him until we can figure out what is going on," Anthony offers.

"But we need to keep this quiet from the others," Harry quickly adds.

"I agree, quiet and guard; we will rotate shifts on watching his pod. I say three-hour shifts will be best: Harry will take the first shift which will end at three, Anthony takes the second which ends at six, I will take the third which ends at nine, and Roger takes the forth that ends at midnight, then we start over." Hank says as he wonders what the Doc is going to say about all that is going on.

"So, I have first and fifth; noon to three and midnight to three," Harry says as he gets things straight in his head.

"Yep, you've got it," Hank says with a smile.

"I sure wish that elevator would come down tomorrow," Roger says as he thinks of Rachel.

"Yeah, me too. Okay, let's get these showers done," Hank says as he hops on the bike and starts pedaling; he knows it is best to sprinkle the seeds he has planted, and not to flood them.

As Hank returns to his pod after everyone is done showering, he locks the door behind him, "Hey, you guys there?" Hank asks as he sits on the edge of his bed.

"We're here, and we have been monitoring the situation, so we are pretty much up to speed," John says in a tired voice.

"Well, what is the plan?" Hank asks.

"We are not going to extract, yet; however, if it gets worse we will have to pull you all out," Robert hesitantly says, "Continue with what you guys are doing."

"If you think we need to extract, just make the call, and we will extract," John declares with a heavy voice.

"I did not see this coming, but I guess that is what this test is for. And don't worry, I will make the call if need be," Hank says as he wrings his hands.

"What issues do you see tomorrow when the elevator doesn't show?" Joanne asks Hank.

"Confusion mostly. For some, it will sink in that the blast was real; for others, they will think this is just a continuation of the test; and for some, they will be confused on if we were to be brought up on the fourteenth day, or after staying fourteen days," Hank states as he recalls all of the scenarios he has played out in his head.

"I never thought about that; I guess I have planned everything around a thirteen-day stay, not fourteen with extract on the fifteenth," John says with a light chuckle.

"It has been a long day, and you have guard duty coming up in a couple of hours, you better get some rest," Joanne instructs Hank as she refers to his drawing of the six to nine shift watching Frederick.

"Yeah, I should take a little nap; night guys."

"Night Hank," they all say in unison as John turns off the mike.

"I can't believe this will all be lost by the snapping of one man," John says to Robert and Joanne.

"Unless he gets violent or suicidal, he is staying until the last day," Robert states as he coldly stares at the monitor.

CHAPTER 34

❧❧

"Aunt Rachel, when is Uncle Roger coming home?" Little Betty asks as she rubs the sleep out of her eyes.

"Come here, little one," Rachel says as she scoots over in the recliner so Little Betty can climb up with her. "Well, I believe they said today. Once I get you off to school, I was going to swing by and ask them when I am supposed to pick your Uncle Roger up," Rachel says as she tries to contain her excitement; these last two weeks have felt like an eternity with Roger gone.

"Yay! I can't wait to see Uncle Roger; I have missed him something awful," Little Betty says with a pout.

"So have I; he will not be allowed to ever leave again!" Rachel says with a resounding, humph.

"Betty, you better get in here and eat some breakfast, that bus will be here before you know it," Grammy Betty hollers as she puts a few bowls of oatmeal on the table.

"Yes ma'am, we're coming," Little Betty says as she hops out of the chair and pulls Rachel to the kitchen with her.

"Is your momma up already?" Grammy Betty asks.

"She already left, she had to head to Knoxville this morning," Rachel informs Grammy Betty as they all sit down at the table.

"Oh, that is right; I would forget my head if it weren't attached," Grammy Betty says with a laugh.

"It would be funny if we could take our heads off,"

Little Betty says with a laugh as she tries to pull hers off.

"No way, I would lose mine!" Rachel exclaims as she grabs her head.

"Same here; let's keep it attached," Grammy Betty says as she grabs both sides of Little Betty's head and pulls down, making Little Betty and Rachel laugh.

"Silly Grammy," Little Betty says as she laughs.

"Hey, why don't I take you to school this morning, it is on my way to your Uncle," Rachel says to Little Betty.

"That would be cool!" Little Betty exclaims.

"Well then, you better eat up and get dressed up, I wait for no one!" Rachel says as Grammy Betty laughs.

"Yes, ma'am!" Little Betty says as she takes a big bite of oatmeal.

"Would you like to come, Grammy?" Rachel asks Grammy Betty as Little Betty eats away.

"No thank you, hun, I need to get a few things done here. Betty, slow down please, so you don't choke yourself," Grammy Betty says with sternness.

"Yes, ma'am," Little Betty says as she puts the last spoonful in her mouth, then hops out of her chair and takes her bowl and spoon over to the sink where she washes it and puts it in the strainer.

"Thank you for taking care of your dishes, young lady. Now be sure to wash behind your ears and comb your hair, and hurry up now," Grammy Betty says in her stern voice.

"Yes, ma'am," Little Betty says as she skips out of the kitchen towards the spare room her and her momma use when they sleep over.

"She is such a doll," Rachel says with a smile.

"She can be, and she can be handful also; I pity the poor man that decides to date her, let alone marry her," Grammy Betty says with a laugh. "So, my boy is coming home today?"

"I think so. Today is the fourteenth day, and it is the day they said, I just don't know what time," Rachel says as she freshens up hers and Betty's coffee.

"Well, you will get that figured out real quick; just as soon as you drop off the whirlwind," Grammy Betty says as they both chuckle as Little Betty comes skipping back into the kitchen already dressed.

"Young lady, what have I said about running in the house?" Grammy Betty says with her hands on her hips.

"No running in the house; but, you never said anything about skipping," Little Betty says with a smirk on her face.

"Really? Well then, no skipping in the house either. And did you brush your teeth?" Grammy Betty says with her head cocked forward and one eyebrow raised.

"Yes, ma'am; and I even used toothpaste this time," Little Betty says as she opens her mouth real wide to show everyone her clean teeth.

"This time?" Rachel asks as she looks at Grammy Betty.

"Don't ask, hun. Grab your stuff and get moving; Aunt Rachel has to go get her man!" Grammy Betty orders Little Betty.

"Uncle Roger!" Little Betty screeches as she runs out the door and to Rachel's car.

"That girl is going to be the death of me," Grammy Betty says with a shake of her head.

"You have already raised two sons and a granddaughter; little ol' Betty is a cakewalk," Rachel says with a rare reference to Grammy Betty's first son.

"That I did. You know what, she isn't a complete fire-breathing dragon child," Grammy Betty says as they both laugh.

"I better get her to school before she tries to figure out how to drive."

"Well, she will need the keys first," Grammy Betty says with a half chuckle.

"She is sitting in the front seat, and I did lock it when I got here," Rachel says as she looks in her purse for her keys.

"Run, girl, run," Grammy Betty says as Rachel spins for the door.

"Love ya, Grammy!"

"Love ya too, hun; now go get my boy!"

As Rachel hops in the car, she says to Little Betty, "Where are my keys, young lady?"

"In the ignition silly, I was trying to save you some time."

"I see Uncle Roger is going to have to take you out for a walk or something; you have way too much energy," Rachel says as she pulls out of the drive and heads for Little Betty's school.

"Yes, we do!"

As Rachel pulls into the parking lot of the Facility, she sees all of the cars are still where they were parked two weeks ago, "Well, at least I am not late."

When Rachel tries the front door of the Facility, she finds it is locked; she knocks heavily on the door. After a few moments, Rachel sees Ms. Camron come out of a side office and comes over and opens the door.

"Ms. Moses, correct?" Joanne asks Rachel as she opens the door.

"Yes, Ms. Camron; Rachel Moses," Rachel responds.

"What can I do for you?" Joanne asks.

"Well, ma'am, I was wondering when Roger was going to be able to come home; today is the fourteenth day," Rachel says meekly.

"Oh, hun; they didn't tell you? Roger and the others signed up to go another two weeks; it is surprising what people will do for more money," Joanne lies with a sly smile.

"Two more weeks? Oh my, I don't know if I can take that," Rachel says as she feels the life slip out of her.

"Don't worry hun, the time will go by faster than you know it. And think of it this way, he is making another two-thousand dollar," Joanne says as she remembers that Rachel and Roger needed money for their home downpayment.

"I would rather have him than the money; but, I must trust he knows best; he wouldn't have signed up for it unless he thought it was for the best," Rachel says as the tears begin to form.

"Don't you fret hun, just have faith in your man. You have a good man there, and I know he wants to see you as soon as this is all over," Joanne says as she feels her own lump form in her throat.

"Yes, ma'am, I, I can wait for him," Rachel says with a smile as she pushes back the tears. "So, when do I come get him?"

"I will give you a call on September third," Joanne says.

"September third, I can do it if he can," Rachel says in confirmation.

"You can do it, hun; now you better get going, I need to get back to the phones," Joanne says as she tries to usher Rachel out.

"Of course, thank you very much, Ms. Camron," Rachel says as she shakes Ms. Camron's hand.

"You're welcome, now get along and enjoy a few more free days," Joanne says as she gives Rachel a little hug, which is very un-Jo like and surprises her.

"Thank you, and God bless," Rachel says as she turns to head back to her car.

"Thank you, and God bless you too dear," Joanne says as she stifles back a tear and heads back in.

As Rachel gets back in her car, she can't shake the

foreboding feeling that has come over her and is worrying her to her core. Rachel says a small prayer, "Heavenly Father, please watch over Roger and the others, please keep them safe, please guide them to You Father, Amen." After a moment, Rachel firmly says out loud, "Roger, you better know what you are doing, mister."

"Was that Roger's girlfriend?" John asks as Joanne comes back into the observation room.

"Yes, she came to pick him up. I hated lying to her," Joanne says with her head held low.

"It won't be much longer, and if Frederick gets any worse, we will pull them early," John says as he begins wondering who else might show up.

"Poor Frederick. John, are we doing the right thing?" Joanne asks with doubt forming in her.

"Yes, I believe we are. The knowledge we gain from this test will help save lives in the future. With the way the world is going, we need to start thinking of survival of the human race. As Spock said, 'The needs of the many outweigh the needs of the few,' and that is what we are dealing with," John says with a sad look on his face.

"How can we stop where we are heading?" Joanne asks, not truly expecting an answer.

"Well, after listening to Roger for the last two weeks, and doing a lot of personal soul searching, I honestly think the only way we can stop the way the world is heading is if we eliminated greed," John says with a blank stare.

"Eliminate greed? I can't see that ever happening."

"No, and that is why we can't fix the problem, only God can," John says as he sits down and stares at the monitors.

"Yea. On that note, I need to head down and get some supplies; do you need anything?" Joanne says as she turns to the door.

"No, I am good. And Jo, thank you for all you do, it is appreciated," John says with a smile.

"You're welcome. Now get back to watching them, we do not need a riot when they realize the elevator isn't coming down today," Jo says as she heads out the door.

"Yes, ma'am," John says as he turns back to the monitors.

CHAPTER 35

̓

"Where are they?" Alfonso asks as he holds his ear to the elevator door.

"They will come, just wait and see; they have to come," Chung-Hee says as he paces back and forth.

"If the elevator doesn't come down by nightfall, what is the plan?" Harry asks Roger and Anthony as they all stare over at the small group huddling around the elevator doors.

"I say we wait two weeks, then attempt to open the doors," Hank says as he comes over to the group as the dread of the upcoming days comes over him; how he wishes he could trade this time for a good firefight.

"Why so long?" Harry asks with anger forming in his voice.

"Because I don't want to be stuck in that shaft if the elevator comes down. No matter what is happening above, it will take them a while to get to us," Hank says as he continues to try and persuade them not to destroy the elevator.

"I will give you today and tomorrow, but that is all I will commit to," Harry says as he stares at Hank.

"Okay, I will take it; we can revisit again in two days," Hank gives in as he chooses his immediate battles.

"The sun is starting to go down," Anthony says as he notices the light dwindling.

"Yeah, and no elevator," Roger says as his heart pines for Rachel.

"Where are they?!" Alfonso yells as he runs over and starts pounding on the elevator doors, again.

"Today is the fourteenth day, maybe they weren't planning on coming down till the fifteenth; or, perhaps they can't come down. No matter what, we need to wait a few days and see," Anthony says to Alfonso as he tries to calm him down.

"Wait and see? They put us down here to die!" Alfonso screams at Anthony as he rubs his bruised hands.

"Hold on, they didn't put us down here to die. We don't know what happened above. No sense getting hysterical," Hank says as he starts to get frustrated with Alfonso.

"I am not getting hysterical!" Alfonso says as he goes back to pounding his fist on the elevator door.

"No, you are not getting hysterical, you are hysterical! Now calm down, we have enough food and water to last a while, so stop worrying," Karen says as she begins to get fed-up with Alfonso.

"What, we are just to sit and wait?" Chung-Hee asks as he comes over to the doors.

"That is pretty much all we can do right now. If they do not come down in two weeks, I will open the elevator doors, and we can climb out then," Hank says firmly.

"Two weeks? They will so pay!" Alfonso says as he turns and heads back to his pod where he locks himself in.

As Chung-Hee watches Alfonso disappear, he looks over at Frederick's pod, and then at Kevin, "Man, this isn't the way it is supposed to be," Chung-Hee says as he heads to his pod.

As Kevin looks around at the group, he slowly turns and walks back to his pod without saying a word.

"We can't give up; we must push forward no matter what we think is going on above; we must have faith that all will work out," Roger says to the remaining group.

"Hard to have faith when you don't know what is going on," Anthony says to Roger bluntly.

"But that is what faith is. **Hebrews 11:1** explains faith as, '**Now faith is the reality of what is hoped for, the proof of what is not seen.**' We must have faith that the Lord will get us out of here, period. That was one of the first verses I committed to memory," Roger says as he remembers his first Bible studies with Momma Betty.

"Like I said, hard to have faith when you are a hundred feet underground, and you have no clue what is going on up above; if there is an 'up above' anymore," Anthony says as he stares at Roger as the knot in his belly twists ever tighter.

"One day at a time; we are not to worry about tomorrow or yesterday, today has its own problems to deal with," Roger says trying to calm the moment.

"True dat, and a few of those problems are in their pods as we speak," Max says as he sits holding Karen's hand.

"Well, we should go in for the night; tomorrow will come soon enough," Hank says as he gets up and heads for his pod; he knows he needs to get this gang to break up and go to bed, and his shift watching Frederick is just about over.

"Good idea, see you all in the morning, good night and may God bless your rest," Roger says as he heads back to his pod. The worries of not knowing what is going on above weigh heavy on him, but Roger knows he must not waiver in his faith, for his faith will sustain him.

"Good night," they all say back in unison.

As Max walks Karen back to her pod, he says, "No matter what happens, I am always here for you."

"Thank you, Max. It is kinda nice knowing my

boyfriend can't run away from me; being stuck down here might have some perks," Karen says as she gives Max a kiss on his cheek.

"I wouldn't run away from you no matter what, don't you ever worry about that," Max says as Karen gives him another kiss and heads into her pod.

"Goodnight Max; and don't worry, I have no plans of running either; tunneling maybe, but not running," Karen says as she shuts her door.

As Max turns and heads into his pod smiling, Anthony feels a lump in his throat and heads back to his pod.

"Well soldier, how was your day?" John asks as Hank locks his door.

"I need hazard pay for this assignment," Hank says as he sits on his bed.

"It has only begun, but be strong and don't take anybody out," Robert says as he sits down beside John.

"I know, no casualties. I am worried about Al and Freddy," Hank says as he takes his boots off.

"Al? What did I miss?" Robert asks with a quizzical look aimed at John.

"He is getting really snivelly and annoying; he might snap," Hank says as he stares at the location of the camera.

"Today is the twenty-first, and we will extract on the second, so twelve more days to go. Oh, Roger's fiancé came by," John says as he remembers Rachel showing up today.

"How did that go?" Hank asks as Robert looks at John for info.

"Not too bad, Jo talked to her and told her that everyone signed up for two more weeks," John explains.

"And she bought it?" Hank questions in disbelief.

"She pretty much had to, and Jo said they did it for an additional two thousand dollars," John says as Robert hangs his head; Roger has never liked deceiving people, and he is beginning to feel like he has crossed the line this time.

"Money is quite the persuader," Hank says while thoughts of past mission's dance through his head; so many missions chasing after evil people driven by pure greed. "Well, gentlemen, it is 9 o'clock, and my Freddy watch is over; I think I am going to try and catch some sleep. Be sure to tell Jo goodnight for me, and good night to you two," Hank says as he peels off his coveralls and slides into bed.

"Will do, and good night soldier," Robert says as John says goodnight and turns off their mike.

"Twelve more days; he is going to need a medal after all of this," John says with a shake of his head.

"I was thinking the same thing." Robert says and then adds, "John, are we going too far? Have we crossed some proverbial line in the sand that makes us wrong?"

"No, we haven't gone too far. The information we get out of this test will save lives down the road, we must remember that " John says as he tries to not only convince Robert but himself also.

"I guess so, but I sure feel dirty."

"So do I, so do I," John says as he turns his eyes back to the monitors and switches on the infrared cameras.

CHAPTER 36

As Anthony awakens to a knock on his door, he can't help but wonder what is going on topside, "I hope you are Okay mom," he says as he slips his coveralls on. Anthony is surprised that his thoughts went to his mother; it has been over two years since he has spoken to her.

As Anthony opens his door, Harry says, " It's three sir, it is your turn to watch Freddy."

"Thanks, I think," Anthony says with a light chuckle, "Is all quiet?"

"As quiet as a graveyard in winter at midnight with no moon," Harry says with a smile.

"Dude, that was not nice," Anthony says as every hair on his body stands up.

"No, it wasn't; but now you will stay awake," Harry says with a chuckle, "For me, I am going to sleep; goodnight Anthony, don't let the shadows get you."

"Goodnight, and sweet dreams of me freaking out all night," Anthony says as he grabs his light and heads out to the table as Harry giggles while he heads back to his pod.

As Hank opens his pod door and looks out to the table as the light begins shining down the tubes, he sees Anthony staring intently at Frederick's pod. As Hank walks over to Anthony to relieve him of his watch, Hank quietly says, "Anthony, are you okay? You look like you saw a ghost."

"All quiet, but Harry messed with my head before he turned in; I have been jumpy all night because of it."

"Well, go get some sleep, it is my turn to watch Frederick, and everyone will be up soon," Hank says as he wonders what Harry could have told Anthony to get him so agitated.

"Yeah, I should," Anthony says just as Chung-Hee opens his pod door and heads straight to the elevator.

"They will be here, they will be coming down soon, we will be going back up today," Chung-Hee says as he stands in front of the elevator doors.

"Well, it won't be for a while; you are dealing with the government, and they don't get started until afternoon at the earliest," Hank says to Chung-Hee.

"They're coming, they are coming, soon," Chung-Hee says as he comes over to the table.

"Just try and relax and wait, don't get yourself all worked up," Anthony says to Chung-Hee as he sits down.

"Yeah, come on Chung-Hee, let's go for a morning jog while Anthony goes and catches a couple more minutes of sleep," Hank says as he hops up and starts jogging in place.

"Okay, might as well, but go slow please," Chung-Hee says as Anthony takes his cue and heads back to his pod.

As Anthony awakens with his pod full of sunlight, he hears Alfonso outside yelling at the top of his lungs, "Where are they? Where are they?!"

"Alfonso, if they are able to come, they will come; try not to get excited, it is not good for you," Max says in an exasperated voice as he tries to calm Alfonso.

"They said fourteen days, and it has been fourteen days!" Alfonso screams as his hysteria ramps up.

"Dude, a bomb went off above, and we are the only ones alive! They are not coming for us!" Chung-Hee screams in Alfonso's face; instantly Alfonso takes a swing at Chung-Hee and catches him on the jaw, sending him to the ground in a crumpled heap.

"No, you don't!" Hank says as he grabs Alfonso from behind and tosses him to the ground. "We don't fight each other!" Hank yells at Alfonso as Alfonso curls up into a ball waiting for Hank to jump on him.

"Come on, I am not going to hit you," Hank says as he lightly grabs Alfonso's arm and helps him up. As Hank sees the tears of fear in Al's eyes, he says, "We have to wait and see what is going on. We do not know what happened above, so it is not good to speculate and get ourselves worked up," Hank says as he glares at Chung-Hee who is shakily getting up.

"We saw the blast, everybody is dead!" Chung-Hee screams as he finally gets up and runs to his pod where he locks himself inside.

"My family, they are all dead. I should have been up there with them!" Alfonso says as he tries to hold back his tears.

"It is not our call on where we are when stuff like this happens, it is fate, deal with it," Kevin says adamantly.

"Preacher, why did God do this to us?!" Alfonso spins around and asks Roger through his tears.

"First, God did not do this to us, but He did allow it to happen. I don't know why God allows things to happen, I do not know His thoughts, nobody does, but I do know that He knows way more than all who have ever lived put together. He not only knows the beginning and the end, but all in between," Roger says as he sits down at the table and opens his Bible to a marked passage, "In **first Corinthians 13:12**, it says, '**For now we see indistinctly, as in a mirror, but then face to face. Now I know in part, but then I will know fully, as I am fully known.**' Here we are being told that we can't see the big picture now, but we will later."

"Why didn't God make the world perfect?" Alfonso says as he sits down, shaking.

"He did. In the beginning, God made everything good; but through sin, all on earth became tainted," Roger says as all sit down and look at him.

"Why did he make sin?" Max asks as he grabs Karen's hand.

"God didn't make sin. Sin is the disobedience of God. God gave us free will, and because of that, we choose to disobey God; we choose to sin," Roger answers Max.

"Why did He give us free will if he wants us not to sin?" Karen asks as she squeezes Max's hand tightly; Max can feel her shaking, so he gives her hand a light squeeze back to reassure her.

"My guess is that God didn't want a bunch of mindless robots running around worshipping Him, He wanted people to worship Him because they wanted to," Roger says to Karen with a smile.

"But why does God let bad things happen to good people?" Alfonso asks as he holds back his tears while wiping the blood from his lip.

"We all have sinned and fall short of the glory of God; nobody is without sin. When we truly accept Jesus Christ as our Lord and Saviour and repent of our past sins, all of our sins are covered by the blood of Jesus, and we are adopted into God's family. And once we have become a child of God, we have eternal salvation in heaven; so even though we suffer and die on earth, we live on in heaven without pain or despair. The bad that happens to us here on earth, it makes us stronger as we go forward in this life; our pain helps us grow, as long as we have the Lord with us."

"Where does it say that in the Bible?" Alfonso asks as he stares at Roger.

As Roger smiles, he opens his Bible to a dog-eared page, "I love this Scripture; it is one of my favorites. Paul tells us in **Second Corinthians 4:7 through 18, 'Now we have this treasure in clay jars, so that this extraordinary power may be from God and not from us. We are pressured in every way but not crushed; we are perplexed but not in despair; we are persecuted but not abandoned; we are struck down but not destroyed. We always carry the death of Jesus in our body, so that the life of Jesus may also be revealed in our body. For we who live are always given over to death because of Jesus, so that Jesus' life may also be revealed in our mortal flesh. So death works in us, but life in you. And since we have the same spirit of faith in keeping with what is written, I believed, therefore I spoke, we also believe, and therefore speak. We know that the One who raised the Lord Jesus will raise us also with Jesus and present us with you. Indeed, everything is for your benefit, so that grace, extended through more and more people, may cause thanksgiving to increase to God's glory. Therefore, we do not give up. Even though our outer person is being destroyed, our inner person is being renewed day by day. For our momentary light affliction is producing for us an absolutely incomparable eternal weight of glory. So we do not focus on what is seen, but on what is unseen. For what is seen is temporary, but what is unseen is eternal.'"**

As Roger sets down his Bible, he solemnly says to the group, "We do not know what happened above, and we probably won't know for a while, if ever; but what we do know is this, we are here, and we are alive. I have a family above, we all do, and I pray they are well; but I know the prince of this world is pure evil, and because of that, death may have come to my family and friends.

However, I know those who have accepted Christ as their Saviour have nothing to worry about if they have perished, for they live on in the paradise of heaven and I will see them later."

"How can you be so sure?" Anthony asks as the thoughts of his mom come back to him in a rush.

"Because the Bible tells me so; and all Scripture is inspired by God and true. I have faith. I must have faith, for, without faith, I have nothing," Roger says as he lays his hand on his Bible.

"I hope you are right, Pastor," Alfonso says as he gets up, "I think I need to rest, I have been up all night."

"Go rest, and we will let you know if anything happens," Anthony says as he looks towards the garden and wonders to himself, *Is this our Eden?*

"Hey, Preacher; you say when we are saved, our sins are forgiven," Max asks Roger as Alfonso goes into his pod.

"Yes, Max; when we repent of our sins and ask Jesus to be our Lord and Saviour, our sins are covered by the blood of Jesus," Roger answers Max as all eyes fall on Roger.

"So, when I am saved I won't sin anymore?" Max asks somewhat pleadingly.

"No, you will sin; we all backslide, but when you do and come to your senses, you must repent fully. When you are saved, and you sin, the conviction of the Holy Spirit is upon you, and you know when you sin, because it does not feel good," Roger says in a calming but convicting, tone.

"I thought all you born-againers were perfect and sinned no more?" Anthony questions.

"That would be awesome, but the flesh is weak. Think of this; the Apostles sinned, and they walked with Jesus," Roger says matter-of-factly.

"The Apostles sinned?" Karen asks as she stares at Roger.

"Yes, the Apostles sinned. The night Jesus was arrested; Jesus told the Apostle Peter that he would deny Jesus three times before the morning came. Peter said, 'no way,' but Jesus knew. Now, for those of you who don't know it, the Apostle Peter is one of the main Apostles; he is considered to be the one who started the true Catholic Church," Roger pauses as he forms his thoughts.

"He denied Jesus? Was he stupid, or what?" Hank asks.

"Scared is more like it. You see, when Jesus was taken away, everyone knew they were taking Jesus away to be killed. However, everyone thought He would bring down His angels or something and show them He was God; they had all forgotten what the Scriptures had foretold must happen. So when Peter saw Jesus bloodied and beaten, his faith wavered," Roger says.

"The chips were down and he coward out," Hank says as his fist clenches; thinking back to another time, another place.

"Exactly; Peter followed his flesh and not his faith. So, Peter denied knowing Jesus three times that night just to save his neck, just as the Lord had said he would," Roger says.

"Man, I wouldn't deny Him," Max says as he squeezes Karen's hand tightly.

"We do daily when we sin," Roger says. "Jesus knew Peter would sin against Him, but Jesus also knew Peter's heart. After Jesus' resurrection, He found Peter and told him He had no hard feelings. Later, right before Jesus ascended back to heaven, Jesus asked Peter if he LOVED Him. Now, the Greek word Jesus used was agape, which means ultimate love, the all capital's LOVE. Peter told Jesus that he loved Jesus, but he didn't use the agape word, he used a word that meant brotherly love. Jesus asked Peter a second time if he agape-loved Him, and Peter said he brotherly loved Him. Jesus asked a third time if he loved Jesus, but this time, Jesus used the brotherly love word, and Peter told Jesus that Jesus knew Peter's heart. Jesus then told Peter to take care of His people. You see, Jesus knew that Peter had faltered because of fear and lack of faith, but Jesus knew Peter would come around and be a good shepherd of God's children; He knew Peter's heart. Peter denied Christ three times, and Christ gave Peter three chances to make it better," Roger says with a smile, then adds, "But we must always be prepared for Jesus' return, we must stay prepared."

"So Jesus forgave Peter for running away, and then put him in charge when He went back to heaven?" Jack asks, confused.

"Yes, you see, back during the Last Supper, Jesus told Peter that Satan had asked to attack Peter; that was back in Luke," Roger says as he flips through his Bible, "Here it is!" Roger exclaims and begins to read, "In **Luke 22:31-34**, Jesus foretells of what is to come: '**"Simon, Simon, look out! Satan has asked to sift you like wheat. But I have prayed for you that your faith may not fail. And you, when you have turned back, strengthen your brothers." "Lord," he told Him, "I'm ready to go with You both to prison and to death!" "I tell you, Peter," He said, "the rooster will not crow today until you deny three times that you know Me!"'**

"So Jesus knew Peter would cut and run on Him, but He also knew Peter would come back," Hank says as he hangs his head and replays his memories.

"Yes, you see, Jesus is always there for us, He will never leave us," Roger says as he feels Hank's heart softening.

"Come on guys, let's go check the garden and see

what has come up today," Jack says as he quickly starts heading for his escape.

"Good idea, let's go look at our blessings; lesson time is over," Roger says as he feels a sadness coming from Jack that he knows needs time to heal.

"Good sermon, Preacher Green Jeans," Hank says quietly.

"Thank you, Hank,, I try," Roger says as a lump hangs in his throat.

CHAPTER 37

ϩ Ϫ

"Colonel Johnson, General Mars here; how are things going?" General Mars speaks into the phone as he stares at the only picture in his office; a family portrait that was taken last Christmas.

"Good day, General; everything is going as well as can be expected," Robert says as he skims the notes from the last couple of days. "Your daughter is doing exceptionally well," Robert adds as he hopes to allay any fears.

"That is good; she is a trooper, she gets that after her mother," the General says as he sets his hand on his missing warhead file.

"How are things going with you, sir?" Robert asks with worry in his voice.

"Slowly plugging ahead. I have confidence everything will work out," General Mars says, even though he is starting to have a tinge of doubt.

"It will, sir; as I have heard a lot lately, we must have faith; you have some mighty good men to count on," Robert says as he tries to build up the Colonel's confidence.

"Very true, Colonel, very true. Well, I just called to check on everyone and make sure my girl wasn't tunneling out. Call me if any issues come up, Colonel, you have my number."

"Will do, sir. Stop by whenever you like, sir, you are always welcome."

"I will keep that in mind, Colonel; take care."

"You too, sir," Robert says as the General hangs up on him. Robert could feel the apprehension in General Mars' voice, and it worries him.

After General Mars hangs up on Colonel Johnson, he immediately dials another number, "General Mars here, I need to speak to Major Harden." Major Harden is the lead on the hunt for Jung and the warhead. "Major Harden, status report please."

"Sir, we are down to the last seven locations on the list, and hope to have those cleared within the next couple of days," Major Harden reports.

"Confidence level, Major?"

"High, sir; if it isn't at one of these locations, it isn't here," Major Harden says with authority in his voice.

"Very well, Major; keep me informed."

"Of course, sir," the Major says as General Mars hangs up on him.

As General Mars sits at his desk, he reaches over and picks up the family portrait, "Baby girl, I will get you home."

CHAPTER 38

CS & SO

"Sixteen days underground; how are they fairing?" Robert asks Joanne as he comes into the observation room.

"Good morning Robert; is it that time already?" Joanne says as she looks at the clock while presenting a spontaneous yawn.

"Afraid so, your shift is over. Do you want some coffee?" Robert says as he stands by the door.

"No, no more coffee; I am floating as we speak. Sit down, sir," Joanne says as she reaches over with her foot and spins the empty chair next to her for Robert to sit in.

"Yes, ma'am," Robert says as he sits in the chair. "So, how are they doing?"

"John is worried about Frederick, and after last night, I think we all better be worried about him."

"What happened last night?" Robert asks with a raised eyebrow.

"Last night he finally left his pod, and it was strange. Around three am, he quietly slipped out of his pod, ran low over to the elevator wall, hugged alongside it as he snuck over to the bathroom, went in and used it, came out and literally crawled straight across to his pod where he locked himself in. Poor Anthony just sat there as he crawled past him; you know they never taught him this stuff in college. Oh, and all I hear coming from Frederick's pod now is a combination of crying and laughing," Joanne says with a worried tone.

"Crying and laughing? What have you been able to see in the camera?" Robert says as he looks at the black monitor.

"I haven't turned it on; I am scared of what I might see," Joanne admits.

With a sigh, Robert reaches over and turns on the monitor, and they see Frederick fast asleep on his bed. "Well, that's not bad," Robert says as he feels a little twinge of relief. "You go rest, and I will keep my eye on him. I will talk to John about him later." Robert is beginning to think they will need to use the extraction option.

"Okay; no arguments from me, I am beat," Joanne says as she gets up, "Don't have too much fun," Joanne says as she opens the door and heads back to her room.

"Yeah, a real barrel of monkeys," Robert says as he switches the yard camera to the main screen while turning up the volume for Frederick's pod.

As Robert watches the recruits slowly funnel out of their pods and begin their day, he wonders what must be going through their minds; fear, apprehension, worry. As he watches, he sees something else; he sees the beginning workings of a team. He watches as Anthony heads over to the showers and begins pedaling the water heater while Hank, Chung-Hee, Kevin, Jack, and Alfonso proceed to fill everyone's canteens and put in the coffee packets; and he watches as Roger, Karen, Harry, and Max head straight to the garden and begin harvesting some radish greens to supplement everyone's breakfast. Robert then watches them all come back over to the table and hand out the cups and greens; he listens as they joke about 'breakfast of champions.' Robert and Hank listen to Anthony quietly tell them about Frederick's late-night jaunt, and Hank says he will check on him in a little bit. Robert sees the beginning of a community, a family, forming.

After everyone finishes their coffee and breakfast, Hank gets up and heads over to Frederick's pod and knocks on his door, "Frederick, it's Hank; how are you doing guy?" Hank asks as he receives only silence in return. Hank turns and heads back to his pod as he shakes his head no to the group as they watch him.

"Jo? Robert? John? Anyone there?" Hank asks aloud after closing his pod door.

"I'm here, Captain," Robert says as he turns on Hanks camera.

"Good morning, Colonel; is Frederick still alive?" Hank asks as he sits down on the edge of his bed.

"Affirmative, he is still with us physically; but mentally, is questionable. The Major watched him commando attack the latrine last night, followed by crawling back to his pod. She said that he cries and laughs at the same time. He is sleeping now," Robert says as he stares at Frederick's screen.

"Yeah, Anthony told me about it; I didn't see this coming from him. Are you going to extract?" Hank says, angry at himself for not identifying and understanding Frederick's mental state; this is Hank's unit, and it is Hank's responsibility to read his men.

"I will talk to John and see what he says, but I wouldn't rule it out," Robert says as he dreads the backlash that will come to the team if they are forced to extract early.

"Let me know what decision you guys come to, don't just gas me without letting me know first."

"Will do son, will do. You better get back out there; it looks like they are heading to the garden. You did great on those light tubes; that garden is doing better than anyone could have expected."

"Thank you, sir; but I think the garden is a combination of all efforts. Once this is all said and done, do you want to go into the private business making underground gardens? I could see quite the market in some areas," Hank says with a smile.

"It is a team effort that is for sure. As far as the retirement job, I think the government holds the patent on your light tubes. Now go forth and weed, young soldier," Robert says with a chuckle.

"Aye, aye Colonel; Hank the gardener out," Hank says as he opens his door and heads to the garden.

CHAPTER 39

☙ ❧

"Hey, Robert; Joanne says we have issues with Frederick?" John asks as he comes into the monitoring room.

"Evening John; it appears Frederick has snapped," Robert says as he turns from the monitors to face John as he comes in.

"Jo told me what he did; it does sound like he has completely packed his bags and checked out, as she put it," John says as he sits down and stares at a sleeping Frederick in the monitor.

"Should we pull the plug?" Robert asks somberly.

With hesitation, John asks, "What has Hank said?"

"Not much; I think he is hoping all will work out, but he knows how quickly this can go south," Robert says as he remembers the Captains last mission.

"That it can. Has he been asleep all day?" John says as he glares intently at Frederick.

"All day; not even the slightest movement. I checked the thermal camera just to make sure he was still alive; he is, he has a heat signature," Robert informs John.

As John stares at Frederick, he slowly finds himself saying, "That is good. I will monitor him tonight; I don't want to extract, but will if need be," John is almost in tears as he sees his study gaining speed as it heads towards the cliff.

"Maybe we can get General Mars to pull the plug; that might save the program," Robert poses the option to John.

"You figure out how to do that, and I will list you first in the study. Go grab supper, I will keep an eye on Frederick; Jo made her turkey casserole, you need to go and get yourself some," John says as he watches the group sitting around the table.

"That is good advice; I love Joanne's casserole. Don't stew too long on this; all will work out, one way or another. I will think about how we can get General Mars to pull the plug if need be."

"All will work out? Robert, you sound more optimistic lately; is Roger wearing off on you?" John says with a smile. Robert used to be the one that would stay up night and day worrying about the smallest things.

"Maybe he is, or maybe I just want some casserole," Robert says with a smile as he walks out.

As John turns back to the monitors, he sees everyone heading back to their pods as the light begins to fade with the setting sun. He watches as Alfonso and Chung-Hee stop and stare at the elevator doors until Anthony comes up to them and puts his hands on their shoulders; they all quietly turn and go to their pods.

After Hank enters his pod, he sits on the edge of the bed and says aloud, "Hey Doc, is he awake yet?"

"Good evening, Hank. Frederick isn't awake yet."

"Is he still alive?" Hank asks with trepidation in his voice.

"As Robert put it, he has a heat signature," John says referring to the thermal image.

"Well, that is comforting. What is the plan?" Hank probes, expecting John to say the study is over.

"I will monitor tonight and decide tomorrow. Right now the Colonel is eating Joanne's turkey casserole while trying to figure out how to talk General Mars into pulling the plug."

"Joanne's casserole, why did you mention that? I am eating MRE's and radish greens, and you go and mention Jo's casserole. I have half a mind to tell everyone about your experiment," Hank heatedly declares as he tries to recall the taste of Joanne's casserole.

"Soldier, remember the mission," John says, half afraid Hank will carry through on his threat.

"The thought of the Major's turkey casserole got me through my last mission; we don't tease about that stuff," Hank says as his anger rises while he weighs his options of going rogue.

"Duly noted Captain McPherson, I will not do it again. I will talk Major Camron into making a special one for you when you get out," John says as he continues to try and save the mission.

"I will talk to Jo, she likes me," Hank says with a quiet jab as he brings his anger down to a manageable level.

"Of course she does, you are the son she never had. And I like you, Hank, I really do."

"Too late to kiss up. Is Freddy moving yet?" Hank asks as he puts his mind back on the mission.

"Nothing," John says as he watches the monitor. "Roger and Harry are having a Bible study; Anthony is sitting back at the dining table; Max and Karen are chatting away in Karen's pod, and the rest are lying down."

"Is Max being good?" Hank asks as he pictures General Mars giving Max his last cigarette as he stands him before a firing squad for touching his daughter.

"Very much so; he has the chair, and she is on the corner of the bed."

"That boy is biting off quite a bit taking Karen on; I am not near that brave. You said Anthony is sitting at the table?" Hank asks, wondering if Anthony is still holding it together.

"Yep. Just sitting in the dark and staring at the garden," John says as he stares at the monitor.

"Gotcha, he is processing everything; don't worry, he will be okay," Hank says.

"How can you be so sure?"

"Simple actually; he is out in the open and staring at the one thing that he feels will sustain them; he is not trying to destroy it; he wants to live. It is Roger's shift on watching Frederick, holler if he doesn't head out," Hank says with a yawn.

"Will do, son; try to rest," John says as he realizes Hank knows psychology quite well.

"I will try, but it is hard when your stomach screams for a casserole that is a hundred feet away, and you can't get to it," Hank says with a final jab at John.

"Sorry, Hank," John says as Hank rolls over in his bed and grunts.

As Anthony sits at the table, he keeps going over in his mind the last time he and his mother spoke, it was over two years ago at his dad's funeral. Anthony blamed his mom for his father's death; she knew he had that bad cough, but she never would insist that he get it checked out. His autopsy said all that needed to be said, lung cancer. Anthony's dad never smoked, but his mom did; that is why Anthony blamed his mom for his dad's death.

As Anthony sits there, he realizes his dad made his own choices; he chose to marry his mom knowing she smoked He opted to allow her to smoke in the house and car; he decided not to go to the doctor, even when he started coughing up the blood; his father made his choices. His mother made her choices too; she chose to continue to smoke and say it was her life; she had no problem letting him know that she smoked when they got married. She chose to ignore her husband's cough and blame it on his allergies; she elected to ignore the bloody tissues she would find in the trash. As Anthony sits there fighting back the tears, he realizes we all have choices, and it is how we react to the choices that tell us who we are. With this newfound realization, Anthony chooses to forgive his mother. As Anthony gets up from the table, he says through the stifled tears, "Dad, if you can hear me, I forgive you. Mom, I forgive you too, and I want to come home," and with that, Anthony heads back to his pod to sleep.

As the night drags on, Frederick doesn't even move; he has been asleep for over sixteen hours.

As Joanne opens the door, John turns and pleads, "Jo, please tell me you will make Hank his own casserole when he gets out."

"Hello, John. Don't worry, I planned on it. You didn't tell him I made one, did you?" Joanne says with her mother stare that burns a hole right through John.

"On accident," John says with his head held low.

"If he doesn't mutiny now, you will pay later."

"I know. I am going to stay up with you and watch Frederick, he hasn't moved yet," John says as he tries to change the subject.

"Fresh pot of coffee is on, go grab a cup," Joanne says as she sits down and stares at Frederick's monitor.

"Thanks, be back in a little bit. Do you want a cup?" John says as he gets up and stretches.

"Not yet, but thanks."

As John comes back with his coffee and sits back down, Joanne looks at John and asks, "Hanks last mission, do you know anything about?"

John stares at Joanne for a moment and says, "Yeah, since we loaned him back to his squad for a test mission, I was involved in his final debriefing.

Hank's last mission wasn't good. Intel said there was

a terrorist group that was smuggling high-tech IUD's into Iraq to use against coalition forces. Hank's team intercepted a heavily armed shipment, and a massive firefight broke out. Many of our guys were wounded as all of the terrorists fought hard, really hard. Once all was said and done, our guys opened up the lone container the terrorists were hauling, and they figured out really quick why the terrorists were fighting so hard; it was an armed suitcase nuke. One of Hank's guys snapped and had a mental breakdown right then and there, the rest almost went rogue; if it wasn't for Hank defusing the situation, who knows what would have happened," John says solemnly.

"Why?" Joanne asks as she tries to picture the event.

"Intel knew it was a nuke but didn't tell them, and they weren't a bunch of rag-tag terrorists as they were told, they were elite mercenaries," John says with a cold and far off look in his eyes.

"Mercenaries and a suitcase nuke? Who was behind that and where did they get the nuke?" Joanne asks surprised.

"Since all the merc's died, nobody was able to positively identify who hired them, but the usual thoughts were there. For the nuke, it was a homemade job; it was scabbed together from Russian and American parts; definitely black market, but extremely well made."

"Good thing the nuke was a dud and didn't go off," Joanne says with a shudder.

"That is the thing, it wasn't a dud; it was armed and only needed the remote to be activated. Hank neutralized the guy with the remote as he was pulling it out to use it," John says as he stares through Jo. John remembers back to the Captain's debriefing, and the level of tension that was present; the anger and fear were real, way beyond anything John had ever had to deal with, but Hank was able to work through it and calm himself down in the end. "When Hank finished with the debriefing, he was shaking."

"Oh my; we have to get him back up here," Jo says with tears in her eyes.

"We will, soon," John says as he smiles at Jo.

CHAPTER 40

☙ ❧

"**K**im! Grab everyone, it is meeting time," Jung yells out to Kim from his office.

"Yes, sir!" Kim says as he heads to the storage room to get Daniel and Cho. "Daniel, Jung wants us for the meeting; where is Cho?"

"She ran downtown to get food. Come on, you can tell Jung that Cho isn't here," Daniel says with a smirk as he walks out of the room past Kim; he knows that Jung doesn't like anybody to leave without notifying him.

"No, today your day to watch Cho; my day was yesterday," Kim says as he turns and leaves the storage room.

"We don't have assigned days to babysit. And why me?" Daniel asks the air as Kim follows him.

"Where is Cho?" Jung asks as Kim and Daniel enter his office and sit down.

"She ran to town to get groceries," Daniel answers as he awaits Jung's explosion.

"What! She did not ask to leave! She knows better! We are too close to victory for her to get us found!" Jung screams as he hops up from his desk, as Daniel and Kim hang their heads, "Very well, we cannot count on her. Go over everything with a fine-tooth comb; we cannot fail tomorrow."

"Yes, sir!" Kim and Daniel shout in unison.

"I am going to check the camera location on Signal Mountain and verify the area is clear; I do not want any surprises tomorrow morning. When Cho comes back, do not tell her I am angry with her; I will deal with her myself," Jung says as his eyebrows scowl into daggers.

"Yes, Sir!" Kim and Daniel both shout out in agreement; they know not to go against their Colonel.

As Jung drives away as he heads for the vantage point on Signal Mountain, his anger boils in him over Cho's actions; he has told her many times that the fate of their country rests on their success tomorrow, and he will not let the Supreme Leader down.

When Jung arrives at the camera location, his anger subsides as he visualizes the world watching his show tomorrow; his family will know that he was the one who fired the first shot of their countries rebirth. Jung smiles at the thought that tomorrow, America will die.

Jung opens a metal briefcase and pulls out a secure phone, takes a deep breath, and dials a number he has only dialed three times in the past; the start of this mission, the acquisition of the warhead, and the death of Park. It was during the call about Park that Jung found out he was to attack on the Day of Songun; this pleased Jung as that was a day Park always looked forward to.

"This is Colonel Jung Yong-chul of the DPRK Special Purpose Force, it is imperative that I speak to the Supreme Leader," Jung says into the phone in Korean and waits. "Supreme Leader, it is my honor to be able to tell you that tomorrow, the villainous America will be struck from within," Jung says in Korean as he stands at attention while speaking on the phone.

As he listens to the Supreme Leader's reply, he continues in Korean, "At precisely noon tomorrow my time, one-thirty AM in Pyongyang, the Supreme Leader's Fist will strike, and you will see it in all of its glory." After listening for a few moments, Jung continues, "Yes, sir. I will leave three hours early after making sure all is ready; you will begin receiving video around eleven PM. Once the camera feed starts, I will head to the extraction point and begin my journey back home. Sir, I thank you immensely for the ability to come back so that I may continue our glorious battle; I will not let you down." Jung listens as his eyes moisten. "Yes, sir; I trust Kim and Kang-Dae with my life; they will not let us down," Jung says as he refers to Daniel by his actual name. "Thank you, sir; the next time we speak to each other, we will be face to face and the imperialist dogs will be on their knees begging for your mercy," Jung says in Korean and then hangs up the phone. "Now, to deal with Cho," Jung says as he puts things away and gets into his car to head back to the warehouse.

CHAPTER 41

As Cho finishes putting the groceries in the car, she stares over at two City of Chattanooga Police officers as they sit eating lunch at the little bistro next to the market, Cho is torn between running to them, or away; what has she gotten herself into?

At first, Cho was all for avenging the death of her brother and carrying out the mission her grandparents, parents, Park, and even she had trained and prepared her whole life for, the preparation for the events of tomorrow; but now, her doubts are getting the best of her.

As Cho slips behind the wheel, she remembers the stories her parents and grandparents told her and Park as they grew up; stories of the atrocities that occurred because of the division of her homeland of Korea at the end of World War Two; a division that was forced on them by the Americans in the south, and Russians in the north. Cho remembers being told that the only way Korea would be reunited as one, is if America was defeated; to defeat America was to save Korea.

To set off the bomb tomorrow would cripple and confuse America, and once crippled and confused, America would fall under the coordinated attacks against her and her allies by the brilliance of the Supreme Leader and the military might of the people of Korea. Cho knows her small sacrifice tomorrow is for the greater good; Cho knows many will die tomorrow, but her people will finally be able to live.

Cho is scared, for she will die tomorrow, her parents will die, her friends will die; Cho could stop all of this by just running to the officers and telling her story. But, would they believe her? Would they find Jung in time to stop him? Would she betray her family and friends to save herself?

As Cho pulls into the warehouse, Jung is waiting for her. As Jung opens Cho's door, he says, "You know not to leave without permission. You could have been followed, and we cannot fail!"

Cho sees and feels the anger flowing through Jung right now, and she knows he is right in his anger, "Sir, I wanted to make us all a special last supper; I wanted us to have a heroes send-off," Cho says as she feels a lump forming in her throat.

As Jung stares at her with his eyes piercing her, he says loudly, "Daniel, do you see anything?"

"No sir, no movements, nothing; I don't think she was followed," Daniel says as he watches the monitors of the cameras outside the warehouse.

"Good. Cho, do not let this happen again; everything must run as planned," Jung says in a calmer voice; he can't afford to lose Cho this close to the attack.

"Of course, sir, you have no need to worry about my future actions. Are you hungry, sir?"

"Yes, yes I am. What are you going to fix us heroes-to-be?" Jung says with a smile.

"It is a surprise sir, now go back to your office please," Cho says with a smile as she shoos him away and grabs the grocery bags and heads for the kitchen.

CHAPTER 42

∛⁏∞

"General Mars; sir, we have high confidence in the whereabouts of Cho Sang-Hun," Colonel Miller says into the phone.

"Colonel Miller, that is great news. What about the rest; Jung, Kim, and Daniel, is she with them?" General Mars asks as he reaches for the warhead file.

"Unknown at this time, sir. She was spotted by one of our observer cameras as she drove into the control zone, then a second camera captured her vehicle as it turned into a warehouse parking lot. We believe she drove into the building; unconfirmed due to the camera angle, but extreme probability," Colonel Miller summarizes for the General.

"If she is in a warehouse, she is with them, and the warhead. Colonel, we can't mess this up; assemble your best team, and we will go in. How much time do you need to get ready?" General Mars says as he stares at Jung's file picture.

"We are already assembled, except for our EOD tech; he is on a flight back from Iraq and will be here and ready to go by ten hundred hours," Colonel Miller says referring to the Army Explosive Ordnance Disposal technician that will be needed to handle the warhead.

"Send me the assembly location and I will be there at zero-nine-forty-five," General Mars says as he picks up the family photo.

"Yes sir, will do."

"Try to get some sleep soldier, tomorrow will come quick enough."

"You too, sir. I will send you the assembly location."

"Thanks, Nick, see you tomorrow," General Mars says as he hangs up the phone and picks up Jung's picture, "Tomorrow we meet; tomorrow I get back what you took from me."

As General Mars dials another number, he takes a deep breath and says, "Mister President, General Mars here, sir. Mister President, we have high confidence we have found the location of the missing package and plan to retrieve after ten hundred hours tomorrow," General Mars says into the phone.

"Yes sir, very high confidence," the General says after listening to the President for a few moments.

"Yes sir, I will be onsite with the team; Colonel Nick Miller is commanding."

"Yes, Mister President, if the opportunity arises to capture we will, but if not, we will neutralize," Frank says, knowing that the only one who they might have a chance of capturing is Cho.

"Yes sir, I will contact you before going in, and once we have the package," Frank says after listening to the President.

"Thank you, sir, good night," General Mars says as he hangs up the phone and begins putting everything away to head home for the night. As Frank closes the office door behind him, he looks up and asks, "Lord, please watch over our baby."

CHAPTER 43

☙ ❧

"Wake up Captain," John quietly says to Hank.

"I don't want to, and you can't make me," Hank says as he pulls the blanket over his head.

"Come on Captain, I need you," John says with more persistence in his voice.

"Let me guess, Freddy believes he is Napoleon, and he is trying to cross the Delaware, and you are going to extract," Hank says as he gets out of bed and starts getting dressed.

"Um, Washington crossed the Delaware, not Napoleon. Freddy woke up around three-hundred hours and started singing show tunes non-stop; Jo is ready to neutralize him herself," John says while staring at Joanne.

"Hank, I know you have seen and heard some scary things in your life, but it is nothing compared to the silence of the night being shattered by Frederick belting out, *'The sun will come out tomorrow'* at the top of his lungs," Joanne says with a shudder. "John jumped so quick I think he hurt himself."

"Not quite, but close," John says as he rubs his lower back.

"Well, how is it going to go down?" Hank asks as he knows this means extraction is imminent. Hank is wondering, and dreading, when he will be gassed; how he hates the headache that comes after being gassed.

"I want to talk to Robert first, but I am thinking of sending the elevator down at noon with a medical

283

team. Send everyone but Frederick up first, followed by Frederick after being sedated. Once everyone is up, begin debriefing and start damage control," John says as he sees his life work crumbling before him.

"Smart move having the Colonel make the decision to pull the plug," Hank says with a sigh of relief in hearing he won't be gassed.

"I know. Actually, Robert was going to speak with General Mars about having the General pull the plug; hopefully that will save the project," John says with his head hanging low, "Robert should be here soon."

"Jo, is there any casserole left?" Hank asks as his stomach growls.

"No, but I will make you a fresh one; I will head down and get the stuff as soon as Robert comes in," Joanne says with a smile.

"I can't wait, and my stomach can't wait."

"For now, go out and keep an eye on everyone; check back around eleven, and I will update you," John says as his stomach growls thinking about the last piece of casserole in the fridge.

"Sounds good. And John, I am sorry about the mission being scrubbed, you are on the right track," Hank says, then adds, "And I forgive you for the casserole incident."

"Thank you, Hank, that means a lot to me," John says as a tear forms.

"Now, let the fun begin!" Hank says as he hops up and heads out into the yard.

"Robert better get here soon, I have a homecoming casserole to make," Joanne says as her own tearful lump forms in her throat; she really misses her boy.

"He should be here by nine, if not, just go ahead and head out; you have a party to get ready for," John says with a smile.

"Yes, I do," Joanne says with a motherly smile.

CHAPTER 44

$\mathcal{CB} \: \mathcal{BO}$

"Good morning everyone, are you ready to write history?" Jung asks as they all sit down for the breakfast Cho has made them.

"Yes, sir!" They all exclaim in unison.

"Cho, thank you for making breakfast; and again, thank you for the magnificent dinner last night," Jung says with a smile.

"Yes, thank you, it was delicious," Kim says as he sits down.

"Thank you, and please sit," Daniel says as he pulls out Cho's chair.

"Thank you, it is my pleasure. Today is a special day; today we avenge the ones we have lost; today we free our people from oppression," Cho says after sitting, "But now we eat!"

"Yes, we do!" Jung says as they all sit and begin eating what they believe to be their last meal.

After they finish eating, Jung stands up, "We all know the plan; I will go start the camera and get into position, you will all get ready and leave at eleven-thirty hours, you will detonate at noon."

"Yes, sir!"

"Kim, have you armed the Fist yet?" Jung asks Kim.

"Yes sir, it is ready for detonation, all that is needed is to push the button," Kim says proudly.

"Daniel, the van is fueled and ready?"

"Yes, sir, everything is ready," Daniel says; Daniel is

always ready.

"Cho, have you memorized the route?"

"Yes sir, along with alternatives in case of issues," Cho says; happy in the decision she had made, she knows Park would be proud of her.

"Good. Now, for the Supreme Leader and for Chosŏn, let the Americans feel the fury of the Chosŏn people on this Day of Songun!" Jung says as he calls Korea by its correct name, Chosŏn, and they all shout praises to their Supreme Leader.

As Jung gets into his car, he quietly tells Daniel, "Keep your eye on Cho, she is our weak leak."

"Always," Daniel says as he opens the roll-up door and Jung drives out.

CHAPTER 45

ᑕᒪ ᑐᑎ

"Sir, we have movement; vehicle leaving," the Sergeant calls over the communication system as Daniel drives out.

"Can you identify the driver?" Colonel Miller asks back as he pulls up the camera feed on his field laptop.

"Sir, positive confirmation; Jung Yong-chul," the Sergeant calls back after his computer confirms.

"Maintain position and let me know of any other movement," Colonel Miller directs. The Colonel switches to a second channel and says, "Captain Marshal, put a tail on that vehicle and do not lose it. We will continue with our mission here; if he does not return before we go in, capture with extreme prejudice."

"Yes, sir! I will put my two best men on him," Captain Marshal says as he motions two of his men over and quickly gives them their directions.

As Colonel Miller looks at his watch, he sees that it is o-nine-hundred hours; the General will be here in forty-five minutes, and the EOD tech's plane will be landing in fifteen minutes. This means show time will be in an hour and they have already lost their secondary target; hopefully, the primary target is still inside.

CHAPTER 46

As Joanne pulls into the market, she can't shake the foreboding feeling that has come washing over her; she keeps trying to shake it off by attributing it to her thoughts on Frederick, but to no avail. As she walks into the market and starts finding the ingredients for Hank's casserole, she stops and looks up and prays. "Heavenly Father, I know I don't come to you near enough, but I come to you now and ask that you look after Hank and all the others with him; Father, I am worried, really worried. Please Father, in Jesus' name, I pray, Amen." Joanne hopes she did it right, she is out of practice; then she remembers something Roger told Anthony just the other day, 'It is not the words you say, it is what your heart says; God hears all.' Joanne feels the apprehension lighten up, but she still knows something bad is in the air.

Joanne looks at her watch, "Nine-forty-five, I better get moving if I am going to have this done in time."

CHAPTER 47

When Hank comes out of his pod, he sees everybody, except Frederick, seated at the table and staring at him.

"Hank, we need to talk about Frederick, and our situation here," Anthony says to Hank as he comes over to the table.

Hank looks around at the eighteen eyes staring at him, "How is Freddy doing?" Hank asks; wondering what exactly is going through everyone's minds, and why his guys didn't come to him.

"I went to check on him and heard singing coming out of his pod, bad singing," Karen says as she stares at Hank.

"Well, bad singing isn't the end of the world," Hank says as he tries to calm the situation for just a few more hours.

"It was the song from that Grease movie, the one at the end where the pretty blonde is singing to Johnny, all bad girl like," Max says as he shakes his head.

"*'You're the one that I want,'*" Karen tells Max.

"Ditto, baby," Max says with a giant smile.

"No silly, that is the songs name Freddy was singing," Karen says as she reaches over and gives Max a little kiss on the cheek.

"Stop the mush and let's get serious," Hank says as his mind wanders to the song as he wonders if Freddy did the '*ooh-ooh-ooh*' part also.

"This is serious Hank; Frederick has completely checked out," Anthony says as the others mumble in agreement.

"So, what do you suggest we do; put him on an ice flow and send him out to sea?" Hank asks as he tries to disrupt the moment with exaggeration.

"No, we need to get out," Harry says matter-of-factly.

"Once we get out, we can go get him help," Jack says.

"From who? We already came to the conclusion somebody nuked us; where do we get help?" Hank says as he continues to try and delay the elevator rush. Hank glances at his watch; it is only eight-thirty, three and a half hours to go before they extract. "The radiation above would most likely kill us all; we need to wait," Hank says as he starts wondering when the Doc is going to gas them.

"So, what is your plan? Stay down here for the next fifty years then try to get out?" Kevin says with a huff.

"No, not fifty years; but we do have to look at this reasonably. How long before they were able to enter the areas around Chernobyl or some of the nuke tests place? Does anyone know?" Hank asks with a firm tone as he hopes nobody has an answer.

"Chernobyl is a bad comparison as it was literally ground zero and had massive fallout, but people started going back to the area shortly after; I think they ran one reactor for a few years after the main meltdown. From what I learned in school, once the dust settles, you can travel through an area, and I figure the dust has settled by now," Chung-Hee says with a matter-of-factly glare.

"It has only been a couple of days; I say we need to wait at least another week before trying to climb out," Hank states adamantly.

"It will take us a month to get through the elevator doors," Harry says as he stares at the elevator.

As Hank stares at Harry, he asks, "And how do you plan on getting through them?"

"We will pry the doors open with the shovels and the picks."

"And if they break; how will we garden till we get out?" Hank asks Harry as he tries to dissuade the group for just a few more hours.

"Why do you want to stay here?" Karen calmly asks Hank.

"I do not want to stay here, but I don't want to act wildly either; I think we need a well thought out plan before we start tunneling out of our safety," Hank says as he tries to edge in a little thought of delay.

"What about Frederick?" Max asks as he tries to get everyone back on topic.

"Anthony, what are your thoughts on him? Do you think he will snap back if given time? Do you think he could climb out of here when the time comes?" Hank asks their resident psychiatrist.

"I really don't know; he might snap out of it, he might be able to climb out, he might just freak out and attack you like a wild dog; none of us knows," Anthony says in blunt honesty.

"Okay, let us do this; let's wait until morning before we attack the elevator. Let's rest up today, take care of the garden, and try and think of a way we can wash our clothes," Hank blurts out without even knowing where the thought of doing laundry has come from.

"Wash clothes?" Roger asks thoroughly confused as he looks around at the others.

"I don't know about you guys, but I am down to only one week of clean underwear left," Hank says with a crinkle of his nose as he decides to go with his outburst.

"You haven't been doing a quick wash of them in the shower? I, myself, am set," Karen says as the group looks at her with awe.

"Really? I never thought about that," Max says as they all slowly shake their heads in agreement.

"Back to the task at hand. Okay, let's appease Hank by waiting until morning to begin opening the elevator, and we can all start doing laundry today; that way we only look unshaven and greasy when rescued, but not stinky," Roger speaks up as a voice of compromising reason.

"Okay, I guess that can work," Anthony says as the rest mumble in confused agreement.

As Hank breathes a sigh of relief, he looks at his watch: nine o'clock, three hours to go, "Okay, I guess we should grab our skivvies and get to washing. I can pedal first, and then we can rotate through."

"Sounds good. I have the least amount of laundry so I can wash while you pedal; I will then pedal for the last," Karen volunteers.

"One question; where do we dry it when we are done?" Chung-Hee asks as his mind has gone back to the basics of life; Hank's seed of confusion has worked.

"I have just been throwing it over the chair and bed frame in my pod; it takes a while to dry because of the humidity, but it works," Karen says as everyone stares at her like she is a genius.

"All right, laundry day!" Hank exclaims as he turns and heads to his pod to get his dirty laundry and wait for the elevator to come.

CHAPTER 48

Ω Ω

"Okay, John, you can take your finger off the gas button now," Robert says to John as Robert realizes John was just a twitch away from knocking out the entire Bunker group.

"Oh my, I didn't realize I had my finger on the button," John says as he slides his hand back, "For a minute I thought they were going to rush Hank."

"It looks like Hank defused with confusion; Hank's dirty underwear," Robert says with an air of levity.

"How does he come up with stuff like that?" John asks in total shock.

"Who knows, but he is about the best I have seen when it comes to fast thinking," Robert says as he remembers some of Hank's missions.

"I am glad he can; I would have melted down. When do you expect Jo back?" John asks as he starts thinking about the casserole to be.

"It is almost ten now; I expect in a half-hour if she wants to get to cooking and have it ready in time," Robert says as he looks at the clock on the wall; nine-fifty.

"Well, we better get everything ready for their return," John says as he gets up and starts for the door.

"Good idea, things are about to get real," Robert says as he follows John out.

CHAPTER 49

⚬

"Sir, General Mars, and the EOD tech have arrived," Captain Marshal informs Colonel Miller over the radio.

"Both have arrived, Captain?" Colonel Miller says in surprise; the tech is early, and the General is right on time.

"Yes, sir; the tech drove in right after General Mars."

"Very well, send them both this way," Colonel Miller instructs.

Almost immediately General Mars and a heavily laden EOD technician are ushered around the corner to the staging area, "General Mars, Captain Franklin," Colonel Miller says as he acknowledges his newest additions to the team.

"Colonel; status update, please," General Mars says as the technician sets down his bag by the Colonel's pickup truck.

"Sir, Jung Yong-chul has left, but I have two of my best men on him," Colonel Miller says with unease.

"He left? Do we know where he went? And what about the rest, and the package?" General Mars asks with slight agitation and great apprehension in his voice.

"Jung is heading up Signal Mountain, but we are unsure of his final destination. For the others, we believe they are still inside with the warhead," The Colonel says.

"We will have to apprehend Jung separate, but that will probably be best. For the others, only one way to find out. Nick; give me a minute to make a call," General Mars says with a deep breath as he steps to the side and phones the President. "Mr. President, sir; General Mars here, sir. It's a go, sir," General Mars says and hangs up, "Let's do it, Colonel."

"Captain, are you ready?" Colonel Miller says as he addresses the EOD tech.

"As ready as I will ever be, sir," Captain Franklin says as he checks his weapon.

"Captain Marshal, are we ready for a go?" Colonel Miller says into his radio as.

"Whenever you say sir, we are ready and in place," Colonel Miller calls back.

"Ready everyone; we go in ten, nine, eight, seven, six, five, four, three, two, one, GO!" Colonel Miller calls over the radio.

With the Colonel's call, the team circles around the warehouse and begins signaling each other. When all are in place, one soldier slips over to the front door and places explosive charges on the hinges and lock mechanism; at the same time, a second soldier does the same at the back door. Once the two soldiers have set their charges, they retreat back around the corner of the building; on the signal, they both detonate the charges and blow the doors clear of their frames. Once the doors are gone, the teams flank the doorway's and toss concussion and smoke grenades inside to disrupt the terrorist.

As the initial explosions go off, Kim is knocked to the ground; Daniel pulls his sidearm and yells for Cho to get to the van. As Daniel fires at the door opening, while Cho jumps in the van on the driver's side, Daniel sees a concussion grenade fly in and land under Kim as he is just getting up off of the ground; the resulting blast kills Kim instantly and throws him to the side. Daniel immediately jumps into the van and screams at

Cho to drive through the main roll-up door; Cho didn't need Daniel's instructions as she was already mashing the accelerator to the floor. As they crash through the door and turn abruptly onto the street, the soldiers on the outside of the building open fire on the van, but Cho is able to get free of the area as she heads towards the highway.

As the van crashes through the roll-up doors, Colonel Miller directs his team to take chase at all costs. As the soldiers jump into their trucks, they continue to fire upon the van as it tries to get away; but with the weight of the warhead and shielding in the back of the van, it is unable to accelerate quickly up the long hill out on the main road, and the soldiers easily catch up to the van.

As Cho drives as fast as the van will allow her too, Daniel fires out of the passenger side window, "Faster, Cho, faster!" Daniel yells at Cho as the soldiers continue to fire upon them.

"I am going as fast as it will go! Once we hit the top of the hill, we should do better!" Cho screams as the soldier's bullets continue to strike the van. As the van breaks over the hill and starts heading down towards the intersection of Pineville and Signal Mountain, Cho realizes that Daniel is not returning fire anymore, Daniel lays slumped over the window frame. "No! I can't do this alone!" Cho screams as she realizes she can't slow down and blows into the intersection out of control; Cho tries to turn but is struck by a loaded semi-truck and trailer which causes the van to go over onto its side in the middle of the intersection, where it slides to a stop with cars barely missing her.

"Van down!" The lead soldier yells through his com unit as his truck slides into the intersection, barely missing the oncoming traffic.

"Secure the van! Do not let them get to the bomb!"

Colonel Miller yells over the com as the rest of the unit blocks the intersection and begins moving towards the van with guns drawn.

As Cho unbuckles her belt, she crawls into the back of the van with the Supreme Leaders Fist; it is lying on its side, but the detonation switch is lying inches before her. Cho reaches for the switch right when a soldier comes to the front of the van and sees her; he aims and fires just as Cho grabs the switch.

In an instant, the van, the soldiers, and everything within a mile is vaporized in a flash of light and an unimaginable burst of heat; in the blink of an eye, over twenty-thousand people are dead, and over fifty-thousand are wounded. As the mushroom cloud reaches into the sky, the blast wave goes forward, shattering windows and destroying structures for miles; the Fist has struck a blow to America.

CHAPTER 50

ॐ ॐ

With a flash and eerie rumble, the Bunker shakes so hard everyone in the yard is knocked off their feet; dust falls from the roof, and a crashing sound can be heard over towards the elevator area. Immediately the Bunker begins to fill with the knockout gas as it pours forth from the hidden pipes.

"What is happening?! Not again!" Chung-Hee screams out as he tries to get back up, only to be overtaken by the gas.

As Hank tries to get to his feet by the elevator, he turns to look at where the crash came from; the elevator doors are bulged out and pushed open from the inside, "This isn't part of the plan!" Hank says as dirt falls on him from above as he gets to his feet. As Hank looks up, he sees part of the ceiling begin to fall; Hank tries to run, but he knows he is too late as the roof falls down towards him; Hank knows he won't make it this time.

As Hank tries to get clear of the ceiling fall, he is struck from the side and knocked clear as the falling section of the ceiling crashes down beside him. As Hank feels a searing pain in his shoulder and right arm, he feels the effects of the knockout gas overtaking him. Hank realizes that he was struck from the side, and not from above; Hank looks behind him through heavy eyes and sees Harry lying under a section of the roof; Hank drifts off to a chemical induced sleep.

As the gas fills the Bunker, nobody stirs as the dust settles; all eyes are dark.

CHAPTER 51

CB ED

"Max, he is waking up; go tell Anthony and Roger," Karen quietly says as Hank stirs and slowly opens his eyes.

"What happened?" Hank asks as he looks around and realizes he is lying on his cot in his pod with Karen hovering over him.

"Don't move. Now, what is the last thing you remember?" Karen asks as Roger and Anthony come into the pod with Max in tow.

As Hank looks around, he tries to piece back his memory, "A blast, earthquake, the roof falling, Harry." Hank says as he remembers being knocked clear of the ceiling and seeing Harry lying in the rubble, "Did Harry make it?" Hank asks quietly.

"No, he was caught by the roof fall. We lost Harry, Frederick, and Jack; Harry was near you, Frederick was in his pod, and Jack was in front of his door when the roof slab crushed all three, and almost you," Roger says with his head held low.

Hank stares at Roger for a moment and says, "He pushed me out of the way. He took my bullet." Hank's stomach twists as the feeling of remorse washed over him. As Hank tries to get up, a shooting pain rocks him to the core as he realizes his right arm is tied to his body, "What the?" Hank says as he looks at the makeshift splint holding his arm steady, "Is it broke?"

"Calm down, soldier. I am pretty sure it is a clean

break of the humerus, but my primary concern is the soft tissues of the shoulder, I don't want you moving your arm around and ripping the muscles," Karen says as she helps Hank sit up.

"Did you say Jack pushed you out of the way?" Anthony asks in bewilderment.

"Far from it, Harry did. I saw the roof coming down and knew I was a goner; then all of a sudden, I get hit by a linebacker and knocked clear. Harry knocked me clear," Hank says as he gets up, confused at what has happened.

"Hold on, you need to rest," Karen commands her patient.

"No, I need to get to the bathroom and then get something to drink; then we need to figure out what happened," Hank says as he musters up his strength and heads out of the tightly packed pod.

Once Hank is outside, he sees the aftermath of the cave in. As Hank looks around, he sees three piles of rubble on the far side of the twisted elevator doors; graves. Hank sees Chung-Hee and Kevin moving supplies out of Frederick and Jack's pods and putting them on the tables. Hank looks up and can just make out one of the gas tubes peeking out from the ceiling. Hank remembers being hit with the gas, and he wonders why John gassed them.

John; where is John? Everyone was supposed to be extracted. Graves dug, people buried, rubble moved, "How long have I been out?" Hank hollers out in confusion to no one in particular.

"Two days; the second blast happened two days ago," Alfonso says as he walks up to Hank with Hank's canteen in hand.

"Two days?" Hank says as he numbly grabs the canteen and heads for the latrine. Hank can't grasp what has happened; is this part of the experiment, or is this real? Alfonso said it has been two days since the second blast occurred; Hank remembers the flash and rumble, but that couldn't have been a real blast, could it?

As Hank comes out of the latrine, he numbly goes over to the table and sits down, "Can somebody fill me in on exactly what happened?" Hank asks the air.

"What is the last thing you remember?" Kevin asks as he comes over and sits beside Hank.

"We had been doing laundry for about an hour; then a major flash of light, brighter than the previous one; earthquake-like shaking knocked me down; got up and saw the roof falling on me. Harry hit me out of the way; Harry lying in the rubble; then passing out and waking up with Nurse Ratchet poking on me," Hank says as he still can't figure out why Harry gave his life for him.

"That about sums it up. Flash, shake, crash, pass out," Kevin says as he stares through Hank.

"We thought we had lost you, too," Roger says as he sits down at the table.

"Should have," Hank says as he thinks of Harry. Little one-hundred and fifty pound Harry knocking him clear of the area with more force than a linebacker; how was he able to do it, and why? "So, two days ago a blast occurred, and now we have three dead and an elevator sitting in its pit," Hank says aloud.

"Yes. You actually saved our lives. If we had been trying to get those elevator doors open or head up the shaft, we all would be dead," Anthony says as he sits down.

"I don't understand, I just don't understand; where did the blast come from?" Hank queries aloud as he tries to fathom the events above, "Did World War Three actually happen?"

"Uh, yea; remember, this is the second bomb we know of," Alfonso says with tears hanging onto the corners of his bloodshot eyes.

"Second bomb; I think I am going to go lay down for a bit," Hank says as he gets up and heads for his pod; confused and disoriented.

"Try to rest, we will be out here if you need us," Roger offers as Hank shuts the door of his pod behind him.

"John? Robert? Jo? Come on guys, talk to me," Hank begs as he digs into the shelving unit where the camera was hidden. As Hank looks at the camera wiring, he sees that the wires have melted together, "EMP pulse?" Hank says aloud as he tries to figure out what has happened. As Frank sits on the edge of his bed, he looks up at the sky tube and quietly says, "Our scenario is real; our fears have happened." As Hank lays back on his cot, he fights to hold back the tears as he realizes his family above, John, Robert, and Joanne, are gone.

CHAPTER 52

☃ ☄

While Hank is lying on his cot trying to figure things out, he hears a knock on his door; when Hank opens the door, Karen is standing there, "Coming in soldier, and don't say no," Karen says as she pushes her way in and makes her way to the chair.

As Hank shuts the door, he says, "I'm okay, no need to doctor me, Nurse Ratchet."

"No doctoring, by the looks of your scars, you have had enough of that," Karen says with a stern stare, "Scars that didn't come from a short stint. Start talking or I start beating on your arm."

As Hank stares at Karen, he realizes he needs to fess up about everything, to everyone; Hank turns and opens the door and walks out with an angry and confused Karen in tow.

As Hank sits down at the main table, Karen sits down across from him, "Everyone, come here please," Hank yells to the group as Karen stares him down.

"What is it, Hank?" Roger says as he sits down next to him.

"Once everyone is here and sitting, I will let you all know," Hank says as he stares back at Karen.

"Okay, we are all here, what is it?" Anthony asks.

"I am Captain Hank McPherson, United States Army Green Beret. Three years ago, as part of my recuperation, I was assigned to the Harrison Research Facility as a special architect in the light tube system you have all marveled about. Since that time, I have been permanently assigned as special liaison and support to Doctor Harrison, Colonel Johnson, and Major Joanne Cameron, while still conducting overseas missions for our government when the need arises," Hank pauses as he lets what he is saying sink into the group.

"A ringer," Anthony says with a stare.

"Yeah, a ringer. I was sent down with you guys to keep you on the missions track, and to keep you from flipping out and killing each other," Hank says as he waits for the next question.

"Great job, Captain," Karen says without taking her eyes off of Hank.

"What was the real purpose of the study? Why send a Green Beret to babysit a two-week study?" Roger asks as his street smarts begin to kick in.

"The purpose was to see how twelve people stuck a hundred feet underground would interact while thinking World War Three was going on above them," Hank pauses and then says before anyone can speak up, "The first blast was fake."

"The first blast was fake? We have three dead, and you say the first blast was fake?" Chung-Hee screams at Hank.

"The first blast was faked; it was faked to see how you would all interact in a major crisis. Fake the blast, monitor for an additional two weeks, then bring everyone out. However, once Freddy checked out, the decision was made to extract early; the elevator was set to come down at noon two days ago," Hank says as he shifts his gaze to Chung-Hee.

"Two days ago the second blast happened; what is with that?" Anthony asks as they all stare at Hank.

"I don't know; all I do know is that it was not part of the mission," Hank says as he looks down at the table, wondering what has happened above.

"You planned all of this?! You planned to kill us all!" Chung-Hee shouts and runs to his pod, slamming the door behind him.

"We never planned for anyone to get hurt; just to get data that might save people in the future," Hank says as the feeling of sorrow floods over him.

"Dude, this is so messed up," Alfonso says as he shakes his head at Hank.

"Hold on everyone, before we lynch Hank, I can actually see the value of this test; I might not agree with how far it went, but I can see the value," Anthony says as he looks over at Roger for a calming word.

"So can I; tests like this are designed to save lives in the future. And think about this: if they had pulled us out at two weeks, we most likely would be dead right now," Roger says as he takes Anthony's cue, but then is saddened at the thought of Rachel's probable death.

"Okay, let's think; since we know the first blast was fake, let's take that out of the equation: so, Mr. Green Beret, who did the second blast, the real blast?" Kevin asks with a glare.

"From the facts we have on hand, I would say we were hit with a direct strike," Hank says as his mind reruns all of his earlier thoughts.

"Facts; what facts?" Max asks Hank.

"From what I can deduce; the magnitude of the flash, and the quake spell a nuke or MOAB going off, and I don't see us being hit by a MOAB."

"MOAB?" Max asks as he try's to grip what he is saying.

"Mother Of All Bombs – MOAB. The largest non-nuclear bomb in the US arsenal; it has the explosive equivalent of 21,000 pounds of TNT and is designed to bust bunkers," Karen answers Max.

"And I don't see a MOAB, I see a nuke. And I am willing to say an actual warhead, and not a suitcase or dirty bomb," Hank says as he tries to envision the blast pattern of each type of weapon.

"Are you saying that you think we have been hit with a direct strike? As in a missile?" Alfonso asks as he stands up and starts pacing back and forth.

"Yes; whatever was above, whatever did this, was big," Hank says with a sincerity that the others have not seen from him.

"How do we know this isn't part of your sick test?" Alfonso demands.

"Because the US government has done some stupid things in the past, but killing off a bunch of students isn't one of them," Karen says as she comes to Hank's defense as she begins to realize he is telling the truth.

"All I know is this; we didn't plan this scenario. From what I have seen in the past few years, I would be willing to bet we have been attacked either by one of many surgical strikes, or a terrorist group launched a nuke," Hank states.

"Surgical strike; how could they do that without MAD kicking in?" Karen asks as she refers to MAD – Mutually Assured Destruction – the theory that if one nuclear missile is launched from one side, all of the nuclear missiles from the other side will be launched in retaliation and vice versa, effectively causing a global thermonuclear war.

"EMP strike maybe; hack of our systems; internal attacks; I have no clue. And maybe it did, maybe the world is on fire above," Hank says with a shake of his head.

"How will we know?" Roger asks as he wonders about his family.

"Did any more blasts occur after the first one?" Hank questions.

"We don't know, we were all out; we figured the initial blast sucked the oxygen away and caused us all to black out," Kevin speaks up.

As Hank thinks of the knockout gas, he decides not to mention it, "Yeah, I can see that happening. Well, the only way to find out is to get up the shaft."

"How? And what if the people above don't speak English?" Chung-Hee says as he returns to the group.

"The how will be just as Harry said we would do it, by getting the outer and inner doors of the elevator open. But what Harry didn't know, is that once we go through the car hatch, there is a ladder on the shaft side we will need to climb up a hundred feet to whatever structure remains, get through any remaining blast doors, and head on out," Hank says as he stares at Chung-Hee.

"That's it? We will be home by Thanksgiving," Anthony says sarcastically as he tries to keep his emotions from overwhelming him.

"We need to take care of that garden, ration what we have, and get into shape," Roger says as he looks at the group, "And we need to thank the Lord that we are not only alive but that we have Hank here to help us out."

"Thank the Lord? Your God just killed everyone above and locked us down here!" Kevin yells at Roger.

"No, He didn't. Evil killed those above, and our saving grace is being down here with a garden, water, shelter, and a person who has the training to help us survive once we get back above. For those above who may have died, if they have accepted the Lord as their personal Saviour, they have eternal life," Roger counters Kevin's outburst.

"Yeah, right. Eternal life while believing in a fairy tale; see how far that gets you when we get above and somebody shoves a gun in your face," Kevin says back to Roger.

"Hold on guys, no fighting!" Karen yells at Kevin and

Roger as Max stands up.

"I don't need to fight the preacher, he will be gone quick enough when he gets above," Kevin says with a huff as he turns and walks back to his pod.

"How long do you think it will take us to make it to the top?" Anthony asks as he try's to divert everyone's thoughts away from Kevin.

"To get through this door, get us all in shape to get to the top, and then through the blast doors; I would say three months," Hank says after a moment of thought.

"So, we need to get the rest of the garden made and planted," Roger says as he envisions the next couple of months.

"And exercise; we must be in top shape to climb out of here," Hank says as he feels the pain in his arm.

"Well, we better get to work; garden first, then doors second," Karen says as she starts for the garden.

"Come on guys, times a wasting," Max says as he follows Karen to the garden.

As Roger gets up from the table, he looks over at the elevator and mumbles through a forming tear, "What path have you set before me now Lord; what now?"

ABOUT THE AUTHOR

⋯⋯

Tim King grew up in a small town in Northern California with a wide and rocky path laid before him; his parents had divorced when he was young, and he and his older brother were raised by their father while his sister went to live with his mother. Growing up a teenager in a mountain town was tough; work was hard to come by, and life didn't have a purpose, survival was the only thought to be had most of the time.

Tim grew to find solace in literature, and he read anything he could get his hands on. Tim read the Bible from cover to cover when he was but fourteen, and attempted War and Peace when he was fifteen; Tim found War and Peace too confusing about halfway through, too many players, and the Bible 'just didn't make sense'. But through books, Tim found a release from reality, a place he could go and not have to worry about daily life; a dreamland. However, Tim found this dreamland was but a temporary place, and when he left it, a void would come back into him, a hollowness that could not be filled, yet.

While growing up, Tim spent time in many different churches of multiple denominations, where he heard numerous and sometimes conflicting beliefs; these experiences coupled with the confusion of his earlier reading of the Bible, pushed Tim into a state where he didn't truly know who his Saviour was.

Tim always professed to be a Christian because he had been baptized as a baby; he was a Christian, no matter what, because that is what Tim had been taught. Tim grew up taking the wide path in life, for the narrow path was not the way a person had to go when they were saved; this is what his peers had taught him. Tim thought God wanted him to have fun in life and live however he pleased, as long as he did not hurt anyone, because all was acceptable in God's eyes if he was saved; this is what society told him. Tim said he had a personal relationship with his Saviour, but he didn't, for Tim was a hypocrite and did not care about his life, and the void grew more pronounced.

After wandering aimlessly through failure after failure, Tim met the woman who would change his life and later become his wife, Mary. Through the passion Mary showed Tim of her love for Christ, she watered the seed which had been planted in his heart many years before, and that seed grew and filled the void that was in him.

Mary led Tim to his Lord and Saviour, Jesus Christ, and in doing so, Tim dedicated his life to the Lord; Timothy stopped trying to do his will, and started doing the Lord's will. Once Timothy started truly following the Lord and stopped being the hypocrite he had been, his life changed; he secured a new job which caused him and Mary to move to Tennessee, and their family grew in the love of the Lord as their new and remarkable life began. Through this new life, this rebirth as a child of God, Timothy found himself yearning to create and express his love for His Saviour through the written word. From this longing to praise His Lord, and through the prodding and guidance of the Holy Spirit, Timothy began writing in the hopes of directing just one to the path of Salvation, one from just surviving, to salvation; for Timothy had realized that every bad decision has a silver lining, the silver lining just had to be found.

Timothy has written three books now, a 90-day devotional, a full year devotional, and a novel; he is presently working on the sequel to the novel, and if his grandson has his way, it will be a trilogy.

Come and let Timothy entertain and teach you through his words; come and find your dreamland.